DESSERTS & DRAGONS

BO HUFFMAN

Desserts & Dragons

ISBN 979-8-9918030-1-4 (paperback)

ISBN 979-8-9918030-0-7 (ebook)

Cover art by Adrian DKC

To Amélia,

the perfect cake we baked.

And to Copa Cabana,

who could best any dragon in any kingdom.

Prelude

Gregor Brimstone came from a long line of tunneling dwarves. His family's lineage traced back to the time when Superstitious Mountain had only one tunnel running from the center of the Earth to the tippy top where the steam and lava spewed out. His ancestors dug the second tunnel, the first intrusion in the great mountain long after it had gone cold, to carve out a cozy little den in the mountain's belly. Over the following generations, Superstitious Mountain became one of the greatest constructs of engineering the dwarf world had ever seen.

Encouraged by his family to be the first to attend university, Gregor applied to the Royal Academy of Engineering and Design in hopes of bettering his dwarven community. To his elation, he received an acceptance letter from a very exhausted, very hungover pigeon, as those flying out of the kingdom of Everdorne tended to be. Gregor tied up all his precious belongings in a baby blanket, hung it at the end of a walking stick, slung it over his shoulder, and bid his family and friends farewell.

After grueling weeks trudging under the sun, Gregor arrived in the capital city of Citeel. He was surprised to find that the address on his acceptance letter, which he showed everyone along his journey, led him not to the titanic, gothic Royal Academy of Engineering and Design, but to the entrance of the royal palace. Once more he flashed his letter, with its royal purple seal stamped as clear as could be, and the guards let him into the Main Hall. There, Gregor was met by a tall, bald man wearing an exquisite robe who tried to tell him he was lost. He shut up as soon as Gregor presented his letter. The address was clearly a misprint, but the man decided this would resolve itself if he maliciously complied. Gregor was beckoned to follow through the maze of hallways and was dumped in front of a door, above which hung a sign that read, *Test Kitchen*. Unaware that he ought to be suspicious at this point, Gregor entered a stark white room, the air within thick with clouds of powdered sugar and palpable fear.

Chef Eclin stood rigid in the middle of the room, rail thin with hollow cheeks dressed in his black coat and a pluming white chef's hat, berating a young man for whipping his cream in a room-temperature bowl rather than a chilled one.

"You expect the peaks to stay fluffy? In *this* humidity? At *this* altitude? On *this* day, with the clouds just *so*? You think we just *whip whip whip* as we please, and the cream does as we wish? No!" Eclin rapped the whisk against the counter, sending his students nearly jumping out of their starched white coats. "Science! You want to take guesses at how things work, go next door to Engineering and Design, where they make models out of sticks and pray to their gods they hold. Not here! We calculate, we measure, we hone in to the precise temperature. When we close the door of the oven, we don't clutch our aprons, praying. No, because we know from *science*, from exact calculations, that we created the perfect formula. This"—Eclin shoved the bowl full of sloshing cream towards the pupil— "was done with no measure, no calculation. *Pathetic.*"

Chef Eclin turned towards Elis, his star pupil. He picked up the pastry before him, assessing it. "Now this crème puff, it is perfect." He didn't have to take a bite—he knew. "But *this*," he said, picking up Noal's, holding it up accusingly to the student's nose, "This is—"

The door creaked as Gregor pushed it further open, interrupting his barrage. Chef Eclin looked over Noal's head and saw the dwarf, dressed in his finest chainmail, gawking from the doorway. "You! Come in. Come taste Noal's crème puff and tell me if it is worthy of His Majesty."

Dumbfounded, Gregor pointed to himself in question, then looked over his shoulder just to be sure. No one stood behind him.

"*Now*," Chef Eclin snapped. Gregor jumped to, nearly tripping over his steel-toed boots as he stumbled in. He dropped his sack by the door and stepped up to the counter, where four very tall apprentices peered down at him in awe. None had seen a dwarf before. The only sight more shocking to them would have been if a woman entered the kitchen. They watched Gregor gingerly pick up the pastry, holding their breath and stealing glances at their instructor, who looked on, stone-faced. "Well?"

Gregor opened his mouth and accidentally inhaled the powdered sugar that dusted the top of the pastry. He choked as it hit the back of his throat. Someone gave Gregor a good-natured thump on the back, bruising his hand in the process from the thick metal that hid under the leather vest. Once he got over his coughing fit, Gregor took a bite. His mind collapsed. He had never before eaten sugar, and this pastry was...*divine*. It was divine by normal, peasant standards, fairly good by royal standards, yet barely acceptable had it been Chef Eclin tasting. The dwarf's tastebuds rearranged on his tongue, and he wept into the pastry before cramming the rest into his mouth. The students stared, shocked.

"Do I pass?" Noal squeaked.

Gregor wiped his hands on his leather vest. Choking back tears, he took Noal's hand and pumped it furiously with gratitude. "That was...the most incredible thing...I have ever tasted."

Four heads swiveled towards Eclin.

"Class. Dismissed."

They scattered, leaving their crème puffs to be judged, their futures as royal pastry chefs hanging on the threads of cream, pastry, and the dust of sugar on top.

The room cleared, Eclin turned to face Gregor. He folded his arms, watching the dwarf eye the rest of the crème puffs.

"Are you...going to eat them all?"

"I don't swallow." Eclin nodded toward the spit bucket.

It took Gregor a moment to understand. He gasped. "What a waste!"

Eclin chuckled. "Not at all, I promise you." His expression softened. He looked over this short man—he forgot the word *dwarf*—and saw himself, all those years ago, peering into the windows of bakeries, dreaming of eating everything in sight. Scrounging coins to finally make a purchase and wondering how many more flavors he could try if only he could take their creation into his own hands.

And so, young Eclin began knocking on bakery doors until one finally took him on as an apprentice. He rose in ranks from washer boy to ingredient measurer and finally to baker. He bounced from one shop to another, each fancier than the last, until he became skilled enough to beg the king for a job in his royal kitchen. He quickly outshone the rest of the pastry department, out-whipping, out-baking, out-fudging everyone else until, eventually, he couldn't even outdo himself. He went on to become Head Pastry Chef for His Royal Majesty King Varundil and, nearly thirty years ago to the day, he baked his first royal wedding cake. Chef Eclin published books. He perfected every pastry known to the kingdom and even invented a few more.

Then everything changed one day when Chef Eclin baked a simple sponge cake. He pulled it out of the oven, inspected it, and decided it wasn't as good as his last one. He tossed it in the bin. He baked another, and another, and then another. While some were better than the last, they weren't as good as that time he had baked a perfect sponge cake, weeks—or years? —ago. He pivoted and instead baked a batch of simple blueberry scones. The scones came out fine. Stupendous, even, his fellow chefs agreed, devouring them before Eclin could toss those, too, in the bin.

Something snapped in Chef Eclin that day. He decided he had already baked the perfect version of every dessert there was ever to be made, and everything from here on out would only ever be second best, and so not good enough. Eclin refused to bake another sub-par pastry. He eventually had to answer the king as to why he wouldn't whip up another batch of cookies or fold another thousand layers of puff pastry.

They would not be good enough for His Majesty.

King Varundil decided the best way to fix this problem was to start an apprenticeship to pass his chef's knowledge along to those who were willing to bake a decent pie. That was how, while still being Head Pastry Chef, Chef Eclin became the renowned and feared instructor of The Royal Confectionary Apprenticeship. It had only turned out a few graduating classes so far, and the program wasn't popular enough to garner the attention of prospective students from across the kingdom quite yet, but the proprietors of local bakeries and pastry shops were eager to subject their children to Eclin's tutelage. Eventually, the supply of local bakers' children ran dry and non-bakers' children began to enroll, which was what this current class was comprised of.

There were rules in Chef Eclin's kitchen, chief among them being that chefs never tasted their own baking, and nothing was ever taken out of the classroom. These were two of many rules, not including the stricter ones he set for himself. He tasted his students' desserts but never ate them entirely. Eclin also preached that all it took was one perfect pastry—that was all a man needed a day.

Gregor Brimstone, Chef Eclin saw, had this fire, this incredible awe for the craft. It was this desire that Eclin wished for all his students to have.

Noal Copperton had the desire, but he lacked all confidence.

Elis Goldstem had the fire, but he was also incredibly cocky.

Brimley Lavra had talent in the science of sugar, one of the hardest skills to master.

Ash Birchwood had craft, always making the prettiest desserts, and no one could match buttercream hues better than him.

But none had the gusto that Gregor had. No one had taken a bite and seen through time and space, transported simply by taste. A pastry was an *experience*, and Eclin knew for certain that Gregor would go wild to make others enjoy them as much as he just had.

"I will teach you in the summer, and you will join the group for training in autumn," Chef Eclin declared, clapping Gregor on the back. "You will be one of the greatest pastry chefs in all the kingdom."

"*The* greatest," Gregor said dreamily.

Chef Eclin chuckled. "Not while I'm alive."

Gregor looked around, feeling a rush of emotions sweep over him. Was this what it felt like to have a calling? "I-I have questions," he stammered.

"Of course you do." Chef Eclin steered him out of the kitchen and into an office where the bald man from earlier waited to get enrollment under way. Gregor watched as the two discussed his future, dumbfounded, his lips still coated with a film of sugar he was afraid to lick, wishing the taste would linger there forever.

It was all so foreign to Gregor. He sat there worrying, unable to concentrate on what was being discussed. Did he have to ask his parents' permission first? What about the engineering school? Was this all an elaborate prank? Did they do this to every dwarf who came to the big city?

At this thought, Gregor nearly jumped up and ran out of the room, but Chef Eclin slid a piece of parchment in front of him to sign and said, "Welcome, chef."

Gregor took the quill with a shaking hand and signed his name, something he had never done on an official document before. As he was led down the hall to the dormitory, he looked up and around the massive, vaulted ceilings and the strangest thought rang through his mind: *I'm home.*

1

Royal Engagement

Dear Mum & Da,

Hard to believe it's been two years since I arrived here at the Royal Academy of Engineering and Design. It feels a bit surreal that I'm in my last week of school before I graduate. I know it's been a while since I've been home. My apprenticeships working on the moat around the palace were hard work, but were good experiences and they need dwarves like me to tunnel, since it's my expertise.

Mum, Noal really appreciated the boulder biscuits you sent, though he did chip a tooth on one. He got too excited and didn't wait for me show him how to soften it up with spit or sweat. Will do better with instructions next time.

The final is making me nervous, but I think I'll be fine. They haven't an-nounced yet what we'll be ~~baking, but I feel confident in my sugar sculptures since Brimley was kind enough to tutor me in exchange for~~

Gregor caught himself, and with a growl, crumpled his letter home. He looked out the window and squinted against the bright light of the morning. Instinctively, he reached into his desk drawer and pulled out the smoky quartz sunglasses Brimley had made for him. Dwarves were accustomed to the darkness and dim lighting of tunnel life. Before Brimley made these for Gregor, he had regular, head-splitting headaches brought on by sunlight. Gregor also wore them in the test kitchen, which was blindingly bright, and generally everywhere that wasn't his dorm. He perched them on his nose and sighed in relief, turning back to the parchment.

It was frustrating, keeping this secret. For the past two years, his parents thought their one and only son was studying angles and arches and stone styles.

As an excuse for not coming home that first summer break, Gregor wrote and told them he was spending the weeks digging a moat that had to get bigger each holiday break. First it had been around the palace. Then it had been around the city. On weekends it was patching up leaks or suspending new bridges. The thought of fessing up to his parents about his true profession made Gregor break out in sweat so bad he had long ago rusted his chainmail under the armpits.

Up until that morning, Gregor imagined he would kick the truth down the line until he was Head Pastry Chef, married to a beautiful and accomplished partner, and they had a child or two. In his daydreams, he took his whole family back to Superstitious Mountain, and while his parents gushed over their beautiful grandchildren, Gregor would casually let slip what he did for work. So casually they would glaze right over it, not even care. Or miss it completely because grandchildren!

Gregor wasn't sure how to tell his parents he was planning on visiting. He considered simply showing up, *surprise*! Then after being fed too many boulder biscuits, he would return to the capital city of Citeel and accept a position as a royal pastry chef in the palace kitchen, an offer all apprentices were extended upon their graduation. He and his roommate Noal already made a pact to work there together until they could earn enough money and a royal purple seal to open their own bakery.

Gregor and Noal lived in the servants' wing of the royal palace, nothing fancy, but it was furnished with all the modern comforts. They became best friends shortly after Gregor arrived after spending a night accidentally locked up in a pantry together. They shared the space atop a flour sack and kept each other from realizing their claustrophobia by telling their histories, sharing their dreams, and confessing they both hated black licorice. By the time they were discovered the next morning by Elis, that overachieving braggart, they were best of friends and didn't even mind dish duty for the month for their technically breaking curfew. Had Elis found it funny and kept his discovery a secret, they might have made a proper trio of friends. Instead, the pair made a sworn enemy, someone they resented but also deeply admired, for he was the best pastry chef in their apprenticeship.

Ash became their unlikely third wheel instead, and at that very moment, he barged into Gregor's dorm. Gregor's hand jolted in surprise and the wet quill struck a line straight through the new letter he was trying to compose.

"He's not here!" Gregor screamed, snatching the rusty chainmail shirt off his chair and clutching it to his chest. "Why don't you knock?"

"It's too hot for donning metal," Ash groaned, flopping onto Noal's makeshift bed. A small cloud of fine white powder plumed out from under the sheet. They had to get rid of their mattresses to make room for their secret cookie business, which they lugged to and from the test kitchen after dark. Gregor slept on sacks of sugar and Noal on bags of flour that had to constantly be beaten into shape for lumbar support.

There was something about Ash that made Gregor uneasy. While Noal was Gregor's best friend, and he believed he was Noal's, Noal was definitely Ash's best friend. This irked Gregor, because the two didn't quite get along. Where Ash was tall and slender with a bob of shiny black hair, a smile on his face as if he was always joking, Gregor was gruff and moody with a full red beard and skin that didn't bode well in the sun. Ash smelled of wide-open fields, grass blades bending in a breeze, and Gregor...well, he was of the Earth. His eyes were hazel, his face ruddy, his arms thick, his torso like a barrel, his legs short, and his shoulders meaty and squared. He could balance a dozen pans in each hand and walk them up the stairs without running out of breath.

He suspected Ash wasn't human at all, but it was rude to ask, and Ash had never volunteered any information. It put Gregor on edge, being so suspicious.

His best friend Noal was gangly, pimpled, and hunch-shouldered, with mismatched teeth he had to talk around. But Noal looked better next to Ash if Gregor was being perfectly honest with himself. They *looked* like best friends, while he and Noal looked like two strangers who kept accidentally falling into step with one another.

But *he* was Noal's roommate, Gregor reminded himself. They were the two who started and ran a business together, albeit secret and illegal. Noal had recruited Ash as their deliveryman, to Gregor's dismay, but they both saw Ash as an employee rather than a partner. Still, when Noal and Ash hung out, Gregor always wondered—though dared not ask—what those two talked about when he wasn't around. Not that he always needed to hang out with Noal. He had plenty to do, like write letters home.

"Are you excited about our final exam?" Ash asked, sitting up. Gregor had turned back to the letter but now peeked over his shoulder to look at Ash. This was...peculiar. Usually, if Ash burst in while Noal was out, he'd wander off to find Noal or else wait crouched by the door to pounce when Noal finally came around. He hardly spoke to Gregor if Noal wasn't around, because why would he?

"Um, er, I was just..." It took Gregor a moment to understand that Ash meant to converse with him. "I wonder what it will be." He set down the quill and turned his full attention, for the first time ever, to Ash.

"Did you hear the princess is getting married?"

"Yes, I did hear about that. It was on a bulletin in the courtyard, was it not?"

"The heralder also came out at lunch with his announcement scroll and shouted the news."

At this, Gregor grew bold. "No, I missed it. Noal and I were proofing bread."

"It's important to keep up with current events and know what's happening around the kingdom. This affects us all, you know. We're all subjects of the princess, and this new fellow, I mean her groom, will be our king."

"King, or consort?" Gregor asked. He still didn't know the order of all the fancy people and their ranks. He really didn't think it mattered to him, a dwarf. In fact, he wasn't entirely sure he was a subject of this kingdom, considering his mountain lay beyond the imaginary moat he was digging. But then, if he was a student here, did that automatically make him a subject? He made a mental note to ask his parents, for surely they would know.

"Why, *king*," Ash sputtered. "It's always been a king and a queen, for as long as this kingdom's been."

"In the mountain, there's a council which advises the reigning head family where wife and husband rule as one. Then if one spouse dies and the remainder remarries, they are always simply consort, to discourage marriage for power.

Queens have ruled Superstitious Mountain for centuries when their husbands kept going off and dying in one battle or another."

Ash's mind whizzed and whirled with this information. "Women can rule? All alone? Huh. I suppose they can do anything a man can do. Even better! You know, I'm shocked they don't allow women in the royal kitchen. I bet they would do well as apprentices. Bring in a sense of creativity and color and such."

"Well, now, I'm not arguing that. I'm just stating how things are. Under the mountain," Gregor sputtered. "Don't go telling people I'm disputing ideas and challenging the Crown. I don't need to be jailed for heresy."

The dorm door burst open, and Noal fell through. For someone so scrawny, he always seemed to have the wind behind him. "Did I startle you? Sorry! Fancy seeing you two getting along." It wasn't a secret that Gregor found Ash annoying, and Ash only put up with Gregor to be around Noal.

"What, we've been apprentices together for years. *Of course* we get along." Gregor rolled his eyes. Noal and Ash exchanged looks.

"Well," Noal said, "did you hear about the royal engagement?"

"We were just discussing it!" Ash brightened. "Isn't it lovely? Er, fun?"

"Chef Eclin will be in charge of the desserts, and he'll need help," Noal wheezed, just about bursting from excitement. "We'll help *cater a royal wedding*!"

Ash leapt up and pumped his fists. Gregor realized, too, what it meant. "Are you sure?"

"We're all going down to the kitchen now! Elis is already taking bets as to what the cake flavor will be."

"I thought the princess didn't have much of a sweet tooth," Gregor said.

Noal reached for a crisp white coat to put on for class. "I heard the princess has a finicky stomach."

"Who'd you hear that from?" Gregor asked, getting dressed as well.

"Me," Ash said, then blushed. "I...hear things."

"Sounds like you really enjoy the gossip coming out of the tower," Gregor remarked, buttoning the last button of his coat. "Ready?"

2

Decree

The capital city of Citeel held the grandest festivals and threw the most lavish banquets in all of Everdorne. Diplomats from kingdoms near and far flooded in to celebrate any and all occasions, and the first wedding in three decades was certainly reason to kick up dust. It was one of the main reasons the kingdom of Everdorne was so powerful; diplomacy was easy when forging alliances took place over the most delicious morsels and scrumptious meals. Great leaders never missed an invitation from King Varundil. It was why the king's chefs were some of the best trained and well paid on the entire continent. Being a chef in the palace was a bit like being a celebrity, and they were often invited to come out during feasts to meet the visiting diplomats and accept their gracious praises.

It was the dream of every apprentice in the royal kitchen to join the ranks of culinary geniuses, and it was even more exciting to be employed in the palace during an actual royal wedding. It was why they put in all those years of excruciating work, learning the power of yeast, the secrets of gelatin, the tempering of chocolate, the layering of puff pastries. How to fill crusts and tarts with exotic fillings. How to torch meringue, prepare fudge, bake breads and sweet rolls and cakes. They knew how to brown butter by smell and blow sugar sculptures. Make bon-bons and sticky-sweet caramel. They learned candy making—lollies and taffies, brittle filled with nuts. They knew how to progress sugar through all the stages of hardening without the need of a thermometer. By the end, they were chemists in the kitchen, the wizards of sugar.

Gregor, Noal, and Ash rushed down to the classroom. They weren't late, but excitement propelled one, then the other, until all three were nearly full-out sprinting down the corridors. Even so, they just missed whatever had Chef Eclin one foot out the classroom door.

"...and to *think*," Chef Eclin screeched. "I have spent the better part of my years—*nay*, the *best* part of my years—whipping up the finest, most decadent desserts for His Majesty. Only to be stifled now because of *ridiculous* requests that no man should have to adhere to. This isn't just creative suppression; this is a barbaric challenge. I will not be humiliated in front of this kingdom and all its guests!"

The three apprentices stood gawking as Eclin whirled away and stormed through them as if they were merely specs of dust in a ray of sun. They shuffled into the classroom and dropped, stunned, onto their respective stools.

Gregor looked around. Elis was sheet white. Brimley clung to the edge of his table as if it was all that kept him from swaying to the ground. The royal heralder began rolling up his scroll when Gregor interrupted. "Hold on now, oughtn't we hear the decree?"

"It-it's—it was addressed to Chef Eclin."

"Right, but the rest of the lot got to hear it, why can't we?"

This heralder had been taught, *they won't shoot the messenger, don't worry*, and so hadn't been prepared to take the brunt of Eclin's outburst. To steady himself, he took Gregor's request and did what he did best. With a crisp whip of the wrist, the scroll unfurled once more. He cleared his throat as if to quiet a crowd of a thousand unruly masses and boomed the words of the decree:

"It is with great joy that His Royal Majesty officially announces the wedding of his daughter, Princess Damora, to Prince Eadwine Norsdorf of the Kingdom of Galloway. He requests that you, Chef Patrice Eclin, as Head Pastry Chef, be tasked with the honorary duty of preparing the most esteemed wedding cake. You shall be compensated handsomely for your time, and your glory will be praised for kingdoms over. The designated guidelines will be listed in this envelope..."

The herald held up the envelope.

"...Although by now you should be familiar with them. Thank the gods for this honor. We trust you will make your kingdom proud."

"What's so wrong with that?" Noal asked as the heralder rolled up the scroll.

"He knows something we don't," Elis said matter-of-factly. "It's been said she's a finicky eater. Say, what's in the envelope?"

"None of your business," the herald muttered, and pocketed it.

"He's mad he's gotten a bit of a challenge?" Gregor tried to make sense of the outburst. "That seems mighty unlike him."

"It's got to be real bad, the way he stormed out," Noal murmured.

Everyone looked back at the royal heralder, who had tucked the scroll under his arm and was trying to discreetly leave the room. He paused, hand on the door, unsure of what protocol was. Peasants and the like would simply turn on each other for answers once he finished speaking, leaving him to retreat unscathed. Every time he declared a decree within the palace walls, on the other hand, everyone felt entitled to a clarification, or a footnote that didn't exist. "I-I just read the scrolls," he stammered and scampered out the door.

Voices sounded in the hall upon his exit; it seemed he didn't escape completely unscathed. After a few moments, the robust figure of Chef Toufie appeared. "I've got a kitchen full of first years trying not to burn hollandaise, so I only have a few moments," he puffed, trying to catch his breath. Chef Toufie shuffled to the front of the classroom and thick, calloused hands set his enormous mug on Eclin's desk. He wasn't quite as tall as Chef Eclin, but his stature was still imposing, with his great big belly straining against the buttons of his black coat. His thick, dark beard hid nearly the entirety of his ruddy face and all other hints of his age. Where Eclin refused to swallow, Toufie did so with glee. He slurped down every sauce, morsel, noodle, dressing, crumb. But then, he wasn't training confectioners, but rather culinary apprentices, in a program that had just been introduced that year to replace all the senior kitchen staff that were drinking themselves out of a job.

"I understand there was a bit of news shared." Chef Toufie looked around the room. "And, well, since I'm minutes away from a kitchen fire, I suppose it's best if I dismiss you all."

Brimley, the young monk who was a wiz at sugar sculptures, raised his hand. "Did Chef Eclin quit?"

"Quit? Quit what? Do you give up on everything just because you receive bad news? Blimey, I've heard the pastry department had mold in their brains, but to hear it!"

Ash raised his hand next. "Does this mean we're still taking our final?"

"This is getting egregious! You're dismissed. I'll see you back on Monday, once I've had time to figure out what you're all supposed to do. Enjoy your day off." Chef Toufie made to leave in a hurry, but it took a moment for his enormous tummy to catch up with the rest of his body as it turned. It swung into place with a slap against his arm. He didn't notice, but the class gawked, half wishing they had chosen the culinary route instead. The man clearly enjoyed his grading periods.

On the way to their dorms, they paused to peer into the kitchen next door, where the fire bell was being rung by a sobbing apprentice. Several others were fighting over the sink, desperate to scrape the burnt mess from the bottom of their pots. Perhaps they had chosen correctly after all.

3
Midnight Mischief

Gregor and Noal tiptoed their way down the hall under the cloak of darkness. Everyone was either at the pubs or asleep in their dorms. Gregor struggled under the weight on his back, and Noal did his best not to rattle the jars in the sack thrown over his shoulder.

When they got to the test kitchen door, Noal opened it with the skeleton key they made the previous year, thanks to Ash. While Gregor's mum sent him boulder biscuits, Ash's family sent him magical trinkets, like the Endless Putty. It held its shape for however long the owner wanted it to, indefinitely if need be, and could be molded completely anew with a single spell. This proved to be wondrously useful. Ash explained that some liked to make jewelry or ashtrays, and when he shared the putty with his friends, Gregor made a pipe out of his lump to gift his father when he finally went home. But it sat and sat on his desk until Noal had the idea that maybe it could be used for something mischievous. They hadn't known for what, but when the concept of their midnight cookie shop was born and the need for a place to bake arose, they quickly pieced together that perhaps magic putty was far more valuable than was given credit for. It oozed easily into the keyhole and hardened at Gregor's chosen magic word. If ever confiscated, the spell could be spoken from anywhere, and the key would melt apart into a puddle of putty once more, swallowing with it their incriminating fingerprints. Noal had an identical key, and they suspected Ash used his lump for something similar.

Inside the classroom, they coaxed Fergis, the classroom Fire Stoker, awake. They walked the rust-red dragon around the room, a cube of sugar trailing in front of his nose, to light the lanterns and the oven, which grew hot and ready as they unpacked the sacks of ingredients Gregor had lugged on his back. They had brought down the last of it, since this was their final night baking, with graduation right around the corner. Noal climbed onto Gregor's shoulders and pulled from the back of shelves miscellaneous ingredients they had collected and stashed— eggs and salt flakes and nuts and various spices. Fergis was paid handsomely for his discretion, always eating the first few batches that inevitably burned as they fine-tuned the oven's temperature. Once perfected, the inscription above the oven was spoken and the magic of the clay in the bricks worked to keep the temperature consistent. Fergis also stood guard, poking his head up when someone—a stray cat, as it always turned out—wandered too close to the door.

Since most rooms in the palace housed dragons, there were no night patrols in the corridors. The domesticated dragons were, from nose to tail tip, about the length of a grown man's arm, of varying temperament and breed. Everyone feared opening a door to receive a face full of fire. Well, nearly everyone. Lucky for them, the first time Noal and Gregor entered the test kitchen after hours, Fergis had been so confused at recognizing the intruders that they managed to stuff a handful of stale ginger crisps down his throat before the flames shot out. Now there was a tacit agreement between the parties in their after-dark activity: silence for sweets.

Twice a week after lights out, Gregor and Noal snuck downstairs to bake. After about an hour, Ash, too, crept down. He was in charge of receiving the orders from the pigeons and boxing them, a dozen at a time. Chocolate chip. Triple chocolate. Nutty brown butter. Chocolate chopped peanut. Toffee walnut. White chocolate pistachio. Cinnamon spice. Vanilla sugar. Ginger molasses. Then, when enough boxes were packed, Ash ran them down the hall to the dovecote, one of many sprinkled throughout the palace.

The pigeons in this hall were the strongest, having been conditioned over the last year to fly cookie-filled boxes all across the palace and the university beside it. Sometimes it took a team of pigeons to get a box to an apartment if there was a party taking place. They were also the best fed pigeons, as they would have fussed to the authorities by this gross mistreatment had they not been cut into the bargain.

All night Noal chopped and weighed ingredients while Gregor, with his ample muscles from a life mining under intense mountain conditions, mixed them and loaded the sheetpans into the oven to bake. Noal sometimes helped Ash package and keep Fergis fed. They pulled in such a tremendous pile of coins during finals and midterms that sometimes they wondered aloud, back in their dorm, why they didn't just quit now and open a real shop.

They knew why, of course.

No one was allowed to open their own shop without the royal seal of approval, which was awarded only after proper training, a list of endorsements, application approval, and "proof of competence," which varied depending on the profession. This purple wax stamped parchment was always prominently displayed in the shop, either in the window or behind the counter. Without it, the business was declared illegal.

Granted, illicit shops like theirs existed all over the kingdom. That was inevitable. But these establishments always had to charge less to entice customers to shop at a place deemed sub-par, and there was always the fear of an audit shutting them down. This just meant they popped up in a new location, but customers were loath to chase a business from one place to the next, and if it happened too often people would give up and finally go to the reputable establishment closest to their home.

Their cookie business was niche, open far later than any other bakery in town. It was safe because no one was going to give up the source of their midnight sugar rush. It was coveted, a thing to look forward to after a night of pub hopping, studying late, or making up after a belligerent quarrel with a sweetheart.

To launch the business, Gregor and Noal had needed capital. So, they took on assistant jobs baking bread at Lorde of Loaves, overseen by the tyrannical Chef Tracy. Each Saturday they woke up before dawn and arrived in town to help Tracy, an old baker who was growing hunched and arthritic, with lifting, weighing, kneading, and baking so that Tracy could do what he did best: catch up with customers and spread gossip. One would not think an old man losing his sight so loved to gossip about the quarrels of the local royals, but he nearly frothed at the mouth with excitement when a new issue of *The Harking Herald* dropped. His regulars would always ask, cheekily, if he'd read it yet.

Now that the cookie business was in full swing, Noal and Gregor no longer needed their jobs at Lorde of Loaves, but they had gotten so used to the routine that they forgot to quit. Plus, they enjoyed deep discounts on ingredients on top of their complimentary daily bread.

Panting, Gregor paused, wiped his brows on his apron, and checked the clock above the door. It was half past two, and they still had a lot of cookies to sell. They were nearly out of the ingredients, which was good, and Noal had begun tidying up and putting things back as if nothing—not even a ghost—had passed through the test kitchen. Fergis was curled up above the oven, toasting his tummy, drooling contentedly in his sleep.

Suddenly, he sat up.

He sniffed the air, and just when Noal, who was counting coins, noticed, the door opened.

No sudden slam, no "Aha! Gotcha!" Just a very confused Chef Toufie, blinking in the doorway in his nightcap and pajamas under an enormous fuzzy robe that was falling open. He clearly did not expect to run into anyone at this time of the night.

"Oh my, I was just...I left my..."

Chef Toufie trudged over to the desk, where hours ago he had left his enormous mug. It was still half full of now lukewarm (it had gone cold, but the baking had toasted it back up a few degrees) coffee. "I woke up fancying a cup of cocoa, and I went into my classroom... Hold on," he said, realizing that the wrong person was doing the explaining. "What are *you* doing here?"

Gregor and Noal stood frozen in place. Their mouths had fallen open in surprise. Noal scrambled over to Gregor, as if being closer would help them think faster. That, and Gregor's pockets were far deeper than his. He sunk the heavy bag of coins into one of them. "We..."

Gregor threw up his hands. "Finals!"

"Pardon?"

"Finals?" Noal squeaked.

"Eclin assigned your finals assignment? Already? And you're doing it *now*?" Chef Toufie's confusion morphed on his face with each question he asked.

"N-no. Not exactly," Gregor backpedaled. He looked over at Noal, who was white as flour. "We were just trying to get our technique perfected in time for finals."

"And...Chef Eclin has permitted this?"

"How else would we have gotten in?" Noal said, finally finding his wits.

Chef Toufie raised his eyebrows. He glanced over at Fergis, who looked equally guilty. Lucky for him, Toufie wasn't good at reading dragons and didn't recognize the emotion so plainly painted on the accomplice's face. Still groggy, Toufie reasoned that the dragon would have reacted to intruders, and since he hadn't, Gregor and Noal were not, in fact, intruding. This was the midnight logic at work. All Toufie wanted was to whip up some gourmet hot cocoa in his classroom, patter back to his room, snuggle down deep in his goose feather bed, and fall asleep the moment the last drop of cocoa slid down his throat. "Alright," he said, but he was cut off by the clamor of the tiny alarm.

Gregor smiled sheepishly and retrieved the batch of cookies from the oven. The smell slapped Toufie awake, making him realize that he had the authority here, *total* authority, and it would be within his rights as chef to... "Let's just see if this overtime is paying off," he said, and snatched a piping hot cookie off the tray. But he was used to putting burning, boiling things in his mouth. In fact, it was a wholly wonderful experience, that bite, and the next, and every single one that made that cookie vanish.

"Well," he said, tucking three more into his robe pocket, "it seems you've mastered this skill. Better finish up and get to bed. And perhaps let's not let this happen again," he added with a knowing glare. Frankly, it would be too much trouble to go tattling to Eclin, should Toufie even know where he was, which he didn't.

Gregor and Noal nodded. "Understood," they said in unison.

"Right." Toufie snatched his mug from the desk, gave Fergis a hesitant pat, and shuffled out of the classroom.

Before they could let out a sigh of relief, the door opened again. "I'll need the key, of course."

"The key?"

"The kitchen key. I'll make sure Eclin gets it back."

"Um, well, you see," Noal stammered. Gregor was at a loss for words, the guilt flaring red across his face. "N-n-nutmeg," Noal stammered, and he felt an odd wetness in his pocket as the key melted into a puddle.

Exhaustion overcame Toufie, and he gave up. "Right. Understood. I mean, we understand, do we not, boys?"

"Yessir."

"Yes. Sir."

Toufie nodded. The door shut. The air stood still a few seconds before finally, *finally*, Noal and Gregor let out the breath they'd been holding. Gregor's came out his nose. Noal's came out his rear end.

"Noal!"

"I was terrified!"

Gregor stepped away to escape the odious gas. "Well, at least now you can finally ask for nutmeg. I can't believe you picked your secret word to be baking related."

"Why, what's yours?"

"Nice try," Gregor said, and went to scoop the leftover cookies off the trays. He was halfway through boxing them up when the door opened yet again. The tray dropped. Ash, in the doorway, nearly jumped out of his skin as well.

"Ash!" Noal yelled.

"For gods' sake!" Gregor growled.

"I'm sorry!" Ash squeaked. "I just saw Chef Toufie go out. Did he catch you?"

"He sure did," Gregor grumbled, scooping the cookies off the floor and into Fergis's lap, although whether he deserved them or not was now debatable.

"Looks like the cookie business has had its last night," Noal said, cramming jars, now filled with leftover cookies, back into his sack.

"Oh no, really? He shut it down?"

"In not so many words, yes." Gregor tied up the remaining bags of flour and sugar, each just enough to be a somewhat decent pillow. He loaded everything onto his shoulders and began the trudge back to their dorm. He called to Ash, "Spread the word. We're done here."

4

Lorde of Loaves

"Perhaps we could do it after hours. We'd stay late, scrub the place clean, clean as a crystal ball, sir?"

Gregor watched Noal run after Tracy, who was shaking his head adamantly at the proposal to let them bake cookies in his shop after closing.

"You don't have a seal!" Tracy roared, mostly compensating for his deafness.

"But *you* do! We'd be a-a-a what did you call it, Gregor?"

"A subsidiary."

"A subsidy! We'd—"

"Sub-si-di-ary!" Gregor shouted, trying to be heard over the crackling of the great oven baking the loaves he and Noal had kneaded all morning. He was sleep deprived, grumpy from the night's adventure, and peeved that Tracy was being such an old cabbage about it all. Why, the bakery would have long gone out of business without them!

"Right, a subsidity. Desserts division. You're not selling sweets, and the closest confectionary is what, four blocks away? That's quite the hike. You'd already have your current customers to sell to, and they're sure to love our cookies."

"They're all diabetic."

"What's that?"

"Can't have sugar."

Noal gasped, clutched at his chest. "No sugar? Why, because they're poor? They don't seem poor!"

"It's a disease!" Tracy roared, a diabetic himself. He didn't have the wife around anymore fussing over his diet, but he ate the breads he baked, which were hearty, nourishing, kept his blood sugar in check, and just a bit too chewy to eat without sopping in soup. It kept him from reaching for all the bad stuff he used to consume, and he peddled the loaves with gusto as the cure for his ailments. The elderly loved it, which meant his clients were all wrinkled and too slow to steal. That's how he wanted to keep it. "Besides, it looks like one just opened up right here."

"What did?"

Tracy nodded to the window. Gregor dropped the ball of dough he was wrestling and followed Noal, who got so close to the glass his breath fogged it. Gregor reached past him and wiped away a circle. "Gods," they muttered in unison.

A sweets trolley had appeared in the patch of grass across from the shop. As they watched, the owner dropped the handles and let the trolley's legs sink deep into the wet ground. It hadn't rained, not recently; it was the effect of chamber pots emptied, bathwater tossed through open windows, and the drunks that sloshed their beer everywhere the night before. It was a softness that never seemed to seize up until the frost of winter finally blew in. That soft mud puckered and swallowed the wooden trolley legs painted a bright, cheery pink that climbed its way up and all around the cart. Its wheels were thick, sturdy, and the canopy above the goods was striped red and white like the peppermint candies the confectioners loved to make around the winter solstice.

The jingle of the door sent Noal and Gregor reeling backwards, clutching their hearts.

It was their classmate Brimley, there to collect the unsold bread to take back to the monastery he had grown up in. It didn't take long for these hearty breads to grow brick-hard, but they had a wonderful way of softening immediately when added to liquid. Day old, week-old, even month-old bread would react to hydration in the same miraculous way. Tracy tried to explain the phenomenon to his customers, but they only ever bought enough for that day and insisted on making the trip down each morning. It made no difference to Tracy, as he had gotten quite good at predicting exactly how much bread to bake each day. But occasionally someone felt under the weather or stubbed his toe in the night making his way to the chamber pot or was surprised with a pastry from a visiting niece and didn't come out that day. So, inevitably, there was always a few loaves left unclaimed. And because Tracy was doing well and the cost of baking bread wasn't much, Brimley always left with those loaves for a few less coppers than was full price. Each a tax write-off, Tracy boasted.

"Oy, do you see that?" Noal gasped.

Brimley, who had gone straight up to the front and was dutifully loading loaves, looked around, confused. He wore his typical monk uniform when not in the test kitchen: burgundy robe tied around the waist by a tasseled rope belt, a wide-brimmed hat covering his tight black curls, and leather sandals. "Did I ignore you? Sorry, I thought I'd said hallo."

"Not us, that!" Noal pointed out the window. With agonizing patience, Brimley finished loading his basket and paid for the loaves. Then he made his way over to the window, where Noal was quite visibly trembling with excitement. "The sweets trolley!"

Tracy also lumbered over.

"Huh. That's new." Brimley stated the obvious.

"I don't see a purple seal," Gregor huffed, eyeing Tracy as he did. Tracy ignored him but did make a mental note of this. He wasn't a spiteful man, and he didn't think this would disrupt his business one bit. There was the matter of principle, of course, and what would the lads think, after he turned down their offer, if he then allowed a seal-less man to sell sweets within his view?

"It must be stopped," Noal hissed.

"Come now, it's not our business to get mixed in other people's business," Brimley chided. He was a pacifist, first and foremost.

"Since when?" Noal snapped.

Gregor gave him a look but didn't dare bring up their illicit cookie operation, which, of course, everyone knew about. In a way, they felt that since they had gotten shut down, it was only fair that everyone should. But if anyone was going to send a pigeon to the king, it would be a man with authority, a man with a purple seal, not his two apprentices.

"It looks like it's got all the usuals," Brimley observed, squinting. "Lollies, toffees, spun sugar even!"

"But what quality?" Noal hissed.

"Noal, you've got a few coppers, why don't you go over and tell us?" Gregor suggested.

"*Me?*"

Gregor rolled his eyes, dug into his pockets, and pulled out a silver coin. "Get something for all of us."

Noses pressed back to the window. Eyes followed Noal as he scampered across the street, then back again. They nearly ran him over when Noal came back, his fist clenched tight around his goodies.

"Well?"

"He's...a strange one." Noal opened his hand, and they inspected the contents of his palm. Each grabbed something different, even Tracy, who decided once in a decade wouldn't kill him.

"It's..."

"Gods, that's good," Tracy moaned.

Everyone side-eyed Tracy, who looked ready to weep. "We should have brought him a cookie to try," Gregor muttered.

"But no seal?" Brimley asked, unsettled by how genuinely good his toffee had been.

"None. I even asked to see it. He simply stuck a few more pieces in my hand and winked instead of answering me. That's bribery, isn't it? Have I just taken a bribe? Oh gods!"

"Come off it." Gregor rolled his eyes. "This is quality, though, Brimley, isn't it?"

"As good as I'd make it. At least the toffee. The nougat?"

A nod.

"The caramel?"

A nod.

"The...what was it Tracy, lemon drop?"

A nod.

They stood in silence, grim, rolling their tongues around their mouths, scraping at the last of the flavor, desperate to enjoy every lick.

"A seal's a seal," Tracy finally said, and they were almost sad to hear it. Confectioneries were as popular as cobblers or jewelers in the city, but few sold individual pieces like this; it was always in bulk, for festivals and other such orders like parties, weddings, and celebrations, with the price of sugar what it was. There was the one shop off Mudd River Ravine, but the caramel tended to glue teeth together, the cookies crumbled a bit too quickly in the hand, and the chocolate bars bent instead of snapped.

"Give me the rest," Brimley said, shaking Noal's palm into his basket. "I'll test to see if there's any funny business about this." Brimley was an incredible chemist. He worked sugar with a craft none of the others had, a gift even Chef Eclin envied. Brimley had apprenticed with an alchemist, then a pharmacist before he got admitted to the pastry apprenticeship.

"Did you get his name?" Tracy asked.

"Alistair."

"Alistair what?"

Noal blinked at him, confused. "That's all he gave."

"Where's he from? When did he get here? Does he make these himself?"

Noal balked at the torrent of questions. To be honest, he'd been so anxious buying the sweets—as if he was fraternizing with an enemy—that he'd been too breathless to ask for more than the man's name. "I suppose I could ask..."

"No, I will," Brimley cut him off. "I'd like to pick up a few more pieces for closer inspection."

Everyone gave a little nod.

"Does this mean...?" Gregor whispered.

"No cookies!" Tracy snapped. "Not with the price of sugar going up as it is. Also...I smell something burning."

He didn't, but this was always the way he ended discussions. Gregor and Noal bid their friend goodbye, and Brimley left. They went about their work, eager for Monday to learn if Brimley discovered anything. It was their last day working at Lorde of Loaves, and Tracy stoically bid them farewell when they finally hung up their aprons for the last time.

"Maybe someday you two will buy me out, turn this bakery into that cookie shop after all," Tracy said with a friendly wink. They accepted the coins Tracy counted out, noting there was an extra copper in their palm. It wasn't much, but the message was sentimental, and they felt appreciated. Gregor and Noal also received a fresh loaf each from the batch they had just baked, and they headed back to their dorm, a bit relieved they could finally faze these breads out of their diets.

Tracy wrote that letter complaining about the lack of seal but didn't post it. Not quite yet.

5

Sweet Surprise

Dear Mum & Da,

We've finished up the moat and I look forward to coming home this summer. It's so sweltering hot already. I never got used to it. I also burn like a scorched tomato, as no one warned me dwarves never evolved the right pigments for protection from the sun. Noal's mum is always fussing about him getting heat stroke, and since she keeps sending him a new one each year, I've taken up wearing his extra hat and light cloak to keep the sun off me. I know wearing the ore we mine from our home is a sense of pride, but the chainmail chafes in the summer and the leather bands holding my breastplate in place get soaked with sweat and start to smell, so I forgo them. I hope you'll forgive me. It's never been so polished, I promise, and no one can tell I'm not wearing it under the cloak. There's a new confectioner in town...

Gregor paused to yawn. It was Monday morning before class, and Gregor had a lot weighing on his chest. He wanted advice from his parents more than anything. They were good at that. When he had a heat conduction question because the caramel kept burning and the chocolate wasn't tempering, he was able to phrase his questions cryptically enough that his parents—who were experts at metal conduction and heat transfer—gave him marvelous advice, placing him first in his class on that lesson. He'd try it again here. After all, engineers could eat sweets from traveling trolleys, could they not? Or would they consider it a frivolous expense?

Money had never been an issue. The apprenticeship itself was at no cost, though technically paid for in unpaid labor they did cleaning breakfast dishes after eating in the dining hall each morning. Gregor and Noal started the cookie business to pay for everyday expenses (like pub hopping). Gregor's mum wrapped a few gold nuggets and rubies or other gems into sweaters she sent him when the winter came each year. Gregor suspected they were meant to be pawned should he need to, but so far, he hadn't. Instead, they lined his dorm shelves as decorations, along with the pebbles and rocks he found and pocketed in his day-to-day. Ash admired them and once asked if Gregor knew their worth or had considered fixing them into jewelry.

"It's customary to court with gifts mined from our mines," Gregor explained, then suddenly felt embarrassed. "But that's not why I hold onto them."

Then Ash said the most curious thing: "I would like it set in a bracelet." Then he blushed and replaced the sapphire on the shelf before scampering off, not even waiting for Noal to come by first.

...and he doesn't have a royal seal. I've told you about the seal, and why it's important. Maybe he's got some royal exception. There's a royal wedding happening, and maybe that will bring in an array of traveling merchants looking to make a little festival fortune. Maybe there's a decree I'm not aware of that allows temporary sales without a seal? I'm just thinking aloud now. Have you heard of the royal wedding taking place? What do you think of it? Does it matter to dwarves? Are we a part of the kingdom? I'm sorry if that is a silly question, but I don't recall you telling me, and I have yet to meet another dwarf in this city.

Lots of love,

Greggy

The knock at the door made Gregor's quill jerk, but not enough to ruin the letter.

"Yes!" Noal sang.

Brimley opened the door. "Sit down," he ordered, and the two fell back into their desk chairs. "I've found something curious."

Gregor and Noal exchanged looks, but before they could speak, Brimley presented two lemon drops. They looked identical. Brimley set them on a granite board he placed on the desk in front of his friends, then pulled a pestle from his pocket and smashed one. He waited a heartbeat before asking, "Anything?"

"What?" Noal asked.

Gregor looked at Noal, then back at Brimley. "What happened?"

Noal looked at Brimley as if he were crazy. "You shattered a perfectly good lemon drop?"

Brimley nodded, seemingly satisfied with this answer. Then he moved the board a bit closer to his friends and smashed the other one. A tiny puff of smoke rose from the center, puckered like a kiss in the air, and popped, flooding the three of them with momentary euphoria.

"Is that...a spell?"

Brimley nodded, quaking with excitement. "He sneaks spells into his candies!"

"But...I didn't feel different eating it."

"You didn't have the lemon drop."

"Who did?"

"Tracy did," Noal said. He remembered the look on the old man's face, an expression he'd never seen before. "He did seem...oddly emotional after eating it."

"What sort of spell is it?" Gregor asked Brimley.

"It's a simple happiness spell. An extra boost of joy. You felt it, didn't you?"

"Yes, but is it just as fleeting when consumed?"

Brimley nodded. "But if you were sad...why, it would be downright addicting."

"It's probably why Tracy didn't march across the way and turn the cart over, to be honest," Gregor said, thoughtful. "He usually has such a lousy temper."

"He shouldn't have had it, he's got the thing!" Noal suddenly looked sick with worry.

"He has got what?"

"The-the—you were there! The sugar disease!"

Gregor went a bit pale. "He's a cheap man, he won't have more."

"Maybe not him, but what of his other customers? What if they start consuming all that sugar? It would kill them!"

"Don't be dramatic," Gregor scoffed, but he caught the grim look on Brimley's face.

"It...could cause a craze." Brimley tapped his temple. "It's a curse, if you dig down into it."

"Let's show someone!" Noal cried. "We'll tell the king!"

"You think the king will care about a single merchant selling his sweets?" Brimley sighed. "Besides, people aren't likely to run a candy man out of town, not when there's poison merchants and assassins slinking around back alleys."

"How is it even possible? Sugar is one of the purest vessels, there's no room to bind a spell in there," Gregor argued.

"Not any spell *you* know. We're not sorcerers or even wizards, we haven't the repertoire of spells many people can cast," Brimley said.

"We can tell your father," Gregor offered, looking at Noal. "He's a noble."

Noal didn't meet Gregor's eyes. Yes, he was the son of a nobleman, Lord of the Royal Copper Mint. He was a self-made man, an artist who was appointed the portrait master of the new copper coins. Eventually, he took over the running of the mint and now basked in the wealth and prestige it brought. In his heart, the lord was an artist, a portrait afficionado. His son, too, was the creative type, and was encouraged to find what made his soul sing rather than take over the family business.

But Noal worried he wasn't good enough.

He wasn't like Gregor, this stranger in a strange land working to make his parents back home proud. He wasn't Brimley, who dreamed of opening a soup kitchen so scrumptious that even the nobles would line up to be served alongside the poor. He wasn't like Ash, who truly, genuinely wanted to serve the kingdom perfect pastries. He wasn't even like Elis, that arrogant snob, also a nobleman's son who baked as an act of pure spiteful rebellion. No, Noal simply wanted to make his father proud by being the best at something. Anything. But he was definitely not the best chef in is class, and he certainly wasn't bursting to bake for the rest of his life. He liked pastries just fine, and was quite good at it now that he was about to graduate, but did it make his heart sing? In truth, it did not. If he was being perfectly honest, he stayed in the program because he wanted to finish what he started, and he loved the company of his friends.

To ask his father for a favor after what felt like a total failure was, well, unfathomable. But this was a chance to do something good, was it not?

"I think...we would need some more evidence," Noal stammered. "He doesn't understand spells. He works in metals and machinery. Magic is just an abstract thing to him."

In fact, this was the reason Noal and Gregor hit it off so well in the beginning. Noal had his collection of retired copper coins displayed on his shelf, each etched with a face from history his father had captured, and Gregor had admired the craftmanship. "Why, this could be copper from our mines!" he'd exclaimed, impressed by the quality.

"Well, he's not the lord of silver or gold," Noal fussed, but Gregor wouldn't hear of it.

"Exquisite! Your father does great work. You must be so proud."

And from that moment, Noal stopped being embarrassed, having been bullied his whole life by the children of other nobles for being the son of the man who coined the currency mostly used by peasants. He finally met a true friend.

"I'll get more evidence," Brimley promised.

They gathered their belongings and made their way down to the test kitchen, falling silent as they walked. They were expecting the announcement of the final exam, which was to take place the next day.

They had settled into their seats when the classroom door opened, and they all perked up to see Chef Toufie, not Eclin, lumber in.

"Where's Chef Eclin?" someone called.

"Is he alright?"

"What about our final?"

"Oh, gods, is he dead?"

Chef Toufie finished making his way over to the desk, onto which he dropped his belongings, including a sack of parchments to grade. He pinched the bridge of his nose with one hand and held the other up for silence. He had spent the better part of the weekend—*his* weekend!—tracking down Chef Eclin to where he'd fled. Then he wrangled his notes from him, met with the king, the princess, and had just finished lunch prep in the royal kitchen. During the long walk down the hall, he racked his brain for a way to announce the final without succumbing to the fallout of the reaction he was sure to get. Where was that good for nothing heralder?

He set his hands on the desk, took a breath, and decided to get it over with.

"For your final exam," he began, and the room immediately fell into a hush. He paused, suddenly enjoying this. It was the first moment of total, absolute silence he'd had since...well, definitely since last week.

Chef Toufie licked his lips. He took a sip from his massive mug. When a soft whimper from Noal broke the tension, he simply raised his eyebrows. A jab in the ribs hushed Noal. Toufie finally spoke.

"A chocolate cake."

Silence.

The apprentices looked at one another, growing more confused with every moment that passed without further instruction. Toufie took another sip in the sublime silence, and then, sure enough, it broke.

"How thick does the icing have to be?"

"Dark chocolate? Milk chocolate? Give us a cacao percentage!"

"Is Chef Eclin coming back? Or are you judging it?"

"Right! Who's judging? What do you know about desserts?"

Toufie took a seat at the great oak desk piled high with recipes, letters, scraps of parchment, warning notes Eclin never sent out, and took another big gulp from his mug. Then another. And another. Until he finally, for the first time all semester, drained it of its last drop. In fact, this phenomenon was so unexpected that when he tilted the earthenware mug to find nothing sloshing towards him, it startled him.

Embarrassed, he set the mug down and found that the class had finally gone quiet again. All blinked expectantly at him. No one even dared prod with a, "Well?"

"It seems Chef Eclin is taking a leave of absence effective immediately, indefinitely." He held up a hand as the rumble began, and it immediately quelled. "Instead, you'll have a surprise judge. And I wish you wouldn't ask who, because I won't tell, and you'll just annoy me. I've got half a mind to hand out these warning slips that are littering this desk. Lucky for you, these misdemeanors"—he picked up a few scraps and read them out loud— "*Opening the flour sack from the wrong end. Breaking egg yolk for the third time.* Noal, really? Three times? What, is the kingdom made of eggs? Anyhow, these pale in comparison to the stuff I've had to scrape, pick, scrub, and melt out of the walls and ceilings of my kitchen, so I'll let them pass—*if* you all solemnly swear to leave me be. I've got beef wellington to make for dinner and I might lose an eyebrow."

Chef Toufie stood up. "Your exam will be given tomorrow. Elis?"

"You'll give us the list of ingredients, won't you, sir?"

"Very clever. You're one more utterance away from a warning note." Chef Toufie gave a wave and the board behind him began to magically populate the time the exam was to take place.

Toufie might have been a novice at teaching confectionary students, but he and Chef Eclin had been colleagues for decades at this point. They had devised the final exam format together many years ago, roaring drunk off mead one fine night. He wasn't about to start breaking tradition now. Not even if Eclin was...well, not without Eclin.

6

Bit Weird

"What are we doing with all these?" Noal lamented, watching Gregor arrange the massive jars of cookies in the corner of their room.

"A closing sale, if you will," Gregor proposed. "We can sell out back behind Tracy's. We've already quit, what's the worst he can do?"

Noal eyed the jars. "Do you think they'll trust us enough to buy it?"

"I'll find out!" Ash announced, and before either could respond, he pranced out of the room.

Gregor watched him go then said to Noal, "Is he a bit of a...?"

"A bit of a what?"

"Oh, it doesn't matter."

"No, say it."

"A bit flamboyant is all."

Noal blinked, confused. "I suppose that's just how elves are."

"He's an elf?" Gregor let out a laugh. "Oh! I knew something was off about him."

"You didn't know he was an elf? All this time? Two years, Gregor!"

Gregor shrugged. "I've just never met another elf. I wonder...if that is a *him* thing, or if they're all like that."

"What does that even mean? Are all dwarves just like you?"

"What am I like? Tell me."

"S-strong," Noal stammered. When his friend rolled his eyes, Noal went pink with anger. "Gruff. You're like a boulder, like those damn hard cookies you once fed me! You never talk about home, and you never invited me to visit over the breaks."

Gregor's jaw dropped. "I've never invited you because I'm here all summer! I haven't seen my family in the last two years. Do you know I've been telling my Mum and Da that I've been digging a great royal moat this whole time? First, it's a moat around the palace. Next, the gators and the crocs got in a fit, so we're making a second ring to separate them. Then the latter moat extended around the whole of the kingdom, that's how outlandish my lie got so that I could stay here and apprentice with Tracy. I'm gruff because I'm exhausted, Noal. I miss my family."

A silence heavy as an anvil settled between them.

Then, "I wonder if your parents know about me or not. Are you allowed to be friends with humans?"

Gregor took a seat on the bag of sugar they had forgotten was hidden under the pile of Noal's not-quite-dirty clothes and dragged his hands down his face, cupped his chin, and peered at his very best friend. "You are my very best friend in the entire kingdom. In the entire world, even, Noal. I would never be shy to tell anyone that, that you are my brother, my kin. But I have had the weight of this secret on my heart so long that I have clammed up even against you it seems. I felt like I've had to hold the secret in against the world."

Noal stood, hands clasped, growing deeply ashamed with every word his friend spoke. While his father took him on trips around the kingdoms during holidays, to lounge on cinnamon shore beaches and explore exotic lands with houses in trees, his friend had been toiling away instead of taking rest.

"I'm sorry," Noal stammered. "I-I know you don't like Ash, and I just don't know why. It upsets me more than it should, but I know it doesn't matter. You don't need to be friends."

Gregor let out a tremendous sigh. "Noal, it doesn't mean we're enemies or anything. We just don't have anything in common."

"You have me in common. And I have lots of things in common with both of you. If you spent any time together, you'd realize just how alike you are."

"There's just..." Gregor's voice trailed off. There was just something about Ash that made Gregor uncomfortable. "Ash is just happy all the time. Infuriatingly happy. He's so giggly, so...sunshine, when I'm the depths of the earth. Does that make sense?"

Noal was human; he walked upon the earth dwarves tunneled and lived under the trees the elves called home. He was the bridge between worlds. That was why he could relate to both, but it seemed to Gregor those two worlds could not relate to each other.

The door burst open. Ash paused in the doorway, panting, wheezing for breath. "They...they're..." He paused, gulped a breath, and tried again. "They're waiting out behind Lorde."

"Tracy will love that," Gregor said, rolling his eyes.

"He's closed for the day," Ash reminded him, and offered to help carry the jars of cookies.

It was the first time Gregor and Noal met their customers, and it was nice to recognize familiar faces. There were acquaintances made at the pub they were regulars at. Others were fellow palace employees they routinely saw in the royal dining hall. Some were even Tracy's regulars, and they paid their coins and took their sugar-laden treats with secretive winks.

When Elis stepped around the corner, dressed in a fine goldthread embroidered tunic, Gregor, Noal, and Ash bristled. While they trained with Elis all day, they hardly saw him outside of kitchen hours. He spent his free time with the athletes, training in fencing, sword fighting, wrestling, his evenings at the pubs around town and under the windows of the girls' dorms, serenading and playing the charming bard. Elis lived in his family's apartment in the palace while the other apprentices lived in the humble dorms. Elis's gorgeous green eyes went wide. "You three?"

Gregor rolled his eyes. "Honestly Elis, who else? You think the royal staff are baking those cookies? They audit ingredients just about every hour!"

Elis chuckled in earnest. He clasped Noal on the shoulder, who nearly crumpled from the force. "Had I known, we might have been friends sooner. I like a clever operation."

"No one would have invited you, Elis," Gregor muttered.

Elis clutched his chest, feigning hurt. "Come now, Gregor. We've been neck-to-neck as heads of the class for months now. Think of the team we could have made! Instead, you went with..." He looked at Noal and gave a little sneer. "He can't even carry the sacks!"

"What are you even doing here? Headed to the pub?" Noal snapped.

"Actually, I'll take some if you've any left," Elis said, eyeing what remained at the bottom of the jars. "I'm honestly surprised. I suspected this little operation was run by one of us, but I fully expected it to be that genius Brimley."

"And *that* is why we're not friends," Gregor said, shoving the last of the cookies at Elis. "Now cough it up."

Elis ran a hand through his thick, luscious blond hair, smiling in a taunting way. He pulled out his purse and plucked out a coin.

"No, no. It's three times that."

"For *cookies*?"

"For *you*." Plucking the other two coins out himself, Gregor gave Elis one of his own claps on the back. Elis stumbled forward, nearly dropping the box. He caught his balance, looked back, red in the face, and forced a smile. "Only for my favorite cookie dwarf!"

"You're the worst!" Ash screamed and chased a laughing Elis down the road.

A twinge of respect bloomed inside Gregor. Perhaps Ash wasn't so bad after all.

Back in their dorm, satisfied that their chocolate cake recipes were perfect—and just the perfect amount of different—Gregor and Noal laid down to sleep. Noal claimed the forgotten sack of sugar while Gregor slept on the two small sacks they had used as pillows. Gregor was too long for his makeshift bed, and Noal's sack was too full, so that his back bowed, sleeping on a hill. It was a terrible night not to get sleep. "I wonder who the judge will be," Noal mused, moments before a full-body wracking yawn overtook him. He turned over, but he didn't have the night vision Gregor had.

"It doesn't matter," Gregor said, shoving his leather gauntlets under his legs, trying to elevate them. "Whoever it is, they'll love our recipes."

"I hope so." Noal rolled back onto his back. "Hey, Gregor?"

"Mhmm?"

"You're my best friend, you know that?"

"I know now," Gregor said. "You're mine, too. You'll come visit the mountain, won't you?"

"Of course I will." Noal smiled into the darkness, feeling at peace.

Gregor wiped at the moisture rolling from his eyes, gave a gruff little cough, and rolled onto his side, snoring happily moments later.

7

The Final

On each prep table was a pile of tools and ingredients: a mountain of sugar, a stack of chocolate nearly as tall as Gregor, blocks of butter, bowls of eggs, heaps of salt and other miscellaneous ingredients, whisks, bowls, pans, measuring tools. These were all hidden under a white sheet, to be revealed when the instructor announced, *"Go."*

The students stood at attention at their tables; Gregor was at the front, on a stool due to his height, beside him Noal, and Ash beside him. Behind them were Brimley and Elis. Behind them stood the great oven, where Fergis paced, excited for what treats he would get that day. Above them, like chandeliers, hung pots, pans, and long, metal utensils from hooks. They all faced the massive oak desk, behind which was the magical green chalkboard, winged by floor-to-ceiling bookshelves stocked full of cookbooks, most of them authored by Chef Eclin.

An invisible piece of chalk wrote along with Professor Toufie as he spoke. Gregor and Noal had often tried to coax the chalkboard to write when they were in the kitchen late at night, to no avail.

You will have two hours to complete your cake, the board read. *Then, the judge will appear. You may not speak to one another. Doing so will result in an immediate fail. Any attempt at communicating with one another will be deemed plagiarism.*

Here, the words stopped etching even as Toufie kept speaking. "Now I'll come by to do the honesty check. Then you may don your coats."

How did the chalkboard know when to write and when not to? It fascinated Gregor, who was not well versed in magic. Sure, he'd picked up a few charms here and there from the streets. Magic was like learning a new language; the books were all there, the spells just had to be practiced. Gregor knew a few spells to coax herbs back from depressed, wilted states only to be cut and trimmed shortly after. But he wasn't like Ash, who, at a look, made the basil and the rosemary in pots by the window spring back to life, who whispered to the mail pigeons and commanded them with ease, and who could call ingredients to himself with a simple flick of the wrist. It now seemed obvious to Gregor that Ash was an elf and not just a wizard. He wondered if that was why elves were so skinny, all that energy burned to cast magic.

Chef Toufie went down the line, instructing each student to roll up their sleeves, and checked for notes, nicks, any form of cheating. Memory, Chef Eclin always emphasized, was a chef's best tool. If something runs out, flip through your memory for alternative recipes, find replacement ingredients, and improvise on the spot. When sugar is rising in temperature is not the time to go scrambling through a cookbook. As Gregor remembered this lecture, he reached his arms out for inspection, and the strangest sensation came over him. Suspicion took over that an unexpected twist would be thrown in during the test. He looked over at Noal obliviously rolling down his shirt, smoothing it down to his wrists. It was too late to warn him. Even if he could tell his friend that he was about to be surprised, what good would it do?

Gregor didn't say a word as he removed his coat from its hook, put his arms through, and carefully buttoned it up. It was an old, permanently stained coat, the only one he owned. Elis's was impeccably white, obviously new and bought for this specific occasion. "There's no extra points for being pretty," Gregor had muttered at last year's final, causing him to nearly be disqualified. The unease grew in Gregor's belly as everyone returned to their stations dressed and ready.

Chef Toufie cleared his throat, and all eyes swiveled to attention.

"To pass this class and earn the title of Royal Pastry Chef to the Kingdom of Everdorne, Keeper of Recipes and Nourisher of Her Subjects, you will need to prove your skills in this kitchen. Not just as a competent follower of recipes, which is why you created your recipe for this final, but as an adaptable, original chef. It is imperative that you work not just under pressure, but with improvisation. Please, reveal your ingredients."

Noal lifted one corner, Gregor the other, and they pulled. As Gregor balled the sheet in his hands, eyes scanning the ingredients, his stomach dropped. He was trained to survey his station quickly, assess within moments. And this station was missing one key ingredient: flour.

"That is why you will now have to make a *flourless* chocolate cake. Your time has started...now. *Go!*"

Noal and Gregor gawked at each other, each reading the panic clear on the other's face. They turned, met the others' looks, saw their reactions reflected in them.

Chef Toufie cleared his throat. "Your time is ticking." The giant hourglass that materialized on the giant desk confirmed this, the sand grains already slipping into the chamber below.

That got them scrambling. Gregor wanted to mutter curses under his breath but didn't dare. He knew Chef Eclin had impeccable hearing, and he didn't doubt Chef Toufic did, too.

While Gregor jumped into action, throwing together ingredients, Noal hunched over a piece of parchment, scribbling a new recipe. The cake would need more structure without the flour, and the sugar and eggs would need to be adjusted accordingly.

In his panic, Gregor had cracked nearly a dozen eggs. The motion calmed him. He was now thinking clearly, soothed by the rhythmic crack, plop, toss.

Flour is structure, Gregor reminded himself. *When mixed with water, the proteins in flour interact with each other to create gluten, the framework of the cake. Without flour, the batter will have a higher liquid content, causing it to spread more during baking.*

Chocolate needs to be shaved.

Eggs need to be separated.

Wet and dry ingredients incorporated.

It will be okay, Gregor told himself. This was a pivot, a side-step from his original recipe. He began to rearrange the ingredients before him, taking inventory. He wondered if Noal would adjust the recipe they had created together the night before in the same way. If Ash would, too. They weren't competing against each other, after all; they were all just trying to pass. There wasn't a limit, as far as he knew, to how many would graduate the apprenticeship and receive the prestigious title. They could all pass with flying colors. Or they could all fail, if this stupid cake dipped in the center, wouldn't cook, or hardened like a rock.

That was the thing with baking; it was mixing ingredients in a dish, putting them into the fire, and praying it would come out alright. Hoping the ratios had been calculated correctly, that the flames would comply, because there was no checking in on it every few minutes. When it was time to take it out of the oven, it was either perfect or it was ruined.

Back and forth, bowls of eggs, blocks of chocolate. Arms reaching over, around, running back to the oven as they raced to complete the task. Someone poked Fergis, who belched a column of fire into the oven. There was time for do-overs. Well, at least one do-over, Gregor realized as he pulled his cake out of the oven and watched the center immediately sink. As Noal pulled his own cake out—having trusted Gregor with the timing—they exchanged horrified glances. They left the pans for Fergis to slurp clean and raced back to their table to try again. Ash grabbed the dragon by the scruff of his neck and dumped him back by the oven, coaxing him to adjust the flames.

Another round of cakes went into the oven, followed by another round of anxious waiting. Gregor watched his own small hourglass, which he used as an oven timer, like a hawk. He didn't dare move or take his eyes off the grains of sand slipping through, and as soon as the last grain fell, he flipped it, made a mark on his parchment. Noal did the same beside him, nearly in unison. When the hourglass expired for the last time, Gregor made for the oven but stopped, catching a look on Ash's face. Gregor stomped on Noal's foot under the table to stop him, gave a fraction of a head shake.

They began to clean up.

Gregor kept watch on Ash from the corner of his eye. When Ash finally made for the oven, so did they, trailing after as inconspicuously as they could. Everyone else did, too, realizing that Fergis would alert Ash when the cakes were ready. Fergis was now scratching at the warm bricks like an excited cat, despite his tummy protruding from slurping up all the failed chocolate slurries.

Sure enough, one perfectly solid flourless chocolate cake came out, then another, then another, until five perfect round loaves were displayed on the tables. They were then iced with frosting or glazed with icing or piped with ganache or powdered with sugar and decorated with flowers or berries or mint.

"Five...four...three...two...one, and...*time*."

The magical hourglass at the front of the class vanished as soon as the final grain of sand slipped through its waist. Chef Toufie gave a flick of the wrist and the flame in the oven extinguished. He scooped Fergis, who had begun to prowl around the room, eyes lingering on the cakes, into his arms and held him firmly against his massive belly. Fergis squirmed until Chef Toufie whispered in his ear. The dragon gave up and climbed onto the chef's shoulder, perched there like a pirate's parrot.

"Please dispose of your coats in the laundry basket. The judge will appear momentarily."

As the students complied, their confidence began to waver. Now came the worst part, the judgment. But by whom?

There was a knock at the door. Toufie lumbered over, opened it a crack, and exchanged whispers. Then he turned back to the class, smiled, and pushed the door open.

Everyone gasped as the mystery judge was revealed.

8

Surprise Judge

"Class, I'd like to introduce to you His Royal Majesty King Varundil. He will be judging your final today."

Everyone watched as the king marched into the room, practically bouncing with every step, and stopped, smiling, in front of that massive desk. He had forgone the fancy garbs, wearing instead a simple tunic, albeit gold-threaded, with well-tailored trousers and impeccable leather shoes. His thinning hair was oiled, and the strong fragrance hit even Brimley all the way in the back. He broke his stance just for a moment to wipe at the tears overwhelming his eyes.

To break the silence—it seemed the collective gasp had drawn every particle of sound out of the air with it—Chef Toufie began clapping. Nervously, everyone joined in until the king was also clapping along, unsure if this was customary. Everyone stopped clapping when he stopped clapping, and he didn't stop clapping until Chef Toufie finally stopped clapping.

"It's such a pleasure—*an honor*—to do this," King Varundil said. He smiled reassuringly, but it was hard to see it under his bushy, grizzled mustache. It was carefully brushed and waxed every morning before breakfast, but somehow always seemed to get a little tousled by afternoon tea. He hoped to put everyone at ease. He knew Mosley, his right-hand man and now wedding planner, really wanted a performance out of this, and he was nervous even though he wasn't the one being judged.

"Chef?" came a squeak. Noal's hand shook as he held it up, asking both forgiveness and permission. "Has a royal always judged the final exam?"

"I'm the first," the king answered. "After all, I'm still looking for someone to bake my daughter's wedding cake."

Had anyone else said this, the usual outcry of questions would have followed. Fearing this, Chef Toufie spoke quickly. "We have decided to allow each of you to compete in the baking competition if you pass your final."

Elis raised his hand and had the rare decency of waiting to be called on before he asked, "What baking competition?"

King Varundil clasped his hands with excitement. "Oh, can I answer?" he asked Chef Toufie, but didn't wait for permission. He was king, after all. "You'll be competing to bake the royal wedding cake."

"Us five?" Brimley piped up.

"And a few others from around the kingdom," Chef Toufie answered. "Pass this round and you'll all be officially entered if you're up for it. Win the Royal Bake Off, and you will be the official royal wedding cake baker."

"Will the kitchen staff be competing?" Elis asked, who hated not being prepared for anything.

"No, they'll be busy making the wedding feast. Besides...they're a bit of a drunken, unimaginative lot."

"They didn't pass this round," King Varundil supplied, eyes twinkling.

"You're not really selling the job," Elis muttered.

"We're still ironing out the details," Chef Toufie said. "Let's get through this round first, shall we?" He motioned the king to Gregor's cake.

A mix of emotions ran through Gregor. He had just mailed the letter to his parents announcing his long-awaited homecoming. He couldn't claim a new moat project now! An expansion atop an expansion? It was getting rather silly at this point. The kingdom didn't have enough enemies to justify such fortification, and the cost to taxpayers! Why, Gregor still wasn't sure if the dwarves were royal subjects or not, but if they were, he highly doubted they would support the cost of an even greater moat. They just might march down and picket the palace, which is what he would do. But the thought of becoming the chef that *baked the royal wedding cake*...why, he would never be out of a job. A purple seal was guaranteed after accomplishing such a feat!

Elis, on the other hand, decided this was fate intervening. *This was his destiny.* His exact moment of birth had been because he was *destined* to be in this room, at this moment, aligning with the first royal wedding in thirty years. It wasn't so much that his family would be proud if he won—rather, they would be so disappointed if he didn't. That was Elis's driving force.

For Noal, this could be the proof his father was constantly waiting for. Proof that his son had, in fact, chosen the right profession and did, in fact, carry an ounce of his artistic genes.

Brimley was consumed with thoughts of recognition. Winning this meant patrons, money for the charity work he'd always dreamed of doing. Serving desserts to everyone and anyone, no matter their class or race.

Ash, well, Ash was just busy trying desperately to avoid the king's gaze. Seeing as how he would walk down the row, one by one, to inspect, critique, and judge not just the cake but the chef, he didn't see how he was going to avoid his gaze for long.

King Varundil raised a dainty silver fork, and a hush fell over the room. They watched him dig the prongs directly into the center of Gregor's cake, testing it, and pull out a heaping scoop. It was a velvety chocolate mousse cake, topped with slivers of almonds arranged like flowers and a generous dusting of powdered sugar. The sugar on top was a direct homage to the first dessert Gregor ever tasted, when he believed powdered sugar was the most magical substance on Earth. He still thought that and believed it to compliment the light, fluffy chocolate below. King Varundil brought the bite towards his lips, which opened, opened...the king inhaled, drawing a cloud of sugar into the back of his throat. Overcome by a vicious coughing fit, he dropped the fork, the piece of cake with it. Gasps rang around the room, which Chef Toufie was getting rather sick of hearing.

Immediately, Ash leapt around the table and presented a handkerchief to the king.

Everyone stared.

Sensing eyes on him, Ash hurried back to his station just as the king was collecting his wits. Tears in his eyes, he held up a hand when everyone began applauding. "Yes, yes, I'm alright." He shooed Chef Toufie away, who had finally managed to lumber over to him. "Now then." He picked up a fresh fork, consciously exhaled, and *then* put the bite in his mouth. He let out a chuckle. "Worth it."

Gregor just about collapsed. He watched the king scratch a note in a little notebook.

King Varundil made his way down the line. He didn't seem to dislike Noal's, who had decorated his with a fresh berry glaze, though the king did remove the sprig of mint before he took his bite.

Ash's cake had fresh orange zest mixed with the dark chocolate loaf, bright yellow icing piped around the edge. The citrus cut the denseness of the chocolate with its bright citric burst.

At Brimley's caramel-drizzled triple chocolate cake, the king clapped the baker on the shoulder with delight, and everyone rolled their eyes. King Varundil scooped a second bite of the chocolate-shaving covered slice in his mouth before moving on to the final cake.

Elis offered to pull the bite of his banana buttercream chocolate cake himself and presented the king with his fork as if he were a victor with a sword. Cue more eye rolls.

King Varundil swallowed the last bite. "Thank you, everyone. This has been a treat." He began clapping. Everyone joined in until Brimley, the bravest, said, "When will we learn our marks?"

Chef Toufie, who was looking over the king's notes, said without looking up, "The good news is you've all passed." He paused here to allow time for the shouts and whoops and backslapping that ensued. "And it seems you're all invited to compete in the Royal Bake Off."

King Varundil grinned. "Congratulations, you've all proven yourselves worthy. I have no doubt you will all put up a fierce fight to win my daughter's favor." He looked to Chef Toufie to make his closing remarks.

"While I'm not surprised you've all passed, I will not force anyone against their will to compete. You are free to withdraw. Anyone?" When no one raised their hand, he nodded. "Very well. You'll hear of the next steps shortly. Meanwhile, my sincerest congratulations. Welcome to the royal kitchen."

Five white chef's hats flew into the air as the new royal chefs hugged one another, ecstatic.

9

Sugar Fiend

It took all of their self-restraint not to whoop and holler the whole way back to their dorm rooms.

When Noal pushed the door open, he stopped dead in his tracks.

Sugar was strewn all over the floor. Gregor pushed his way past Noal, who stood frozen in shock, and made his way over to the smaller bag of sugar. It had been torn open and was still…wiggling around?

Gregor grabbed a poker from the fireplace. He crept up to the bag, noticing the footprints in the powder as he did. A dragon.

"Stab it," Noal hissed.

"Then do what with it? Skewer it, broil it for dinner? I'm going to chase it back up the chimney it came from."

"Drats, did we leave that open?" Noal skirted around the room to their fireplace and checked. Sure enough, the vent was open, either pried or forgotten. The last spring chill had long left, but a few brisk dawns had them tending a low fire some mornings. "Well, it's time to close it for sure."

"Not yet, I'll tell you when," Gregor instructed. He edged around the spray of sugar, and when he was sure the path to the chimney was clear, began beating the wriggling bag.

A dragon the size of a well-fed alley cat scooted bum-first out of the tear it had made, immensely rotund from having gorged itself. He was muck brown, not like the vibrant colored pets kept around the royal palace. He hissed at Gregor and wheezed, trying to run, dragging its distended belly. Gregor set his hands on his hips, watching the thing struggle to escape.

"Na-ah, up the way you came," Noal chided as it made for the door. "Last thing we need is a little snitch giving away our secret."

"And tell your friends the next one's getting poked and strung up, so don't come back for more," Gregor added, and began tapping the floor behind it with the poker to hurry it up.

It did its best, it really did, but the tresspassing dragon wasn't in any shape to go at top speed. He waddled to the chimney and wriggled his way up, leaving a spray of soot as he scrambled up the flue.

Noal pressed his ear against the brick and waited until the scratching stopped before he flipped the vent shut. "There. Nothing like the first vermin of the summer."

Gregor reached for the broom and dustpan and made quick work of sweeping the place clean. "Out in the country, they can get as big as palaces."

Noal snorted. "You're exaggerating."

In the city they never got bigger than a horse, though most were small as cats and were as bad as mice, colonizing any hole and hollow they could find, camping in attics and barns when they could. Long discarded pets that bred and bred.

"No, I'm not," Gregor insisted. "They have their own territories, like panthers. Only crossing into another's to mate. My mountain, Superstitious Mountain, is in a cursed zone. Every year a dragon comes to lay her egg at the top. It started many generations ago, with the Mother Dragon, who laid her egg on the mountain right as us dwarves settled in. A brave dwarf grabbed it and journeyed with it to the other side of the continent. Mother Dragon followed him the whole way, scared if she attacked it would hurt her baby. The dwarf left the egg on a sandy beach, where it was reunited with its mother, and the dwarf returned a hero. They thought that was the end of it, but then *that* dragon hatched and flew back to the mountain to lay *its* egg. This time it flew ahead and waited at the place it had met its mother, and sure enough a dwarf arrived, carrying the egg, just in time for it to hatch. And so that baby returned, and so on and so forth down the line until it became an instinct bred into the offspring, and every generation the egg is laid in the sacred hatching spot. Each time, we hold what's called 'The Luck of the Draw,' where a dwarf is selected to make the journey to reunite the egg with its mother."

"Why don't you just boil the egg and be done with it?"

"You mean kill the dragon?"

"Why, sure. Then there won't be another dragon coming back to your home."

"If we kill her baby, she'll just lay another one. And probably smoke up the mountain and get rid of us in turn."

"It's not bothered by you moving its baby?"

"It's since turned into a symbiotic relationship. Mother lays egg and flies off, egg gets taken from the mountain through Citeel down to the cinnamon shores where its mother waits, and we get to live in peace for a few decades until baby has her own baby."

"Ah, the call to a quest," Noal said.

"What does that mean?"

"Many species require the completion of a migration or a great task each generation. Kelpies, for instance. They hatch in lochs. Once they hit puberty, they make their way to the ocean to find a partner. Once mated, they return to the lochs to give birth and raise their young. It's why we know to stay away from lochs; kelpies are very protective of their young and can get aggressive. Say, what happens to the dwarf that returns after they've gotten rid of the egg?"

"They become King of the Mountain," Gregor said. "The last one was my father."

Noal's eyes went wide. "You're a prince? Why didn't you tell me before?"

"Not really," Gregor hurried to explain. "There's no lineage like with human kings. Every dwarf child is raised as if they could someday contend for the Luck of the Draw, and so anyone can claim the title of king. The council chooses who it will be when the time comes, and if I were home, I'm sure my name would be thrust in the ring as well. Obviously, I don't want that. I'm a chef, not a hero."

"When was the last Luck of the Draw?" Noal asked.

The knot that had been sitting in Gregor's stomach for the last two years now doubled in size. "Nearly thirty years ago," he confessed. "A new egg is due any year now."

Gregor finished sweeping up the dragon's mess. Then he changed, stripping off the undershirt he'd completely sweated through and pulling on a crisp green dressing shirt that brought out the green of his eyes. He oiled and combed his beard, which he paused to admire in the mirror. It had grown long these years, and he took great pride in it. He routinely trimmed it with careful precision, as if faceting a gem, and braided it elegantly, twisting tiny silver and gold beads into it here and there. Many dwarves did this, though most had enough metal and precious stones embedded in their beard and hair that it resembled a helmet, protecting them from falling debris down in the mines. It would be too hot and heavy to do so himself, but Gregor liked the tradition, and so kept these bits of his heritage. He wrapped fresh leather strips about his calves, his forearms. His chainmail he'd rusted useless, but the leather of his original outfit he'd repurposed. It was soft, rich, and reserved for special occasions such as this.

When he turned, he saw Noal had also dressed in his very best finery. They smiled at one another in approval. "Ready?"

"What are we going to do with the sugar?"

"Throw it out, obviously," Gregor said, looking disgusted.

"*Obviously*. I'm talking about the other sack. Do you think Darce will take it?"

"What's a pub owner going to do with a bag of sugar?"

Noal threw up his hands. "Maybe we'll get a pint or something out of it, I don't know. It's worth a try."

Gregor let out an exasperated sigh and made to pick up the sack but stopped. He retrieved the tin of salt he kept on his dresser and sprinkled a ring around the fireplace, just for good measure, should anything decide to find their way back down the chimney. Salt didn't keep out spirits, but it sure did keep out sugar-obsessed dragons. "Let's go," he said, and tossed the sack of sugar onto his shoulder.

10

Badger & Bard

Badger & Bard was one of many watering holes in the kingdom and the favorite of students and palace staff. For one, there was no cover charge, unlike the other pubs that hired entertainment. This was because Badger & Bard's entertainment was a constant rotation of thespian students, singers of the Royal Choir, and traveling musicians. They showed up early, signed up on the parchment, guzzled their free pint, and put down their hats as they took the stage to put on the show they dared not share in the light of day.

It was also where the apprentice mead makers sold their experimental batches, served out of the wonky practice mugs fired by beginner ceramicists. It was a place mentors and mentees could mingle and the former didn't have to worry about being harassed concerning grades. The beer was cheap and terrible, the entertainment familiar, and it was the place every palace guard told visiting pretty girls to go to. Elis was also one of their top recruiters, with his thick blonde hair and fine, expensive clothes.

Gregor and Noal knocked on the delivery door with their sack of sugar and quickly began arguing with the manager.

"For a few pints of ale!" Gregor insisted. "It's good! It's Tracy's. You know us, Darce, we've been coming here since before we knew the difference between a scone and a biscuit."

Darce, the general manager, was in over his head tonight. Elis had rounded up an especially loud bunch of gals, and with this wedding looming, a lot of strange faces had pushed their way through the doors that evening. Many of them were strangers who had tasted far better beer in their lives and were causing a fuss. "They don't understand the culture," Darce spat, and had already kicked a group out rather than refund them. That only made room for the next crowd outside the door to shove their way past the orc bouncer, who was also nearly at his wit's end.

"Look, Gregor." Darce ran a hand down his face, exhausted. "I'll give you a quart of ale, and that's the best I can do."

"You're a gentleman and a scholar!" Noal shouted and did his best to help Gregor heave the sugar sack onto a shelf. They'd just been robbed blind, but it was better than nothing. They carried their mugs and the pitcher to the table where Brimley, Ash, and occasionally Elis were, when he wasn't making his rounds about the tables, clapping everyone on the back, acting like he owned the place.

"But he does," Brimley pointed out. "His father does, at least. A share of it. Another share is owned by the king's right hand, that Mosley fellow."

"You've got to be joking," Gregor moaned. "Why doesn't Elis just marry the princess and be done with it? The kingdom's richest, most charismatic, most infuriating man, ladies and gentlemen!"

"Here, here!" Noal raised his mug, and they all joined in. As infuriating as Elis was, as egotistical and narcissistic as he could be, he was *one of them*. They had watched him blossom from the shaggy, nervous lad to the strapping lord he was now. He made being a chef *sexy*, and for that they were grateful. They owed him something for that, even if it was just a seat at the table in any pub they happened to find him at. Currently it was his turn on the mandolin, and most of the room was swept up in the chorus.

Badger & Bard had three levels, four if the rooftop was counted. The pub was dug into the side of a hill, the inside cavernous and spacious, which was why Gregor especially liked it. It smelled of earth and sweat and yeast. Inside, it was illuminated by torches, their flames sustained by Fraun, Fergis the dragon's older brother. Booths of once-fine leather, now an unknown color from all the spills they absorbed, were placed around the perimeter of the room. In the back was the bar, long and glossy, from behind which Darce ruled, he and his other bartenders pouring from seemingly endless barrels, commanding the brightly colored levers. The stools at the bar faced an enchanted mirror that made the seer appear far more attractive than they actually were. Ash picked up on this immediately, and it was only after they bullied him into casting a detect magic spell that Noal and Gregor begrudgingly admitted to it.

In the center of the cavern was the raised stage, where there was a performance of some sort every night: dancers, jugglers, bards, poets, the whole lot. Everyone wanted to be noticed, and although sometimes the performances fell flat, for the most part they were grand. And if they weren't, well, Darce would grab them by the collar, show them to a seat in the shadows, offer a pint and a kind word, and politely ask them to never grace his stage again.

The second and third floors were balconies scattered with tiny tables paired with two chairs each overlooking the first floor. It was hard to get a seat on these levels, which were coveted once claimed, as they were excellent places from which to watch the show. An iron spiral staircase in each corner of the pub—corners was a loose term, as the room was mostly round—accessed the upper floors, and eventually the rooftop, which was the grassy top of the hill. Here, couples nuzzled each other under the performance of the stars and the view of the palace lit up at night, the shadows of the stardust sweepers dancing over the roof. It was quiet, as a rule; no loud voices here, and it was Fraun's job to ensure this. He slept up there, along with anyone else who had too much to drink that night, and he was the one who rounded up the stragglers in the morning and made them pay for lodging by cleaning up trash, mopping the floors, and shining the glasses behind the bar. A cheap price to pay for what was always considered by everyone a wonderful time.

At this point a lutist joined Elis, then a lyrist, and the three of them kicked up a ruckus with the drinking song, "Ey-oh the Stinking Hag." Mugs pounded tables, sloshing drink over their lips, heels stomped, and voices shouted.

When the final note rang out and everyone erupted in applause, Elis returned the mandolin to its owner, took the mug that Darce offered him, and fell heavily into the seat waiting for him at his friends' table. His hair was shiny and slicked back with sweat, and the top few buttons of his silk shirt were undone. He was panting but grinning broadly. "Any requests, lads?"

A harpist took to the stage and plucked a ballad from the strings, giving everyone a chance to calm down, catch their breaths, and refill their drinks before they demanded another familiar tune.

"I suppose you're staying to compete?" Brimley asked Elis.

"Of course! Who amongst us is giving up this chance at glory?" When no one volunteered, Elis raised his mug in a "told you so" and took a long drink. "Besides, this is the fastest way to get a royal seal."

Gregor frowned. "What do you mean?"

"Win the contest and you'll get one," Elis said.

Everyone sucked in a gasp.

"You don't know that," Noal hissed. "We get to design the royal wedding cake, that's all."

Elis shrugged. "Sure. Believe what you want to believe."

The waitress arrived with a massive tray on her shoulder, from which she began expertly unloading the plates of dinner they'd ordered while they cheered her on. She rolled her eyes, pocketed the coins, and scoffed at Noal when he asked her to bring another round. "On a night like this? You're lucky I remembered to bring your supper."

Noal gawked at her retreating back. She peeked over her shoulder and winked, causing Noal to blush and Brimley to thump him so hard on the back he nearly fell out of his chair. "You'll get her someday," Brimley teased.

"I don't...I mean she's just...she just works here!"

"Turning up your nose at the working class?" Ash accused.

Noal couldn't manage a word he was so flustered, and was thankful when Gregor said, "Shut up and eat."

They dug into their food, the table going silent as they gobbled down the bites. While Gregor and Noal worked part time at Lorde of Loaves, many of the culinary apprentices worked here. They might not have perfected hollandaise sauce, but they knew how to grill sausage and bake perfectly crisp seasoned potatoes.

To Noal's horror, the waitress came back, this time with a tray of cake, which she began doling out onto their table before they could protest.

Gregor was the first to gulp down his mouthful of potatoes. "We didn't order these."

"Yes, well, we need to get rid of it. We have twelve cakes sitting back there going stale. Eat up!"

"How funny that we're getting served chocolate cake," Noal said, and took a bite. "Ooh, it's good!"

"Is this...*flourless* chocolate cake?" Brimley asked, giving the slab a sniff and a poke. One bite confirmed it. "Wait, are these our cakes?"

"No." Elis rolled his eyes. He jabbed a finger over his shoulder without looking up. "They made the cakes."

They all looked at where Elis pointed and spotted three former royal apprentices huddled around a table: Harlowe Langston, Gale Wynd, and Lance Lorence.

Harlowe was a wizard. Ten years ago, he pivoted professions and attended the royal pastry apprenticeship with the goal of helping his cousin's struggling confectionery after graduation. Lance came from a chocolatier family and graduated a few years after Harlowe. He too worked at Harlowe's cousin's candy shop, now much improved. Gale graduated the same year as Lance and worked in his own family's bakery.

"What are they doing here?" Noal asked, recognizing them.

"They're our new rivals," Elis said nonchalantly. "Right before our final, there was an open-call baking competition right here in this pub. The winners are going to compete against us to make the princess's wedding cake. Those are the three who passed."

"You knew about this?" Ash asked, incredulous.

"Of course I did. Found out after our own exam finished. Haven't you got a mirror?" Elis raised his palm to reveal a small device clutched in his hand.

"A what?" Gregor snatched it out of Elis's hand. It was, in fact, a mirror. But it wasn't. It was enchanted, like the mirror behind the bar, but Gregor definitely wasn't looking at a handsomer version of himself. "What am I looking at?"

"You're looking at the past, my friend," Elis said, grinning over his shoulder.

Sure enough, Gregor watched the replay of the *other* baking competition. The stage of Badger & Bard was set up with prep tables, buzzing with a dozen bakers that fluttered about, measuring and mixing and tossing their hopes and dreams into the great oven meant for scorching meat pies. It belched out flourless chocolate cakes of varying success. Gregor caught occasional glimpses of Fraun prowling around the base of the oven, the same excitement in his eyes Fergis had during their final as he awaited to dispose of the failed cakes.

"I figure we'll be introduced as competitors tomorrow at the coat ceremony," Elis interrupted, prying his mirror back.

"Elis, you already know them," Gregor said incredulously. Though the city was big and busy, the baking community was a small one. Shops were always willing to lend sugar or exchange eggs for chocolate with one another if a shipment was late or if something spoiled right before an order was due. And the bakers all knew who the latest crop of apprentices were and hired many of them to work in their shops in the summers or after they graduated their apprenticeship.

"I know, I'm not an idiot. What do you want me to do, go fraternize with the enemy?"

"Hardly enemies," Brimley chided. "Let's not let this turn into something nasty."

"There can only be one—"

Elis was interrupted by Noal's chair scraping against the floor. They watched Noal weave through the crowd, unsure if it was the stickiness of the floors or his drunkenness that made him sway. Fearing the latter, Gregor pushed off his seat and pursued his friend, who had forced his way over to the table they had just been staring at. Gregor pulled up to the high top and looked around to find not only Harlowe, Gale, and Lance, but three *girls* blinking down at him from the table. He blushed harder than he probably ever had in his life, and muttered a flustered, "Uh, hallo."

"We *are* competing," Harlowe was assuring Noal. Harlowe had a flowing beard and luscious brown hair he kept in a braid that went down just below his shoulders. He wore a light blue summer cloak, and his twisted oak staff was propped against the wall behind him. Noal blinked at Harlowe incredulously before throwing his arm around Harlowe's neck and pulling him into a choking hug. Harlowe grimaced and awkwardly patted Noal on the back until Noal unlocked himself.

"Doesn't seem fair," Gregor said, trying to ignore the girls. "You're no longer working in the palace, and this is for the *royal* wedding."

At this, everyone else seemed to finally notice him.

"And you cheated your way in," Gale shouted from across the table, which wasn't long enough to be shouted across.

Gregor cringed. Gale, a halfling, made him uncomfortable. His skin freckled as easily as Gregor's, his eyes were dark brown, and his short hair spiked every which way, as if it had never met a comb it liked. Gregor always thought they ought to be friends, seeing as how they were nearly the same in stature, but Gale was as arrogant as Elis. While Gregor was strong in the way an ox was, heaps of muscle under it all, Gale was strong in the Elis way, all muscles and lines, but for show; Gregor doubted he would survive a frying pan to the abdomen. True strength lay in the core, the glutes, not in the arms and calves. Still, because Gale thought himself pretty, he thought himself better. While he was cordial with Gregor, he never took up an offer for a drink, and Gregor had long ago stopped asking.

"Feeling worried we'll beat you all, since you're still novices?" Lance asked. He was human, like most citizens of Citeel, and a very average looking one at that. Forgettable, even. He was the fidgety type, and he twiddled his barely-there goatee. "We're the ones working in *real* bakeries." His friends tried to shush him, eyeing the girls, who were starting to lose interest.

"Fellas, relax," Harlowe coaxed, and glared at Gregor. "Getting ourselves riled up for nothing, are we? What's done is done."

"Bet your cakes are goblin snot! Bet they're absolute troll cheese!" Gale hurled.

"I've got to take a leak," Noal announced. At this, the girls pushed away from the table and left without a word, followed by the bemoaning of everyone except Noal, who was very focused on where he was going.

"Your friend's got the weakest bladder in the kingdom," Gale announced.

"Come off it, he's just finished his final. He's had a bit more than he should have."

"Bet he hasn't had more than me, and I'm half his size!" Gale let out a tremendous laugh at this, one of his favorite jokes to make.

Gregor forced a smile. "Congratulations to you all, by the way."

"To us," Lance cheered, and they clinked their mugs together.

Gregor pushed away from the table and scanned the crowd, looking for his friend. He spotted Noal at the bar, talking to a stranger. This would have been curious, except for the fact that the town seemed to be full of strangers these days, trickling in for the festivities. They would soon be coming in hordes, to be sure, as the royal wedding approached.

The shape of the man sitting at the bar speaking to Noal seemed oddly familiar, but Gregor couldn't place him, not even as he walked up and looked him in the eyes. Noal threw an arm around Gregor's shoulders when he arrived, pointing excitedly to the stranger with his mug. "Gregor! Meet Alistair. He's the candy trolley man!"

Alistair smiled broadly and offered a hand, which Gregor shook, struck with awe. It was like meeting a celebrity, in a sense. Alistair was tall, dark-haired, with grey eyes that crinkled at the edges with his smile. *Handsome.* And he had all his teeth!

"How do you do?" Alistair asked in a smooth, silky voice.

It dawned on Gregor that this man could sell him absolutely anything with a voice like that. He gawked another moment before he replied, "I'm Gregor."

"Your friend was just telling me quite the tale," Alistair said, putting a finger to his nose and giving a wink. "A Royal Bake Off, eh?"

Gregor shot Noal a glare.

"What? It's no secret."

"It's a bit like competing for the princess, isn't it?" Alistair said. "So romantic. A shame she's marrying a lousy man."

"Who's a lousy man?" Ash asked, walking up to the bar.

Noal threw his other arm around Ash's shoulder and, thinking he was whispering, yelled right in his ear, "This fellow thinks the princess is marrying beneath her."

"What's wrong with Prince Norsdorf?"

"For one, what a name, and secondly—"

"What's *your* name?" Ash asked, cutting Alistair off.

"Alistair, his name's Al-is-tare-*eh*," Noal crooned.

"Seems a bit bland. No culture in that name, Alistair. Who are you to come into our kingdom, insult our princess, and have the nerve to poke fun of a prince's name? What do you do? What kingdom do *you* rule?"

"He's the candy man!"

At this, Ash, who was inches from Alistair's nose as he berated him, broke away to look at Noal, confused. "A what?"

"He's the man with the new candy trolley. You've never seen it?"

"I—don't get out much," Ash muttered.

He turned back to Alistair, but before he could say another word Noal added, "He's got no seal. No purple seal. He's *illegal*."

Ash just about burst with excitement at hearing this. Noal had just cocked the arrow in the bow. Ash pulled back the string with a grin and fired. "So, you're a foreigner coming into our kingdom selling sweets without a royal seal. Who do you think you are? You ought to get run out of town. We've earned our places here, we've worked hard. We're the ones who deserve to sell sweets in this town, not you."

At that, the front doors of the pub burst open. In walked four royal guards in full uniform. They looked around, surveying the room, locked eyes on Alistair, and marched directly toward him.

11

Sore Loser

G regor, Noal, and Ash all held their breath, staring with rounded eyes at the approaching figures. The guards marched to the bar, stopped right behind them, and removed their helmets. The one in front looked right over their heads and beckoned to Darce. "Four pints, would ya?"

"Off for the night, lads?" Darce asked, grabbing the mugs from the shelf above him.

Realizing they had not, in fact, come to arrest him, Alistair leaned back a bit, looking rather pleased with himself. "I bet if I won that contest of yours, I'd get a seal," Alistair said, now completely ignoring the guards who were removing their shiny badges.

"You couldn't! You can't compete!" Noal lamented.

"Says who?"

"Alright, alright!" Gregor grabbed both his friends by the shirttails and pulled. "Off we go."

"Hold on now," Noal protested.

"We're just having a chat," Ash insisted, trying to wriggle free. Gregor got his arms behind their knees and heaved them up, one over each shoulder, and carried them back to their original table. He saw the other competitors staring. Their expressions changed, amused smiles appearing on their faces. Gregor rolled his eyes and dumped his friends in their chairs. "Alright. Brimley, these two are far gone, and I'm tired. I'm taking Noal back to our room, can you get Ash home?"

"I'm fine," Ash fussed, straightening his tunic.

"If you go back there, so help me, I'll be on the candy man's side when the punches fly," Gregor threatened.

"Isn't that *the* candy man?" Brimley asked, nodding towards the bar.

"It's Alistair," Noal corrected. "Yes."

"You spoke to him? What did he say? Did you ask about his seal?"

"Hasn't got one," Gregor said, taking a moment to drain his pint, which had gone flat. "He's a curious fellow. Shady. No good. Best we stay away."

"I already got that feeling," Brimley said. "I suppose he's seen us all together now. I can't go ask him how he sneaks spells into his sweets."

Gregor looked over to see Alistair, who was obviously staring at them, finally turn his back. "Best keep your distance. Noal, let's go. We've got to look fresh tomorrow for the coat ceremony." Gregor grabbed his friend by the elbow, bid everyone goodnight, got a friendly pat on the head from Elis on the way out, and made it all the way back to the dorms without getting any throw-up on him.

"Trust me, you're happy now but you'll be miserable in the morning. Drink it," Gregor coaxed, shoving the flask of water into his friend's hand. Then Gregor collapsed onto the sheet on the floor, exhausted. He closed his eyes, watching the stars behind his lids dance and start to swirl.

"Gregor?"

"Hmm?"

"I don't want to be your enemy."

"What?" Gregor sat up so he could hear better, but he did so with some difficulty. "Why did you say that?"

"The competition. I don't want to compete against you. I don't want us not to be friends."

"We'll always be friends."

"What if you're a sore loser? *I* might be a sore loser. I've never done anything like this before in my life. What if it brings out the worst in us?"

Gregor fell back down. "Noal, listen to me. If you win, you'll make me your apprentice when you open shop. If I win, I'll make you mine. Your glory will be my glory. We'll share the win. We'll share everything but the title of winner. How does that sound?"

"Do you promise?"

"By all the ore under the mountain, I promise."

"By...all the copper in...the kingdom, I, too, promise."

That was good enough for Gregor. It was apparently good enough for Noal, too, who started snoring a moment later.

12

Luck of the Draw

*D*ear Mum & Da,

I know I told you we finished the moat as part of graduation and I'd be home, but they've added an extension! I should only be about another month, and then I'll be home. I miss you lots and I'm excited to see you and everyone else. We've got lots to catch up on, and I hope all that I tell you will make you proud.

Lots of love,

Greggy

Gregor stared at the note. He had tried to put quill to pen with truth behind its grip, but sweat broke out all over him, his heart began racing, and he thought he would pass out. *I ought to write a note and not send it, just keep it,* he thought. *Write it and rewrite it until I have the courage to send it. Yes.*

But in the end, he wrote this note, lit the wax candle, dripped a few drops on the fold, and sealed it with his family's seal ring. He got up and made his way down the hall to the pigeon coops, where the mail was taken and sorted into little cubbies. He was pleasantly surprised to find one in his; his parents tried to keep up with letters, but getting a pigeon in and out of the mountain was tricky, and so they usually only received and sent mail when they broke the surface, about once a week or so but even less often in the winter or if the weather was bad. Gregor fastened his note to a pigeon and sent it off before heading back to the dorm, reading his parents' letter on the way.

Dear Greggy,

So many questions! Your father and I will do our best to answer them all.

Firstly, we're so proud of all you do. It must be the nicest moat in the kingdom! Why, by the time you're done with it, we might see it from our mountain. We're technically outside the kingdom, adjacent to it, but far enough that we don't pay taxes. We engage in trade, and we like the monarchy, for the most part. They don't bother us, and we don't bother them. However, if you choose to stay in the kingdom, your father and I will understand. We miss you terribly and we'd like you to visit before you make such a permanent move. We'd even like to come to the citizenship ceremony if you opt to become one. Superstitious Mountain will always be your home, but it's getting crowded, we can all see that. Pretty soon it will all be cousins atop cousins, and frankly, we've already talked to the elders about branching out, mingling with other dwarves from other mountains. It's a shame ours is just one big one, instead of a whole range like the Amethyst Cloud Mountain range—they have such a sense of community. In fact, your father and I were thinking of taking a diplomatic trip to the range this summer. We'd be happy to bring you along if your work gets done in time and you're hankering to meet others of your kind. Maybe find a nice partner, settle down. Of course, your father mentioned you might have already met someone, which is why you've been so distant, but I'd like to think we're open-minded about anyone you meet. While it's nice to be with a dwarf who understands your way of life and culture, we know you are acclimating well there and might have other standards in a partner, which we'd be happy to hear about upon your homecoming. After all, the princess is marrying a foreigner, why shouldn't we all? Mix it up a bit, I say.

A bit of home news: the Mother Dragon has been spotted circling the mountain, so she should be laying her egg any day now. In preparation, tonight we'll be holding the first Luck of the Draw in thirty years! Your father's ready for retirement anyhow, although he wants you to know he's sad you're not here to be entered for the drawing.

We've heard of the royal wedding and thought about getting a few of us together to purchase one of those magic mirrors. Your father insists that what goes on outside the mountain isn't any of our business, but I keep reminding him that you're outside the mountain, and may very well stay there a while, and it would be so nice if we didn't rely on drunk pigeons (have you noticed an influx of these? We have.) for correspondence. As for if it matters to us…well, not really. But it's sort of fun, isn't it? Seeing what all goes on around there? I'll admit, I wasn't much for venturing out either until you took the leap. My brave son! Have I told you we're proud of you? So proud!

Kisses,

Mum

& also Da

Gregor wished he had read this note first before he sent the other one off. If there was ever a moment to disappoint his mother with the truth, this was it, seeing as how she'd ended on such a high note. He was her son who went beyond the mountain, and that was what she was most proud of, was it not? He made a mental note to *write that damn letter.* Tell them about his day to day; mention Lorde of Loaves, where he worked for the past year baking healthy breads. Tell them about living with his best friend and their now defunct cookie business. Gregor imagined his parents' shock, then his mother's laugh. She *would* enjoy the stories. His father might grumble, get elbowed by his wife to fess up, isn't it funny? Gregor found himself smiling at this image. He decided to let Noal read the letter from his parents.

Noal was in their room when Gregor got back, sitting on the now bare floor, pulling breakfast from a sack.

"Thank goodness, I was about to start gnawing on your boot," Gregor said, dropping beside him. He reached for the hunk of cheese and a roll of sausage. "That took longer than I thought."

"Sorry, I had to swing by Ash's dorm to make sure he was okay."

"What do you mean? He's in the same dorm we are, isn't he?"

Noal's eyebrows raised, going over in his head what he'd just said. "Y-yes," he stammered. "But…he was at a friend's celebrating…"

"Oh. I thought Brimley took him back. I suppose they made a detour."

"Right, what a night," Noal rushed to agree. He broke off a piece of bread—light as a cloud!—and handed it to Gregor, who devoured it.

"I want you to read this letter." Gregor offered the note to Noal, who accepted it once he wiped his hands on his trousers. It took him longer than Gregor to read it, not being accustomed to the loopy scripture and having to rely on a lot of context clues, but he absorbed the gist of it. He let out a frustrated sigh at the end. "You *have* to tell them."

"I know," Gregor groaned. "And I already sent a letter telling another fib!"

Noal frowned, unsure where to go from here. "Listen," he said finally. "My father wasn't thrilled about what I wanted to do, but I'm doing it myself, on my own accord. I know you come from a long line of dwarves who live in the mountains and there's pressures there that I can't relate to, but I think at the end of the day your mum just wants you happy and self-sustaining, right?"

"You're right, you're right," Gregor grumbled. "Did you read the part about the mirror? They're going to find out!"

"Write a letter *now*." Noal jumped up, seized by excitement.

"I don't have the time," Gregor lamented, and stuffed the rest of his cheese in his mouth. "We're due in the Throne Room for the coat ceremony. I'll do it after. I *promise*."

Noal's eyes lit up. "How did I forget?!"

"Cheap beer," Gregor reminded him. He felt fine this morning; he had gotten his heavy drinking done in his youth, down in the mountain. Dwarves loved ale and grew up on it. It was the city liquor that hit hard, the fancy drinks in their delicate glasses that Gregor kept accidentally smashing in his powerful grip at all the places Ash and Noal took him to before they made Badger & Bard their usual watering hole.

"I suppose it's time to bring back the mattresses," Gregor said, looking around. It felt like the end of an era, though it was on the precipice of another. Still, it didn't quite feel like things were beginning, not yet.

"You don't think Brimley will put up a fight, do you?"

"He'd be a bad monk if he did," Gregor said, and they snickered. Brimley *was* a bad monk, in a lot of ways; he drank, didn't shave his head, and spoke too loudly all the time. He was also a pharmacist, an alchemist, a horticulturist, and, for the last year, a monk who didn't sleep on the dirt floor like the rest of the inhabitants of his monastery.

"I live my life to serve humanity," Brimley had once told Gregor. Although, how making gold helped humanity, Gregor was still scratching his head about. When he found out Brimley had been an alchemist to try to make gold to feed the poor, Gregor had offered to just give Brimley gold, as they had buckets of it back home. To this, Brimley retorted, "I could *buy* the herbs at market, but I'd rather grow them myself."

"What's the fun in that?"

"What's the fun in mining gold?"

"It's what we do. It's what we live for."

"Exactly," Brimley said, and Gregor had left it at that.

Gregor often thought back to this conversation; digging for gold was what he did, just as toiling to serve others was what Brimley did. Now they both baked. But digging would always be a part of Gregor. He still hunted around the palace courtyard for rocks to collect or to use for target practice with his sling. And Brimley still volunteered at the monastery garden in his free time, pulling the weeds and picking the carrots even as the monastery made a handsome profit in all their business operations.

Gregor wondered if he was relinquishing some fundamental part of him by replacing the shovel with the spatula. He was still a dwarf, there was no hiding that, but he felt the distance between him and his dwarvish community growing. Who would he relate to when he returned home? Would he truly return home? After this apprenticeship, he and Noal had agreed they would take the offer to work in the palace kitchen for a few years. Then they could apply for the purple seal and open their own shop.

Would dwarves visit, knowing there was a newly opened dwarvish pastry shop?

Gregor had tried his very best to explain sugar and desserts to his parents through his letters, sometimes even copying the text from cookbooks verbatim to get it right, but short of shipping a box home how could they understand? But it sometimes stretched weeks between his parents' letters, and Gregor was sure that any desserts he sent home would be harder than boulder biscuits by the time they made it to the mountain. And unlike boulder biscuits, the magic would be lost in the staleness.

The future intimidated Gregor more than he admitted to Noal, who freely and often confessed his terror of the unknown. Gregor knew this was all just the beginning of their confectionary journey, but it felt like the edge of a cliff was fast approaching. The enormous expanse of time stretching ahead suddenly made Gregor feel as if he was lost in a pitch-black darkness, no end in sight. He grabbed the back of his chair to steady himself and used his other hand to wipe the film of sweat that had broken out on his forehead.

"Maybe it'll hit once we have the coat," Gregor muttered.

"What will hit?"

Gregor shook his head. "Nothing. Ready?"

13

Coat Ceremony

The Great Hall was enormous, draped in red from floor to ceiling; red carpet crept into red walls that bled into red drapes that were swept aside and tied with gold tassel cords. So many that Gregor lost count as he walked soundlessly beside his fellow apprentices, their footsteps consumed in all that plush everywhere. Above them, massive chandeliers made of polished crystals housing stardust lit up the walls, the ceiling, making it feel as if they were promenading through a tunnel of fire. The Great Hall served as the reception area for guests waiting to see the king in the Throne Room, where they were being led by a lavishly dressed Mosley.

Mosley was, by his own words, the king's right-hand man. He was the one who bustled into the royal bedchamber each morning and pulled the drapes aside and ordered the king's breakfast to his room; the one who briefed His Majesty on the day's agenda and laid out ceremonial outfits if the occasion required such finery. And Mosley was now the planner of the royal wedding, a task he felt he was owed considering the hand he had in orchestrating the engagement. Part of the planner's duty was to stage this new baking competition that the king had so marvelously sprung on Mosley at the eleventh hour. Mosley took the slugs with a grin and a curt, "Of course, Your Majesty."

The ornate doors were already flung open, awaiting their arrival.

Gregor saw before they entered that the Throne Room was far more intimate than the Great Hall. The thrones sat squeezed together atop a dais, under a baldachin. Where two usually sat now there were three. The third throne was more of a chair, on which the soon-to-be prince sat, shifting anxiously in his seat. Beside him was bride-to-be Princess Damora in her queen's throne, and beside her, in the grand throne, was her father King Varundil, grinning ear-to-ear. Where in the test kitchen he dressed modestly, here he was dressed in full ceremony regalia.

"Mosley!" the king shouted and jumped up once the doors were shut behind them. Unable to contain his excitement, he ran down the steps to greet the group as they walked in. "What a day! Five new confectionary graduates. I do hope some of you will stay in our kitchens. It's always such a shame when parents want their children back in their family business. I've still got plenty of teeth to lose to sweets," he joked, and the chefs couldn't keep their own smiles off their faces.

Brimley was in his usual crimson robe and leather boots, Ash in the nicest tunic he owned, Noal and Gregor in their second finest pair, and Elis in an outfit that outshined them all, probably purchased just for the occasion. "He must have a live-in seamstress," Noal muttered under his breath, and Ash snickered.

"Welcome," Chef Toufie boomed, standing at the foot of the dais in his black dress coat, smiling at the graduates lined up before him. Princess Damora wore a simple, elegant dress, paired with white gloves that went up past her elbows. Her hair was another matter, with all its braids and curls coiled all around her head. Nothing on her flashed or twinkled in the light, no jewelry on her save the newly bestowed engagement ring on her finger. When she came down the steps to stand beside Chef Toufie, they stood close enough that Gregor could scrutinize it, a simple square of moss agate set in twisted silver. Gregor admired the handiwork, but decided it was too frou-frou, something an elf artisan must have made. No dwarf would fuss over such tiny details, creating the ivy leaves that clasped the center stone. Their eyes met and she gave a reassuring smile. *Sweet* was the word that came to Gregor's mind. *Gentle. Calm.* "The princess and I have the great honor of awarding you your royal chef coats. Congratulations on your great accomplishment. You are joining a league of kingdom-renowned chefs. This prestige is recognized by all the citizens of Everdorne, proof that you have completed exceptional work and are the most talented pastry chefs in our kingdom. We look forward to all you will accomplish with the knowledge you have gained in these palace walls."

Princess Damora read off the first name. "Elis Goldstem."

Elis stepped forward, flashing her his most dazzling smile, and slipped his arms into the black coat she held up. When he closed the flap and began to expertly thread the buttons through the holes, they saw the embroidered emblem of the royal purple seal on the left breast, over his heart. It wasn't *the* purple seal, just the image of one. Still, it was a sight to behold; two river otters twisted around each other in the hexagon, the words "Fides Et Sapientia" smiling up from the bottom. Faith and Wisdom, represented by the twin otters, like the ones that used to swarm and swim the river the city had been built around, allowing trade to boom as it carried goods through the city and beyond. Those otters had long been replaced by dragons, who unfortunately ate all the otters. Now those otters were only ever spotted on the royal seal.

Elis shook Chef Toufie's hand and received the certificate from him as his classmates cheered. Then he turned back to Princess Damora, who pinned the royal pastry pin onto the collar of his jacket: the royal crown floating over two crossed golden whisks.

Elis stepped back into line, beaming.

"Noal Copperton." Noal stepped forward and did precisely as Elis had.

"Gregor Brimstone." Gregor thought he would faint from excitement before he heard the sweet, twinkling sound of his own name. He found courage and stepped forward. He stuck his arms through the stiff new coat and buttoned it same as the others had, feeling as if he was joining them on the other side of a chasm. There was a brotherhood here, one that would last their lifetimes, he knew. He couldn't keep the grin off his face as Noal beamed at him, and he felt alright. He felt like he *belonged*. When he accepted his certificate, he shook Chef Toufie's hand so hard Toufie had to reach over and pat him on the shoulder to *let go*.

"Ash Birchwood."

"Brimley Lavra."

When Brimley stepped back in line, Chef Toufie motioned for everyone to cease their clapping, which they did immediately, glad to give their palms a rest.

"Congratulations to every one of you. Now, for the Royal Bake Off, where the winner bakes Princess Damora and Prince Eadwine Norsdorf's wedding cake.

"King Varundil decided it would only be fair if the competition was opened to all the willing bakers in the city, which was why yesterday a contest identical to your final was held at the Badger & Bard to see if anyone else qualified. I'm pleased to say we had a great turnout, and I think we're adding a great bit of talent to this pool of already excellent chefs. Mosley, please present the other competitors."

Mosley pulled the door open, and familiar figures filed in. Mosley introduced them as they stepped into view. "Harlowe Langston, Lance Lorence, Gale Wynd, and Alistair Alimar."

Noal audibly gasped at the sight of Alistair, and Gregor stomped on his foot to shush him. Alistair smiled that dazzling smile. "You remember me."

"From the candy cart," Noal said.

Alistair's smile wavered. "From last night?"

"Last night?" Noal looked at Gregor, confused.

Gregor leaned in and whispered, "I'll explain later. Just nod."

With the full cast of competitors lined up before the dais, Mosley took his post beside Chef Toufie and cleared his throat. "Welcome! His Royal—"

He suddenly stopped, remembering something as he looked around. He went over to a wall and pulled a tassel. The velvet curtain pulled aside to reveal a mirror the size of a large portrait, aimed right at them. Mosley swiped across the surface of the mirror before hurrying back to his post. He cleared his throat again and resumed. "Welcome! His Royal Majesty the King of Everdorne is so very thrilled to host you all in the Royal Bake Off.

"There will be two additional rounds. Your next challenge will be to make your finest single-layer cake. One the princess can eat," he added, in a way that felt very clearly ominous. "You will be judged on edibility, flavor, creativity, and of course, presentation. We will meet Monday, bright and early. Good luck."

Mosley gave a satisfied nod and hurried back to the mirror, swiped his fingers across the glass again, and pulled the curtains back across the front of it.

Princess Damora went down the line of competitors and handed each a compact mirror set in a polished shell case that closed with a little gold clasp. The king's monogram was stamped on each. A gift, but not really a gift.

"Consider these your diaries," she said. "Feel free to use them at will…"

Noal fumbled as he opened the case, and a small piece of folded parchment fell out. He stooped to grab it, burning bright red with embarrassment.

"…the runes to command it are on the parchment."

"Unlock, lock, transmit, receive…" Gregor read under his breath. He looked at Brimley, who surely knew what this was. Brimley met his gaze and nodded, understanding they would discuss this later.

"Tell us how you *feel*," Mosley added, and everyone just stared at him blankly. He gave a little nod, as if that would suffice, and added, "*Good luck.*"

They all shuffled out the door after him, feeling a bit dazed. "Let's go get a drink," Gregor suggested, and they stayed out nearly the entire night drinking, singing, and toasting with friends and strangers to their accomplishment well earned. They had the week to whip up a new recipe and gear up for the next round. But tonight, they would get even drunker than the night before.

14

Compelled to Compete

Choosing competitors had proven to be quite the challenge. No confectionary in the city wanted to part with their help, not when there was money to be made at a time like this. Especially not the sweets dynasties, those families who were famous through multiple generations for their festival faire. And Mosley hardly had time to send a heralder around the whole kingdom to round up competitors on such a short notice. While the wedding had time to be planned, it had been assumed that Chef Eclin would be the one baking the cake, no question. When he turned down the offer, it had been a scramble to find a replacement. Chef Toufie was an accomplished culinarist and as such knew the basics of baking, but his sweets skills weren't of the caliber of Chef Eclin. Toufie gave Mosley one hard glare and Mosley regretted asking him to bake that cursed cake.

And so, Mosley had to send out just about every pigeon in his menagerie to all the bakeries and confectionaries he could find on the city map. Those who had hands to spare did so, begrudgingly. From the sparse volunteers of chocolatiers, candy makers, and bakers, Mosley whittled it down to three. Well, only three cakes didn't fall apart, so the judging went rather quickly. Then the stranger happened to show up.

Mosley hadn't been completely keen on letting Alistair compete. "We can't just throw this stranger—literal stranger, from foreign lands—into the mix. It would upset everyone!"

"I can see it's upsetting *you*," King Varundil said, raising his eyebrows. "Let's not forget, Mosley, *we* were once strangers."

Mosley, were he a man with more diplomatic background, would have argued that all are strangers since birth, but he knew better than to take up philosophy with the king, who so loved petty squabbles.

"Sir, I just worry about inviting a foreigner into the palace. What if he's a spy?"

The king clapped. "He could be. Think of the thrill!"

Life had become a bit dull since his wife left him to be a witch in the woods. No wars, no feuds, not even duels! His wife had forbidden it, casting spells around the kingdom to protect it. Oh, they were still on talking terms—wonderful friends, even, since they shared a daughter—but the queen wanted to let down her hair and pick mushrooms and open an apothecary for pilgrims. What was he to do, stop her? As if! She was far more beloved than he, and as they liked to say, she ruled from outside the gates, he from within. Princess Damora saw her mother plenty; on holidays, during festivals, and anytime she fancied a bit of a mushroom trip in the countryside. She updated her mother on how her father was doing and noted after her engagement that it seemed he was feeling more bored than usual. Lonely, perhaps. Her mother was the one who proposed giving him permission to orchestrate this competition. *As long as the wedding goes unhitched, let him.* Besides, with Chef Eclin gone missing and no one to bake a wedding cake, this was turning into quite the important task, and the king took it to heart.

Mosley gave up. "Alright, Your Majesty. I'll reach out to this...confectioner. The one that showed up after the three winners were announced. He's got a cart, you say?"

"My spies have kept watch on him for days. He arrived with a sweets cart and just started selling. He produced a foreign seal, and frankly he probably won't be here long enough to make applying for our seal worth it. I think it would be fun to offer him the opportunity to earn it this way."

"Alright, alright." Mosley watched a dragon crawl up the back of the throne and onto the king's shoulder. Fergis let out a little yawn and settled into the crook of the king's neck. The king reached up absentmindedly and scratched Fergis behind the ears, used to his little pet. "Do we...want him to win?"

"What's the fun in that!" King Varundil let out a burst of laughter. "We can't rig this game. I know, I know, we have such fun pulling strings, but this is my daughter's wedding. We really do need the perfect cake. Her mother's coming," he added, and his eyes shone with excitement. "I imagine if we had had more children she might come up more often. Alas..."

He scratched Fergis again, who blew a little breath of smoke. The king reached into his robe's pocket and pulled out his pipe. He placed it between his lips and Fergis blew a tiny flame into the bowl, and now there were two streams of smoke swirling around the king's head. "Oh, do you mind?"

"Not at all," Mosley said, slowly lowering the hand he'd instinctively put in front of his nose. He despised smoke. And dragons.

"I've been so stressed with the preparations. Are all the mirrors in order?"

"Ah, yes." Mosley brightened, eager to move onto a topic he was prepared for. He hurried over to the wall, where something large was covered in a velvet cloth. He yanked the rope to reveal a shattered mirror.

"Gods! Who delivered that? We must fire him at once!"

"No, no, Your Majesty." Mosley grunted as he wheeled the massive mirror in front of the king. Once in position, he pointed at each of the fragments. "It's not one piece shattered, it's a mosaic. All the different pieces have been enchanted to transmit from their twin. I have a menagerie of animals that will be outfitted with mirrors who will transmit to these..." Mosley pointed to several mirrors the size of tea saucers on the mosaic that were simply reflecting their own faces back at them, not yet activated. Other mirrors showed the hallways around the palace, the inside of common rooms, the test kitchen, the main kitchen where the usual mayhem was breaking out, the library, the study, the Throne Room, the fencing gym, and one even showed a view of the courtyard, the summer blooms bursting in their plant beds.

"Astounding," King Varundil murmured. He leaned in close, inspecting each individual piece. When he sat back a sensation of vertigo came over him, and he closed his eyes, let out a breath. "It's going to take a bit to get used to it."

"Of course," Mosley said, staring at his creation, in awe of his own brilliance.

His eyes still closed, King Varundil said, "And the public?"

"We are selling hand mirrors as we speak. There's a gem in the center of the handle that lets the users turn them on and off. Quite the update from the rune-controlled ones, which are more sophisticated but have a bit of a learning curve. Citizens can also arrange for one of our sorcerers to come by and enchant their current mirrors at home."

"These mirrors of theirs, once enchanted...the spell can still be traced?"

"What do you mean, sir?"

"I mean, can we see into the mirrors ourselves?" The king gestured to his mirrors. "Perhaps replace the view of the library with a live feed of, oh, I don't know, the opera?"

"If everyone could just tune into the opera, how would the opera make money?" Mosley asked, puzzled.

"Only *I* would. And I'm a patron. I'll up my fee to them. But that's just one of the places I'd like to peek into. Other places wouldn't be so fancy, say, local pubs?"

"Wouldn't that be a huge breach of privacy, your grace?"

King Varundil opened one eye to give Mosley a knowing look. Mosley turned away to throw the cover back on the mirror. He realized the gravity of the situation. "Your Majesty," he said, turning back, "I know it's not for me to say, but I am worried that maybe there is some overstepping here."

"There are criminals, even convicts in the kingdom. You know this, even though you're not on our Official Outlaws Board. They need to be kept an eye on. They love the excitement of a festival and tend to use celebrations as catalysts for mischief."

All sorts of people and creatures were flocking into the kingdom at this time. Royal officials and guards would wander into establishments, meet fetching new characters, get a little too comfortable, spill a few too many secrets...there was always a period of political heat after festivals like this, so many tempers to pacify, rumors to dismiss, officials to reprimand. Short of banning all royal personnel from leaving the palace, there was no way to ensure secrets stayed safely on this side of the drawbridge. Already there were rumors of elevating certain taxes, ripples of civil unrest. After his only child's wedding, King Varundil wanted to do nothing but lounge for several weeks and sleep off what he hoped would be a tremendous hangover. These mirrors would be a way for his spies to keep track of people of interest and to ensure peace and order long after the wedding was over.

"Mosley, I hear your concerns, I do. But let's let kingdom security stay with those who have that specific expertise."

"As you wish, Your Majesty," Mosley grumbled. "Will that be all?"

King Varundil gave a gleeful clap. "Yes. Wait, do you have one of those handheld mirrors that controls all of these?"

Mosley produced one and showed the king how to flick the glass to switch between channels. "Marvelous. I'll practice on this until I can work up to..." King Varundil gave a little wave at the wall of mirrors, aware that Mosley was monstrously proud and didn't want to hurt his feelings. "Good job, Mosley."

Beaming, Mosley left the king's chamber, certain that everything was in order.

15

Mead Monastery

The Knights of the Full Table lived at Mead Monastery, a homesteading monastery dedicated to the worship of Gidea, the goddess of the home. The monastery itself was once a fortress that sat on a hill at the edge of the city. It had long ago been converted into the home for the homey monks. Their crusade was to end hunger, and they did so by devoting themselves to the arts of beer brewing, cheese making, gardening, sourdough perfecting, and beekeeping, amongst other crafts. On Sundays they loaded up a wagon and old Dimitry the donkey shuffled into the palace's courtyard, where they set up a market to raise money for things like medicine for the poor and upkeeping projects around the monastery.

Brimley was the youngest member of the brotherhood, charmed into joining as an orphan after he saw a painting of Gidea—on a beer label, no less—and fell in love. The orphanage didn't hesitate at the chance to put a child to work and traded him for a wheel of cheese. Not even their finest wheel.

Brimley loved it there. Anything he wanted to learn, they taught him, and when no one was there to mentor him, they sent him around the kingdom to learn. No skill was too outlandish, hence the alchemy stint, and now the chef apprenticeship. No one worked harder than Brimley, though talent wasn't always on his side.

He dreamed of opening that soup kitchen, training people to cook wonderful meals for themselves, serving others, and making sure no belly went empty, like his used to. Now his belly was nice and round from plenty of beer and bread and cheese. With his Royal Confectionary Certificate, Brimley could now ask the Abbot to begin plans for his kitchen, and he was already scouting the best wing to set it up in.

The day after their coat ceremony was a day of rest for the newly graduated pastry chefs. After sleeping in to recover from their hangovers, Gregor and Noal decided to make use of their free time and go retrieve their mattresses. As they followed Brimley down the halls of the monastery, Noal and Gregor all but held their breath, unsure if this was a *church* church or not, even as Brimley happily chatted the whole tour.

"And peas! You would never guess how many varieties there are. Just an absolute endless number of soups you can make with them, too," Brimley droned on, nervous and excited to have his friends in his home. Also a bit sad, because he had rather liked sleeping on those mattresses.

"You're sure they'll let us take the donkey?" Noal asked again.

Monks sat on stone benches, sipping their pints of ale, laughing, arguing, saluting them boisterously as they passed by. Gregor couldn't keep the grin off his face.

"Dimitry's due for some exercise," Brimley assured, and finally pushed open a door to reveal his room.

It was an absolute jungle. A skylight shone sun into the room, which was packed with plants. Gregor closed his eyes and inhaled, enjoying the cool, earthy smell.

"The oxygen in here is *incredible*." Brimley beamed. "Breathe deep!"

Noal and Gregor dropped onto their mattresses, which were stacked on the ground, no frame, no fuss. The sheets were made from the bamboo that encircled the perimeter of the property, a natural privacy fence, and it was a cool, sweat-wicking cloth, Brimley explained. He poured them pints from a barrel in the corner of his room.

"We should just come here instead of Badger & Bard," Noal joked, taking the offering.

"Actually, we host brewing apprenticeships here. The beer at Badger & Bard is from our practice runs. Drinkable, but we keep the best batches here." Brimley winked.

Gregor drank deeply, closing his eyes to fully immerse himself in the taste. It was wonderful here. Monasteries had a reputation for being stiff, quiet, solemn places. Some were. There were plenty of gods and so plenty of monasteries around the kingdom and the countryside beyond, though none quite like this one. It was completely different than the mines he had grown up in, which were crowded, confined, broiling, rife with competition, and so unbearably loud. Perhaps if dwarves broke the surface more often, they would be a more mellow bunch, Gregor thought. Looking around, he felt at peace. He couldn't imagine moving back home, not now after all the adventures he'd had. The places he'd been to would fade into tales he told when prompted, memories that no one else shared. Gregor knew in his heart that while he would visit home soon, he was now a city dwarf.

"How are the experiments going?" Gregor asked. "With the candy?"

"Well, you saw. I figured out there are spells in the candy."

"And?"

"And then I ran out of candy."

"I'm confused," Gregor said. "Doesn't he have a trolley stand? Can't you just go buy more?"

"I can't, because it's not there!" Brimley sighed, exasperated.

"Where is it?" Noal asked, incredulous.

Brimley shrugged. "It seems as if he's abandoned that endeavor in favor of the competition."

"No one just 'gives up' their business," Noal argued.

"What about for glory?" Brimley countered.

Gregor tugged his beard, thinking. "I'm sure he's stuck it somewhere he can retrieve it after this whole competition is over. He'll either win the purple seal and open shop under its protection, or he won't win, and then he'll take that trolley and leave town."

"We don't even know there's a purple seal to be won," Noal lamented.

"We do," Brimley said, looking at the parchment he'd just unrolled, the one they had assumed was the offer for employment, which was presented to every graduate. It was, but rolled inside of that parchment was a second slip of parchment, which Brimley was reading.

"What's that?" Noal asked.

"What does it say?" Gregor asked, getting up from the mattress.

"Alright, alright!" Brimley started from the top. "It says, 'Welcome to the Royal Palace! You are here to compete to be The Official Cake Baker of the upcoming royal nuptials. There will be two rounds, after which the winner will be chosen. The winner will be given the honor of baking the official royal wedding cake and the chance to be awarded the royal purple seal for a job well done. This competition will be transmitted via magical mirrors. You must consent to the use of your image, likeness of your image, and your voice to compete. To consent, please sign below. Good luck.'"

"Sign for what?" Noal grabbed the page from Brimley's hand.

"For marketing purposes," Gregor grumbled, and grabbed the parchment out of Noal's hand.

"It's sign it or be disqualified," Brimley concluded, and after they had each read it, agreed this was the case. They didn't quite understand what it meant but understood they would have to sign their own slips once they got back to their room.

"Are you accepting employment in the royal kitchen, Brimley? Gregor and I are. We figure we'll put in our two years and then open a shop."

Brimley shook his head. "I'm opening a soup kitchen here. You'll have plenty of help if Ash and Elis accept, which I think they will."

Disappointed, Noal pivoted the conversation. "This whole mirror business is funny, isn't it? And what's with the runes? Have I got to learn them all?"

"Honestly, I'm not messing with it," Gregor said. "It seems like an infringement of privacy."

"It can be. Mirrors are strictly forbidden in the monastery," Brimley said.

"I thought that was because you're not supposed to be vain or whatever," Noal said.

Brimley made a face. "You should come more often. Take a cheese and wine pairing class. Open your mind a bit."

Noal looked offended, and Gregor interrupted by circling back with, "So what you're saying is, you can't experiment without more candy, and without that, we have no proof of malicious intent and Alistair is still competing."

"Right," Brimley confirmed.

"Seeing him was a shock. We absolutely need to get him disqualified, or who knows what he'll do with the cake," Noal insisted.

"Why are we assuming he'll do anything to it?" Brimley asked. "Just because he can, and had, doesn't mean...alright I'm hearing myself aloud now."

"He's nefarious," Noal said, completely confident in this.

Brimley looked at Gregor, who shrugged. Brimley sighed. "Alright."

"The plan is, we make friends with him, get him to trust us, and then weasel all his secret intents out of him," Noal said conspiratorially.

"We get him drunk and force it out of him," Gregor suggested.

"Then we catch his confession in the mirror!" Noal jumped up with excitement. "It's the perfect plan."

"You don't even know how the mirror works," Gregor reminded him, taking another gulp of his ale. He wasn't nearly as excited as Noal. His plan was to simply beat Alistair, fair and square. Alistair wouldn't dare show his face after a loss. Maybe it was the ale, maybe it was the freshness of graduation, but Gregor felt invincible. He had spent the last two years of his life training for this. He wasn't about to let a nobody beat him. Gods, is this how Elis felt, *all the time*? It was amazing!

"You sure you didn't spike this ale?" Gregor joked, feeling the warmth spreading up from his belly.

"You've been drinking the rejects for too long." Brimley beamed. He tipped back his mug and drained it. "Alright then, let's get these mattresses loaded up for ya. Then you'll help me load up the apprentice beers. We've got a lot to get rid of."

16

Mirrors, Mirrors

The palace dungeon had long forsaken its original purpose of holding prisoners and hosting their ensuing punishments and night-long tortures.

It was turned into a crypt for a while, but the royals didn't seem to be dying fast enough.

Then it was a bunker in case the skies opened and rained down hellfire.

When Mad King Jolson died, the paranoia went with him, and the next king cleared out the rat-chewed cots, the cobwebs, the expired preserved foods, but kept the bottles and turned it into an impressive wine cellar.

His son turned the dungeon into a gymnasium, though it made the place smell quite rancid.

The next princess turned it into a concert hall for secret performances. She was forced to practice the flute and harp but really wanted to beat drums and blast the cornet. The secret auditorium didn't stay secret long.

Next it was a woodshop, which replaced a lot of the sturdy furniture in the palace with crooked, flimsy, wobbly works of "art" which eventually ended up as firewood.

Then came the art studio, since it already had all that paint lying around, which it remained still to that day. The fumes vented out through pipes that had been added during the gymnasium period and was quite cozy with the added scented candles and cushions.

Mosley was down there fashioning pieces of mirrors into desired sizes. Beside him sat his cousin Celeste, a high-ranking lady-in-waiting of the princess, knitting tiny little sweaters onto which she stitched the pieces of mirror Mosley prepared. Her heavily painted face was pinched in concentration.

"It looks like pigeon armor," Celeste mused, holding up what did, in fact, look like avian battle gear. She was the tallest of all the ladies-in-waiting, an imposing fair-haired figure. She was the schedule setter and thereby the most kissed-up-to lady in the palace, after the princess of course. By being Mosley's relative she was bestowed an authority she did not abuse but loved to wield.

"Nonsense, this is purely peaceful," Mosley snapped. He took the garment from her and looked it over, admiring it. "It would be a shame if these got ruined."

"The squirrel ones are precious. No dragons?"

"They're not as inconspicuous."

"Oh, because mirrors flying above reflecting the sun, blinding people, will be so subtle," Celeste snorted. This wasn't the first time Mosley recruited her for a stupid game; the whole courting of the princess had been one trick after another, one sneaky idea planting after the next. It had been exhausting, but also exciting, far more fulfilling than Celeste's day job. Sewing holes in royal undergarments paid the bills but was horrendously boring. She tried stitching little swear words and that amused her for a while, but either no one noticed or didn't dare say anything, so the big altercation she had hoped would come of the cheeky business never took place.

"One bird here, one squirrel there. It won't be like a cloud of mirrors descending on them. This needs to be *inconspicuous*."

"They'll catch on before long. You know, I heard nearly half the kingdom has opted to enchant their mirrors by now. There won't be a pub or gambling hall in the city that won't be transmitting."

"It's the king's wishes to have this up and running in time for the royal wedding, and then the royal coronation. It's not about the Royal Bake Off. That's just the dry run."

"Something tells me the others are just dry runs as well," Celeste muttered.

"What's that?"

Celeste dropped her knitting in her lap. "Darling Mosley, you still take me for the fool, after all these years?"

Mosley scowled. "I wouldn't, Cousin."

"But you do! Or else you're fooling yourself. You think, honestly, that the king has no ulterior motive? You think he's just so generous, gifting the kingdom a glance into the private happenings of the palace? No ruler gives up privacy for free. He's paranoid. He's going to enchant every mirror until he can peer into every single house and establishment and keep an eye on every person."

"Not in front of the mirrors," Mosley hissed.

"Are they already enchanted?"

"Not these…"

"You're paranoid already! You and the king are one and the same, mad as can be," Celeste accused. "And look at me!" She held up a tiny squirrel sweater. "How idiotic is this?!"

"Suppose there's an assassination attack!"

"There's been no such attempt in years, Cousin."

"Not since the last wedding."

"And not then either!"

"Alright, that is true. But we weren't the kingdom we are now! There's civil unrest, you know, with the coming of this new prince. He's got ideas. He wants to tax the rich to feed the poor…"

The knitting needles hit the floor, and a long, tapered finger pointed right in Mosley's nose. "You'll remember, Mosley, that we were once two church mice. Or have you so easily forgotten?"

"We've since worked hard!"

"Because the church lent us its roof, and the king offered us employment. We have been living off the charity of tithes and taxes. Have we not?"

Mosley harumphed. "Not everyone does as well as us."

"And you could not do anything at all without some help. Now knit your own stupid sweaters."

Celeste made her way to the door, but Mosley jumped up and beat her to it. He fell to his knees and clutched her beautifully embroidered dress hem, the likes of which must have cost a year's worth of salary to some in the dungier part of the city. "Please, dear Celeste, you make a fair point. You are wise, but you speak too freely! Do you really believe if we become suspicious there won't be reason to turn us out? We have no alliances in this palace that wouldn't snitch on us for a few nubs of gold. I've worked so hard…*you*'ve worked so hard."

Celeste rolled her eyes but enjoyed the groveling a few seconds more before she shushed Mosley. "Alright, alright! But you admit you're becoming paranoid, and you're not even the one being spied on. Those poor chefs, they'll be out of their minds with mirrors hunting them down."

"These are so subtle," Mosley insisted, picking up the knitting needles and handing them back to her. "They're *brilliant*."

They're something, alright, Celeste thought, but she kept that to herself. She motioned to the shards of mirror scattered across the table. "You have one that can see into all of these?"

"Yes, of course."

"But is it also enchanted to be impenetrable?"

"What do you mean?"

"Every window can be peered back into, unless you lock it iron-tight with a spell no one can break. Do you trust your magical abilities?"

"No, that's why we had the royal sorcerers enchant them."

"Then they can break in."

"Why would they?"

"Because they don't work for *you*," Celeste reminded him. This sent a chill down Mosley's spine. It was fine if he was surveilling everyone, but the thought of someone watching him? Mosley's mind darkened with worry. Celeste noticed and simply said, "I'm sure you can find someone. For the right price."

From the way she said it, Mosley suspected she already had. What he knew for sure was that she wouldn't give up her source, would never admit it aloud, certainly not in front of mirrors, enchanted or not. Because it was illegal to personally enchant a mirror the king couldn't tap into. But now that he knew such a sorcerer was out there, Mosley had to find him. After all, he wouldn't be the king's right hand if he couldn't.

17

Letter Home

Two days after their coat ceremony, it was back to work for those who had accepted jobs in the royal kitchen. Before they left their dorm, Gregor and Noal signed their royal work contracts and privacy releases, though they were still not entirely sure what it was they were agreeing to. Gregor made to leave to take the letters to the pigeon cot to mail them, but Noal bullied him back into his desk chair and forced a quill into his hand.

Dear Mum & Da,
I've kept a secret from you. Worse. I've lied to you both.

Gregor's quill began to quake. He set it down and rubbed his favorite chunk of sapphire that sat unpolished on his desk, his thumb brushing circles on the smooth side. He thought of the candy Tracy had tasted and wondered if Alistair could make one laced with courage. Gregor gritted his teeth and scolded himself for the terrible thought. He picked the quill back up and wrote with newfound fury:

I'm not working on a moat. I'm not even an engineer! I'm a pastry chef. A really, really good chef, because I've been apprenticing at the royal kitchen for the last two years and just graduated. I haven't been home in the summers because I've been working in a bakery and running an underground cookie business to work on my craft. And also avoiding you, because I've been afraid I'm a disappointment. I should have told you ~~sooner~~ as soon as I was accepted. I didn't even apply, there was a misprint on my engineering acceptance letter that led me to the wrong building, and I was admitted on the spot. I don't even remember how I managed it.

I love the work, I really do. And I'm very good at it. Baking is in my bones. Please be happy for me?

I'm competing to bake the royal wedding cake, and my face has been transmitted in those enchanted mirrors, so you might already know all this. I've got high hopes that I will win.

Root for me?

All my love,

Your Greggy

Waxed and sealed, Gregor took both his and Noal's letters down the hall and inspected the pigeons, half of which were knocked out in a drunken stupor, snoozing, refusing to rouse no matter the shakes. "And you still get bread and bed!" Gregor grumbled and fastened his letter to a drowsy one, but in an early-morning haze sort of way. What was the rush? Besides, it might take weeks for the letter to get to the mountain. Maybe it wouldn't even get there at all? Gregor couldn't tell if he was hoping for this outcome or worried about it.

He made his way down to the royal kitchen to join Noal where he was plunging another plate into the giant sink, sloshing suds onto his chin. Baking competition or not, they still had to earn their room and board. He and Noal assumed that passing their apprenticeship meant getting more glorified jobs in the royal kitchen. Instead, they were on dish duty, meant to stay out of the way until after the royal wedding, its menu having been planned months ago, and prepping duties already allotted. Lucky for them there was never an end to dishes, and Chef Toufie was too overwhelmed to redistribute the duties. Except to Elis, who had managed to weasel himself onto breakfast duty, kneading biscuits and scones, still drunk from the night before. He barely napped before he changed out of his fineries into his fresh black coat. They all felt more grown-up, wearing the black uniform of the royal kitchen versus the white one of the apprentices. Ash was on evening duty, and Gregor felt relieved that he wasn't around, at least not these next few shifts.

"I did it," Gregor announced. "I sent the letter!"

Noal elbowed Gregor in the stomach good-naturedly. "Good on you! How long will it take to get there?"

Gregor shrugged and loaded another pile of breakfast dishes into the rinse sink. "Dunno. Days, maybe weeks. Sometimes they come regularly, sometimes not. But it's out there. It's in the gods' hands now, I suppose."

"Well, the pigeons do alright," Noal said, trying to sound reassuring.

"That's what I'm afraid of," Gregor grumbled.

"It must be a weight off your mind. Ow!" Noal winced, shielding his eyes. Gregor looked up and he too caught the mirror's reflection in his eye.

"Can someone get that damn thing down?" Gregor hollered, and it only took a moment for someone to comply. Gregor blinked and saw it was still up, but angled away so that the rising sun didn't shine directly into it from the window. "Oy, it's staying?"

"King's orders, because of you ruddy lot." Rubyn the sous-chef scowled, stirring his sauce. "You're going to make us all famous, don't worry."

"It's a violation of our privacy," Noal lamented.

"Who pays your wages?" Rubyn retorted.

"Is it me, or are they popping up everywhere?" Noal asked.

"The mirrors? Aye, maybe," Gregor grumbled. "Just ignore them."

They tried to, they really did. But they noticed them fastened to the ceilings in the great halls, in the corners of rooms doing their very best to be inconspicuous. Gregor caught Noal playing with the compact mirror they had been issued, and Noal pretended he was just moving it around his desk, guilt written all over his face.

"*I* don't care. You were the one worried about your privacy," Gregor pointed out. "Just keep that stupid thing aimed well away from me."

"See, I've figured out that you can receive transmission without projecting," Noal said, launching into an explanation as if Gregor had invited one. "I can see everything! The rooms in the palace, inside of artist studios. There's even a mirror in Badger & Bard. Look!"

Gregor shoved Noal's hand away and Noal nearly dropped the mirror. Noal looked hurt. Gregor rolled his eyes and apologized. "Look, it's just, I feel anxious that my parents are going to see me before they read the letter I sent them explaining it all."

"But I just told you, no one can see us."

Gregor gave him a skeptical look. "Where there's windows there's peepers."

Noal's looked horrified, and he snapped the case shut. "Fine. I'll do it elsewhere."

"Good idea," Gregor agreed. "Say...is anyone else using them?"

"Oh sure, Elis blabbers into it every night. Sits there shirtless combing oil into his hair while he talks about his feelings on the baking contest, the future, and sings the praise of the king and princess like a proper brown-noser."

"Who's he talking to? You? The princess? Can you turn the volume up?"

"Anyone. Everyone. Maybe even the royals. See, if you do this rune..." Noal procured the instruction parchment and pointed to a symbol from the list of rune keys. "...then it basically lets anyone find your mirror and watch. And if you flick the glass like this..." Noal demonstrated, and images appeared, flickering by as fast as his finger swiped the mirror's surface. "...you can see everyone projecting. And then if you do this..." The volume increased and it felt as if the person were right there in the room with them.

That was how three hours passed by in the blink of an eye. Gregor finally looked up and realized the sun had gone down. He jumped up, panicked. "What time is it?"

Noal squinted at the clock. "Gods, we've been staring at this thing for hours."

"Put it away, I never want to see it again," Gregor ordered. But there had been underground dragon races they had cheered on, a cosmetic witch teaching a lesson on how to apply foundation and find the perfect shade of red, which had them sucked in for at least half an hour before Gregor cleared his throat and reminded them they didn't wear makeup. "Sort of makes me want to," Noal confessed sheepishly. "It's an art form, it really is. I'm going to be staring at lips for days now trying to discern who's wearing the right shade and who's not."

They had even come across Elis's mirror, and they hooted and hollered with excitement before they settled down to listen and grew uncomfortable to find they shared the same worries he did about the competition. "Let's change the channel before I feel sorry for him," Gregor grumbled, and Noal obliged.

There were mirrors in glass blowing studios, blacksmith shops, the bakeries they had frequented, and Noal even recognized a few faces as former classmates. "I ought to get one inside the copper mint," Noal whispered, dreaming of how some might find the inner workings of the business as fascinating as he happened to find lipstick matching.

Gregor made Noal swear on the spot he would give up the mirror. "It sucks time, and look, we've wasted the whole afternoon. This is a nightmare. We have things to do!"

Noal grumbled an agreement and peeled himself off the bed, which they had been laying on together, sharing the mirror. It had been so long since they had anything comfortable to lay on, and it had been so addicting, this new form of entertainment, but Gregor was right. There was baking to be done, techniques to be practiced, shifts to work at the royal kitchen.

Noal quit the mirror, or it at least seemed so to Gregor, though he did suddenly start taking longer bathroom breaks than usual.

18

First Round

The days were spent poring over cookbooks, scribbling recipes, running down to the test kitchen after scarfing down a quick lunch to test the recipe, tweaking the ingredients or replacing them completely. Scratching out this, adding in a pinch of that, recalculating measurements until Gregor and Noal woke up and realized they had run out of time.

On the day of the baking contest, Noal nearly shook himself out of his seat at breakfast.

"For goddess's sake, drink this," Brimley said, and handed Noal a flask.

"For breakfast?" Noal looked aghast. "You might look into having a drinking problem."

Brimley rolled his eyes. "It's herbal tea. We don't just drink ourselves blind at the monastery. And if that's what you think—"

"Yes yes, I'll come by more often to pray." Noal swiped the flask out of Brimley's hand and took a swig, made a face. "Ugh! No sugar?"

"Sugar's getting expensive." Brimley took his flask back and took a sip himself. "You get used to the taste."

Ash dropped into an empty seat beside Brimley. "What's that?" He didn't wait for an answer before swiping the flask out of Brimley's hand and taking a long drag. He made a face. "Oh yuck, I thought that was spirits."

"Why does everyone assume that?" Brimley asked incredulously. He offered it to Gregor, who shook his head.

"Not after their reactions."

"Fair enough." Brimley pocketed the flask.

"I heard you complain about the price of sugar," Ash said, pulling the plate of meats toward him. "Is that why we don't like the prince?"

Gregor's eyebrows raised. "We don't like the prince?"

"It's his stance on the health of the kingdom," Noal said.

Everyone blinked at him, expectant. "Well, don't just leave it at that," Gregor coaxed.

"Oh, well..." Noal gave a little shrug. "He's thinking of putting a tax on sugar."

"Are you trying to get the man poisoned?" Brimley hissed. "You just told a group of sugar fiends that their future king is thinking of banning sweets!"

"Not ban, I don't think. Tax it."

"We can't have that," Brimley said vehemently. "Sugar is a basic building block of life. It feeds yeast in bread and beer. It's not just for festivals and weddings. It's what makes life, life."

"There's no way the princess will get behind this," Ash insisted. "I've never read of this policy. We're getting all worked up because of a rumor."

"It's a bit more than a rumor," Noal grumbled. "They won't tell you the truth in your gossip pages."

Gregor raised his hands to quell the tension. "We're all getting very excited for nothing. We've already got enough to be worked up about this morning."

He basically had to dress Noal, who couldn't find his pants, then when he found a pair had in the meantime lost his shirt, and when he found that his shoes went missing, until Gregor slapped a smooth stone in his hand to fidget with and collected an outfit for Noal himself. "You don't do laundry enough," he complained and finally pieced an outfit together that didn't have sugar dusting on the elbows or hems. He was anxious too, but seeing Noal losing it brought a calmness to him. It turned to excitement. Gregor decided it would be less of a test and rather a chance to prove himself. After all, he had done just that at their final; surely he could do it again? And better this time, no doubt. And if by now his parents owned a mirror, by gods he was going to put on a show for them.

The chefs finished up their breakfast and marched down to the test kitchen. Walking in, they found the other contestants already there, and Mosley was right behind them.

"Pick a station, please!" Mosley made his way around the room, pulling aside cloths, revealing mirrors arranged around the room as the competitors pulled fresh, crisp coats off the walls and donned them.

Elis squeezed between Ash and Brimley by the coat hooks to whisper to Ash, "Say, where are you staying?"

"What?"

"You heard me," Elis hissed. "You're not in their room"—he nodded at Gregor and Noal—"and you're not rooming with any of the other chefs now that you're hired on. I've checked. I'm trying to switch rooms. They're bunking me with snoring Rubyn! What strings did you get your daddy to pull?"

Mosley clapped, garnering their attention. "I'm not forgetting this," Elis snapped before taking his station. Gregor watched him out of the corner of his eye, having overheard the conversation. There was definitely a secret to Ash, he was sure of it now. But what was it?

Mosley went behind the great oak desk to the enchanted chalkboard, which was covered with a sheet. He pulled a tassel on a rope as thick as his forearm to reveal it had been replaced by a giant mirror. All the contestants blinked in wonder, especially those who had spent the last few years in that room scribbling notes from that very chalkboard.

"Are we transmitting already?" Brimley asked, trying to push down his mop of hair. Elis flashed a dazzling grin, just in case.

"In just a moment." Mosley looked over at the clock on another wall and mumbled something about hurrying.

Moments later, the door opened. In filed a troupe of people and a dog, who were, as Mosley exclaimed, "Ah! The judges!" He gave a swipe to the mirror and went to take his place before the great oak desk, which had been completely cleared, and behind which four cushioned stools had been placed. As Mosley introduced the newcomers, they gave a little curtsey or bow and took a seat.

"Princess Damora, Lady-in-Waiting Celeste, Chef Toufie, myself, of course, and this..." He gestured to the black, wolfish dog with massive, pointed ears and a stick of a tail that rhythmically slapped the leg of the desk it was wagging so vehemently. "Stop it," Mosley hissed, and the rhythmic thudding stopped. Mosley gave a relieved sigh. "...is Arosco, the royal taste tester."

Harlowe and Lance exchanged a charmed smile; Elis looked as if rotten fish had been dumped in front of him. "Must we really?" he asked.

"Elis, is it?" Mosley asked, his sharp eyes locking on the pretty boy. "Yes, I suspected so. I was warned about you. No complaints. Or you'll be disqualified." Mosley said this rather gleefully, perhaps because he knew Elis's father, who wasn't the easiest to get along with. Mosley wasn't one to bully, but shutting privileged people down...well, that was a bit of a hobby. He turned back to the competition with a renewed sense of flourish.

"Welcome to the Royal Bake Off!" Mosley shouted into the mirror, making everyone flinch. "For this challenge, you will be making your very best single-layer cake. All the ingredients you could want are in the cabinets and pantry behind you. You have two hours. Fergis will light the oven when you are ready. Ready, set, *bake your best*!"

An invisible gong rang through the room so loud they all jumped. Simultaneously, a half dozen or so little sheets they hadn't noticed before fell like petals, revealing even more mirrors.

Mosley clapped with excitement as he watched them all startle and scramble for the cabinets. He walked around with a hand-held mirror, occasionally speaking into it, looking entirely gleeful as he flashed it at contestant after contestant and then back to himself, rapidly speaking into the glass.

Gregor, Noal, Ash, Brimley, and Elis decided all at once that almonds were the best flour alternative and fought over the massive jar until they finally agreed that if one ground enough for all of them, they could all have it and not waste time arguing. That was how Gregor, the strongest, ended up grinding almonds while Brimley and Noal took turns fetching him the other ingredients he asked for. He started first with a massive mortar and pestle until Elis discovered a coffee bean grinder while hunting for piping tips, and that sped the business up an awful lot.

Noal listed off the gathered ingredients. "Almonds, sugar, vanilla, milk..."

Ash walked by and hissed under his breath, "No milk."

Gregor and Noal, standing side by side, looked up, shocked. "No milk?" But Ash was already back at his station and wouldn't look up at Noal. They were competing, were they not?

"Make it without milk," Gregor whispered.

"No milk from what? Cow? Goat? Sheep? Werewolf? That's the most useless hint ever!"

Gregor looked around. Elis was beating butter and sugar together. Well, either Ash knew something they didn't or was trying to sabotage them. Almonds finely ground, he moved on and busied his hands grinding sugar into powder as he watched Ash like a hawk. Sure enough, there was no milk at his station, but he was soaking whole almonds in water. Brimley also noticed and looked around in confusion until he caught Gregor's eye. Gregor shrugged, trying to pretend it wasn't anything, but Brimley began wrapping his block of butter back up in its waxy paper. As he did, he nudged Elis—on purpose or not, Gregor could not make out—who looked up, annoyed. He saw what Brimley was doing, had his own realization, and muttered a curse as he looked past Brimley and saw Ash soaking almonds.

"Replacements!" Gregor hissed under his breath, and that seemed to snap Noal out of his panic. The giant hourglass at the front was daunting, and it was easy to get flustered when a cake—a moist, delicious delicacy—could not have dairy. Or flour.

"Oil!" Noal nearly snapped his fingers with excitement, then remembered himself. Oil to replace the butter, and the milk...well, maybe it was cheating, maybe it wasn't, to copy Ash. Others would catch on to the oil as well, and they did; Elis nearly snatched the jug out of Noal's grip, but Brimley slapped his hand away, and Elis remembered himself. A tacit collaboration ensued, and the oil jug was passed around, as was the jar of almonds again, but it was up to each contender to decide how much of what to use. And what flavor cakes to make.

"What next, no sugar?" Noal muttered.

As he worked, Gregor watched the other chefs, who seemed completely oblivious to what was happening at their end. Gregor worried that either they were right, or very, very wrong as he watched them beat buttercream silky smooth, using so much dairy it would have put someone lactose intolerant clear into the grave.

As the cakes began to come out of the oven, Mosley made his rounds again, stopping before piping hot, uniced cakes. He hem-hawed and wiggled his eyebrows, which was probably comical to the viewer on the other side of the mirror but spiked everyone's anxiety in the kitchen.

"What? Is it okay? Is it?" Lance called after him once Mosley had moved on.

A burst of light flashed, followed by a puff of smoke as Harlowe instantly torched the meringue on his cake.

"No magic!" Mosley shouted, running towards Harlowe with his mirror.

"He could have stated that in the rules," Ash muttered, and, while Mosley was still distracted, hurried to ripen the strawberries he had before him to perfect plumpness with a touch. He caught Gregor's glare and rolled his eyes. "*Fine.*"

Gregor tried his best to tune it all out and focus on smashing hazelnut after hazelnut with a rolling pin. He knew chocolate was safe, sugar was safe, flour was not, dairy was not...and so he'd wracked his brain until it settled on a chocolate icing hazelnut cake. He figured leaning into the nut theory wouldn't hurt. For the icing, he mixed the finely ground powdered sugar with cocoa powder and a bit of water to pour over the top. It dribbled down the sides of the loaf in long, teasing tendrils, hardening into a shiny shell. The cake ended up perfectly moist and dense and packed with bits of coarsely chopped hazelnuts, which also decorated the top.

"*Time!*"

19

Edibility

Piping bags, sugar sifters, jars of dried fruit, nearly empty bowls of icing, and utensils of all shapes and sizes clattered onto countertops as everyone immediately dropped whatever was in hand. They took a step back, clasped their hands behind their backs, stepped their feet hip-width apart, and fixed their gazes on the front of the room, which, in this case, bore their own reflection. In it, they could survey everyone else's cake without obviously gawking, and the variety impressed them.

"When called, please step up and describe your cake and slice it for us."

Gale was the first to be called up, and he steered his cardamom carrot cake topped with cream cheese frosting to the great oak desk. Everyone's eyes trailed him as Gale finished cutting five slices and served them to the judges. Before they even reached for a bite, the dog raised a paw. Everyone—excluding the princess—devoured their slices with relish.

Gale stepped back to his station and waited as notes were scribbled.

After much whispering, Mosley stood and made sure to smile into a mirror as he said, "Flavor is very good, not too sweet. Well done. Presentation is simple and a bit lacking, as is the creativity. You've played it safe, Gale. As for edibility, zero."

"Zero?" Gale blinked in confusion. "But she just gobbled it up," he said, motioning to Celeste.

"Yes, but I'm not the person you're supposed to please. It's the princess."

Princess Damora cleared her throat, looking uncomfortable with how blunt Mosley and Celeste were being, though this wasn't out of character for them. "Unfortunately," she said softly, "due to some ingredients, I can't eat this."

"Why not? What can't you have?"

Celeste's eyes flashed. "You can't speak to the princess like that!"

"Like how?" Gale wailed. "I asked a simple question." He slapped the back of his hand into his palm repeatedly for emphasis.

Harlowe approached his friend and put a hand on his shoulder, whispered something into his ear. Gale seemed to crumple. "Thank you," he told the judges and shuffled back to his table.

"I'd like to go next," Harlowe volunteered. "I used flour, eggs, butter—"

"No, no, no," Mosley protested, but the princess raised a hand for him to hush. "No, let him," she said. "You mentioned no rules against this."

Harlowe relaxed a bit and eagerly listed off the rest of his ingredients. "...to make a mascarpone lemon meringue cake. Please enjoy."

They liked the taste, creativity was there, presentation was lovely—"Look at those peaks!"—and yet, that dog's paw was up, and so Harlowe only got a polite smile from the princess, and a zero for edibility.

No one volunteered next, and so Mosley called on Ash, who brought up his strawberry lemon oat loaf and sliced it the same as everyone else. This time no paw was raised, and the princess took her first bite of the competition. Her eyes lit up and defeat shaded Gale and Harlowe's features.

"Ooh, it's tart." Princess Damora puckered her lips with delight.

Chef Toufie kept diligent notes and chewed slowly, swishing each bite around his mouth for optimal flavor exposure.

Ash said nothing. Everyone's eyes bore into him in the mirror and at the back of his head as Harlowe and Gale stared expectantly at him, waiting for a list of ingredients. Still, nothing.

After Mosley polished off his slice, he addressed the tension. "You're not taking after Harlowe?"

"It's a competition," was all Ash said, and the air nearly combusted behind him.

High taste, good presentation, low creativity, but edibility was there.

Next, Elis presented his coconut raspberry cake. Coconut shavings like fresh snow powdered the top, dotted with dollops of raspberry jam. If the princess could have eaten it, it might have been her favorite.

Brimley presented his lemon lavender loaf. The cake itself was lemon flavored, poked with holes into which sugar syrup boiled with lavender was poured to soak the flavor through. Lemon slices and lavender sprigs crowned the cake. No bite. The rest of the critique didn't even seem to matter.

Gregor presented his chocolate hazelnut cake, completely unsure if it would meet the criteria. So far, only Ash's cake had been eaten, and while he now confirmed dairy was not edible, he wasn't sure how Brimley's cake—which seemed void of dairy—hadn't passed. His didn't either, which baffled him, although Chef Toufie ate this one with great gusto.

Alistair's white cake was flavored with almond extract; he'd seen all the almonds and assumed the princess loved almonds. It was topped with vanilla icing that had a hint of cherry juice. It was a bold choice, but Alistair knew cherry candies were all the rage right now. The cake was slightly pink and very moist from the cherry juice he had sprayed lightly over it before he iced it. He was told it was the prettiest one so far. Still, it was not eaten.

Noal presented his poached pear with honey drizzle cake. Uneaten.

Lance was last. He was profusely sweating, an absolute mess, unsure what to make of all the cakes. No one besides Harlowe mentioned ingredients, but he decided to as well. Maybe it gave everyone an advantage, but it was an act of solidarity with Harlowe, and perhaps they could work together to figure out the mysterious allergy ingredients. Harlowe was a wizard, after all. That made him smart, right? After Lance listed the ingredients of his angel food cake, he walked his cake up.

He'd nearly made it to the table when he tripped over his own feet.

Lance didn't go flying, but he did lunge forward, and the cake slid from the tray. He slammed a hand on top of it, which kept the cake from plummeting to the floor, but also made a crater in the center of it.

Gasps rang out and Mosley nearly exploded with delight.

Burning with shame, Lance did his best to cut around the dented top, slicing off chunks from the edges. So much for presentation.

It was still yummy, but inedible. Inedible and with the worst presentation. *Inedible.* The word pounded in Lance's mind. He stepped back to his station, looking as if he would cry.

Lucky for him, Mosley concluded the contest with, "We won't be eliminating this round. We have tallied points that will be combined with the final round next week to determine the winner."

Elis couldn't help himself. "Who's in the lead?"

"I think you can conclude who's not," was all Mosley said and got the reaction he'd been hoping for: Lance burst into tears. Gregor couldn't be sure, but it seemed to him as if every mirror in the kitchen swiveled in the direction of the spectacle. Harlowe did his best to comfort his friend. The princess hurried to clear her throat, and that scared Lance into swallowing his outburst.

A respectful hush fell over the room. "I *so* enjoyed this," she said, catching Ash's eye. "I look forward to tasting *all* of your cakes next week."

Ash blushed and stared holes into his splattered workstation.

"Next week's challenge is a vanilla cake. But there will be a surprise," Mosley said.

"What is it?" Elis asked.

"It will be *a surprise*," Mosley repeated, looking baffled that Elis didn't understand that this meant, *I'll tell you then.* Elis did know this, but he figured it was worth a shot to ask anyway.

"A vanilla cake *the princess can eat.* It will take place here a week from today."

Their feet dragged as they left the kitchen, each chef suffering from varying degrees of shame. They *had* to do better next week.

20

Secret Revealed

The tension boiled over in the hallway when Elis grabbed Ash by the collar and dragged him around a corner. He pushed Ash up against a wall and bared down on him. Noal and Gregor, who saw this, hurried after but kept their distance when they saw Elis no longer had his hands on Ash. Frankly, they were very curious about what was about to take place.

"Spit it out, then," Elis hissed. "You knew the secret and no one else did."

"I did." Ash pushed Elis, who was caught off guard and stumbled back a few steps. "Why should I tell you the secret? We're competing against one another, aren't we?"

At this, Elis didn't have a comeback.

"I don't owe you friendship, Elis. Not when you never gave it before, and certainly not now, when we're literally at the end. You chose who to make allies with long ago and trying to bully me into letting you in on a secret won't help. Go butter up that dog, that might get you further."

Elis threw his hands up in frustration but caught sight of the spectators. He dropped his hands and said to Gregor and Noal, "You see there's something suspicious, no?" With that, he stormed off.

Ash tried to give a reassuring smile, but Gregor stepped in between him and Noal, arms crossed. "Elis is right, there's something off about this. What are you hiding?"

"What do you mean?" Ash easily looked over his head at Noal, but Gregor grabbed Noal by the shirt front and pulled him down to his level, forcing Ash to lock eyes with him.

"Gregor," Noal pleaded, trying to tug himself free.

Gregor turned. "What? Do you know what's going on?"

"We...we should talk," he said, looking back at Ash, who let out a reluctant sigh but nodded. "Let's take a walk."

Gregor let go of Noal and fell into step behind the two. He wanted to walk between them but couldn't keep pace with the length of their legs. Still, he was easily within earshot should they try to converse. They didn't. They made it all the way into the royal courtyard without a word.

"Go on," Noal said, taking a seat on a stone bench. "It's time he knows."

"How do I even..." Ash wrung his hands. "I'm not staying in your dormitory wing. I never was. Your dorms only allow men."

"Sure," Gregor said.

"*Your* dorms."

Gregor frowned. "You're not staying in our dorms...?"

"Because I can't," Ash finished. He let out a tremendous groan and closed his eyes. "I'm a lady-in-waiting."

Gregor looked at Noal, confused, who stared at his shoes, beet red. "They let men be ladies-in-waiting?"

"I'm a lady!" Ash shouted. He—she—sunk onto the bench beside Noal. "I'm a girl. I've been a girl this whole time. I'm also an elf so I'm tall and flat and I cut my hair short and keep my voice low."

It took Gregor a moment for the understanding of this confession to hit him. "You've been a *girl* this whole time?" He looked between his friends and could barely get the words out between sputters. "You kept this a secret from me?" Gregor fell into the seat beside Noal, the heels of his palms in his eyes. He turned to look at Noal. "Her, I get. But you?"

"It's not my secret," Noal said defensively. "Besides, if anyone found out, they would have expelled her. And that's not fair! She can bake as well as the rest of us, she did her time at the apprenticeship same as we."

"How did you not get caught? What about when the princess judged?" Gregor asked. "She didn't recognize you?"

"I think...well, I'm not like, a top lady-in-waiting or anything like that, so maybe she didn't realize. Or maybe she did, and she's a bit more...progressive than her father. In any case, she let me graduate."

"Is Ash even your real name?"

"It is. It's short for Ashlynn."

In the next moment, Gregor realized then that Ash was no worse than him. He who had been lying to his sweet, supportive parents the whole time he was training. One lie to get through it all. Gregor stood up and extended his hand. "I'm sorry. I did not mean to offend by my reaction. I did not mean to imply that your gender had anything to do with your skills. You are an excellent chef."

Ash shook his hand, the peaceful offering of starting over. "I'm sorry I lied to you. I only told Noal because he asked if I would be his roommate."

This blow hurt most of all. Gregor looked at Noal, who held up a defensive hand. "Only in case you said no! You were my first choice."

"Hey!" Ash cried.

"Oh, come off it, both of you!" Noal lamented. "All this time, I've been in a terrible spot. You're both my best friends, but I'm each of your best friends, and I feel like I'm the rope in an eternal game of tug-o-war. I live with Gregor, and he was my business partner, and I spent the summers with Ash. There! You're always going to feel like you have to fight for my favoritism but I'm doing my best to be just with my time. It's truly unfair that the two of you have found this to be a point of quarrel instead of coming together to be close friends."

"I always felt a bit uneasy around you," Gregor confessed to Ash. "I think, deep down, I might have known you had a secret. I was always suspicious."

"I don't know that I would have had the courage to confess it sooner," Ash said. "I apologize."

"We've already shaken in friendship, that's behind us," Gregor said, trying his best to truly get over the uncomfortable ache within him. He would, he resolved, do better. For Noal. "Now, this cake business."

Ash looked even more embarrassed. "I couldn't well have told you both the secret allergies of the princess, could I?"

"What was the last thing? What was it that you put in that I didn't?" Noal asked.

"It's what *you* put in that I didn't. Eggs."

"I-I hadn't seen eggshells, so I just assumed you had already added them." It was Noal's turn to feel betrayed. "Eggs? Really? No flour, no dairy, no eggs?"

"That's it," Ash nodded.

"That leaves...well, just about nothing," Gregor said, flabbergasted. "What did you keep the cake together with? A coaxing charm?"

"It's a miracle she hasn't died yet," Noal said, referring to the princess.

"She's just not a big sweets person. Also, the royal taste tester helps," Ash said.

"Do we tell Brimley?" Gregor asked.

Ash shook her head. "No. We're still competing. Part of the challenge is figuring out the secret allergens."

The clock tower bell tolled the hour, making them all jump.

"I'd better get back to my duties," Ash announced.

"Come out for dinner," Noal urged. "Now that this is all out in the open, I'd like you two to get better acquainted."

Ash gave a little laugh. "I'm not a new person, Noal."

"No, but now we can speak freely, truly, for the first time! Besides, it's been such a day, let's go to the pub and complain. Scheme. We can't do that in the dining hall, can we?"

"You're right," Ash said, thoughtful. The servant's dining area was large enough to accommodate all the staff, but she had always gone at calculated times, sometimes with the ladies, sometimes with the apprentices, and never did the two groups mingle. But now with the mirrors...it put Ash on edge. No one would be looking at her, why would they? When there was a wedding and betting halls to tune into and the royal dressmaker making frantic updates each morning from under a comically large pile of tulle. "Alright, let's."

21

Badger & Bard, Again

Badger & Bard was in full swing that evening despite the summer thunderstorm rolling in, threatening to break any minute. Gregor and Ash took a seat at a newly cleared booth and Noal went to order beers at the bar.

Gregor picked up the menu and fanned it a few times, looking over the top at Ash, who was still Ash, but not really.

Ash glanced up. "What?"

"It's just a bit weird, is all," Gregor said. "Suppose I suddenly told you I'm a fairy, you'd look at me funny for a week and a half."

"I was determined to become a royal chef and do anything to get there. It's unfortunate that there are certain rules in place. Imagine they decide not to let you in because you're a dwarf. Would that not be unfair?"

"I wouldn't dress up as a fairy and try to get in if that was the case."

"Then you just don't want it badly enough."

Three mugs slammed onto the table, and Gregor grabbed one, gulping greedily. He pulled away and made a puckered face. "Think how much money they could make if they actually sold the good brews."

"Brimley told me that part of their income at the monastery is beer tourism. So not likely," Noal said. He took a drink and mirrored Gregor's face. "I've been ruined."

Ash, who hadn't tasted the beer alternatives, drank it easily and let out a tremendous belch. "What?"

Gregor tried his best to blink the shock off his face. "It's not very la—*well done*." Ash grinned at him. "Now, tell us how you replaced the egg in that cake."

***

At a booth across the pub sat three other competitors, feeling rather sorry for themselves.

"Where's your trolley?" Gale shouted at Alistair, who was all the way at the bar and out of earshot. Harlowe patted his hand. Gale pulled away, not in the mood to be soothed. "He just saunters into our kingdom and gets handed an invitation to compete for *our* princess's approval? Have either of you even had his sweets?"

Harlowe and Lance shook their heads.

"He doesn't have a purple seal," Gale added. "To think! My family has spent generations building our business and he just *rolllllls* up with a trolley and plants it in the ground like a flag. He ought to be run out of town, not welcomed into the palace." Gale drank from his chipped mug. "My great-grandad was a dwarf," he added before either of the others could cut in to change the subject. Gale's eyes went far away. "Passed through the kingdom on his way to deliver a dragon's egg."

"What was he doing with a dragon's egg?" Lance asked. "Was he stealing it?"

Gale gave a wave. "It's called Luck of the Draw. Each generation a dragon lays an egg on a mountain and the bravest dwarf goes on a quest to return it to its mother. The journey goes right through this city. As he was passing through, he met my great-grandma and got her good. Surprised they didn't scramble the egg into an omelet then and there."

"Isn't that the reason the city's run over with dragons?" Lance asked. "I heard a dragon was born here and was so admired it made having a dragon fashionable."

"Hold on, I think you're right," Harlowe said, realization dawning on him. "That's why your bakery is called The Golden Egg, isn't it?"

Gale drank from his mug, burning bright red. He certainly didn't want to be *blamed* for the dragon overpopulation.

"Why aren't you friends with Gregor? Seeing as you both have dwarf in you," Harlowe asked.

"The newbie?" And from the way Gale said it, Harlowe could just about gather the reason.

"We were all strangers here once, you know. You just told us your great-grandad was a passing-through dwarf! How do you think her parents felt when your grandmother announced she was loving on a stranger? Did he even stay?" Harlowe asked. He cradled his mug of hot toddy sans lemon, sans water.

"Of course he did," Gale huffed. "He gave up being King of the Mountain for her."

"So romantic," Lance murmured, looking dreamy.

"See? Not all foreigners are bad," Harlowe concluded.

"So go buy him a drink then," Gale huffed, waving his mug in Alistair's direction.

"Come off it, Gale. You being sour isn't going to do anything but waste time while that one"—Harlowe nodded towards the bar—"schemes."

"I'm getting another," Gale announced, scooting out of his seat.

"Don't, you'll only get in a fight," Lance groaned.

"I'll go," Harlowe offered, and eased a coin from Gale's purse as he slipped by. It wasn't magic, pickpocketing, but it was a fun trick, handy to have. He elbowed his way to the bar, at the opposite end of Alistair, lest he be a lesser man and lose his temper as well. "Three Dragon's Breaths," Harlowe shouted after scanning the enchanted chalkboard menu a moment. He wasn't much of a beer drinker, but the hot whiskey was hitting his belly something fierce.

Darce nodded and began to tip mugs to the lip of the beer tap. Harlowe looked past him at the mirrored wall lining the bar behind the bottles and instead of seeing his reflection, he saw Gregor's. Which was fine, and cheered him up even, but then he realized Gregor was in his chef's coat, and he wasn't at the bar at all, but rather...the royal kitchen?

Harlowe looked around expecting himself, for one panicked second, to be back in the kitchen. He saw the inside of the pub. He whipped back around to the mirror to find Noal, sweating profusely, watching a forkful of his cake being lifted to Celeste's mouth.

"My gods," Harlowe whispered.

"It's the rerun from earlier," said the man beside him. "Made damn fools of themselves, the whole lot of them."

"Everyone can see this?"

"Everyone with a mirror."

"Not true," Darce said, overhearing. "I had the mirrors enchanted just this morning. Mirrors won't do anything unless they're cursed or enchanted."

"Who?"

"Who what?" Darce asked.

"Who enchanted the mirrors?" the man asked.

"A royal sorcerer."

"You're letting the government come in and spy on you?" The man looked incredulous. A few others around him hushed, curious.

"What! It's for entertainment. It's the new age, Steu! You want to wait for a drunk pigeon to bring you the paper still, that's on you, but I've got customers who come here for the gossip and the news. I want to be the first to show it."

"Is it two-way?" someone asked.

Steu swiveled in his seat to face him. "What's that mean?"

"Meaning, we can see what they're putting out, but can they see us now?"

This got everyone chittering anxiously.

"See what? The ruddy drunk lot o' ya staring, salivating, and swearing? What's the king got to do with that?" Darce barked, getting irked. "No one's watching you, Steu, and I don't want you starting rumors that my bar is bewitched, or you won't be welcome here no more."

"I didn't say *bewitched*," Steu stammered, but Darce cut him off with a look. He turned to Harlowe and suddenly remembered the beers he was supposed to be filling for him. "Sorry, I'll finish those."

Harlowe went to say it was fine, take his time, but Darce had already turned away.

"Oh good, I was going to bother your friends, but they're squabbling like a flooded pixie colony." The owner of the feminine voice slid in beside Harlowe, so close he had to pull his foot back so that she was no longer stepping on the toe of his boot. An elegant hand extended toward him. "I'm Harper Leewood from *The Harking Herald*."

Harlowe shook the hand and then immediately wiped his down the front of his shirt, suspicious of spells, powder, and saliva. "I'm sorry I don't read the...?"

"*Harking Herald,*" she repeated, leaning in close to be sure she was heard. The woman had short, raven-black hair cropped shorter on the sides, the top kept long and plumed up like a crest of black feathers. Her cheekbones were sharp like the little teeth she flashed when she smiled, and her grey eyes were sunken deep behind a hooked nose. She wore a violet cloak that clasped at the throat and closed completely, hiding everything beneath it. She looked frightening, but Harlowe couldn't place why. He wanted to pull back, but there was no room behind him at the crowded bar. He looked over at Darce, panicked, but Darce was yelling at someone to come exchange the barrel that had run dry. Harlowe wanted desperately to let him know that anything—*anything*—could go into those mugs. Blood of Ogre was good, Wolfsbane Elixir, Belladona Tonic, Oatsby Red, Tattle the Tankard...any beer would do!

Harper opened a compact mirror, set it on the bar, and nudged it so that it angled towards Harlowe. "I was hoping to catch a few words. We're all so eager to discuss your thoughts on the final round. Or would you rather fill your followers in on what went wrong today? Not as uplifting a topic, for sure, but perhaps you'd rather reminisce?"

"Darce!" Harlowe bellowed, not taking his eyes off Harper.

"Almost! I had to change the barrel!"

"Anything, man, anything!"

"I'm not mixing Dragon's Breath with Oatsby, that's rancid! It might even detonate the mug! No, no, just hold onto your britches, I'm about to tap it now."

Harper smiled that tiny sharp-toothed smile at Harlowe. She pushed a strand of her curls back, revealing tiny feathers wisping around her hairline. "Maybe I should have bought you a drink? I'm sorry, I don't mean to be rude, it's just been a while since I've done interviews. I had a gossip column and then was doing aerial coverage, mostly weather, but they wanted someone who could—"

"There!" Darce shouted, slamming four mugs on the bar. "And an extra for the lady. Press drinks for free. Don't be unfair to me, Harlowe, it's a busy night. I've got a lot of foreigners who don't know beer and haven't exchanged coins yet. I'm running to the back trying to calculate exchange rates on coins I don't even know are legit."

"Alright, alright," Harlowe muttered, pressing Gale's coin into the out-stretched palm. "Keep the change."

"Does it pay well, being a chef in this city?" Harper asked, snatching up her mirror.

"I'd rather you not trail me," Harlowe said as Harper did just that all the way back to his table. His friends turned, their smiles wavering at seeing the stranger. Harlowe offered no explanation as he took his seat, burning a deep shade of mortified red.

"Who's this?" Gale asked, motioning with his refilled mug.

"I'm—" Harper went and grabbed a stool from the next table and settled onto it. She gave a relieved little huff, opened her compact mirror again, set it casually on the table, and resumed. "Harper Leewood from *The Harking Herald*. I'm covering the Royal Bake Off. I figured you'd like to tell your side of the story first."

"First? Who's telling it at all?" Lance asked. "Is it Alistair? What's he blab-bering about? Say, what's his story? That's what you really ought to be covering. Mysterious man appears in town, selling sweets without a royal seal. You know about the purple seal, don't you, Harper?"

"Uh, well, I'm not really covering trade and commerce, if that's what you're implying."

"What are you looking for then? What's the angle? Gossip?" Gale asked.

Harper clasped her hands together. Her nails were long and curved. "I'm covering politics. The royal wedding is causing all sorts of stirs in the kingdom. I'm wondering how you three"—she pointed to each one of them in turn—"fit into the fold. What's your angle? Why win this? Will it bring glory? Riches? That royal seal?"

"We're winning so *he* won't," Gale snapped.

Harper pointed her mug at him as if it were a gavel. "I want to know what your strategy is."

Lance took a swig of beer and shrugged. "We need to figure out what the princess is allergic to. Do you have any clues for us? After all, you're asking for a story with seemingly nothing in return. This could be a bit of a, what would you call it, quid-pro-quo?" He wagged a finger between himself and Harper. "A little nudge to get us going. Then, as the winners, we'll give you an exclusive first interview."

"There can be only one winner."

"You're right! Fellas, what do you say? Harper here gets us a list of the princess's secret allergies and in exchange whoever wins will give her the first interview. *Exclusive* interview. That seems fair, doesn't it?"

"And if *he* wins?" Harper pointed at Alistair at the bar, deep in conversation with a balding man.

"Fine, go make the deal with him then," Lance said with a shrug. "See how easy he is to talk to. I can assure you, he's tighter than a deep-sea mystic shell."

Harper decided this would be much easier to milk than elbowing her way back over through that crowd. She motioned for a waitress, ordered another round, and made sure to gently nudge the compact mirror in the direction of the speaker as they took turns chatting.

22

Sweet Secret

"Two—no, three of whatever you have left." Ash stood at the swamped bar of Badger & Bard, squinting to read the labels on the barrels and failing. Nearly all the names on the enchanted chalkboard were crossed out, and it was hard to tell what was left. The pub had gotten more and more crowded as the evening crawled into night and more customers strayed in.

The mirror behind the bar didn't faze her. That one wasn't a threat. She worried of the ones that appeared overnight in all the halls and common areas of the palace. Ash knew how they worked; the princess had an enchanted mirror in her room that chimed sweetly to get her attention when there was a call for her to take, either from her father or a lady-in-waiting announcing the bath was drawn, the breakfast was ready, or the horse was saddled and ready to straddle for her morning ride.

In fact, Ash had been offered an enchanted mirror on many occasions by her parents, who wanted to speak with her regularly. She declined each time, already unable to keep up with their incessant letters. She occasionally used the mirrors around the palace to place a call to them but kept the chats brief, citing that they were royal mirrors to be used only for official business and that using them was a privilege she could only enjoy sparingly.

It had been tricky, enrolling in the apprenticeship after she arrived to be a lady-in-waiting. Being an elf had advantages; she was tall, slim as a board, no feminine features filled in yet, and if she applied immediately, wouldn't fill out until quite a while after graduation. She trimmed her hair just long enough to cover the points of her ears and hid the length under a headdress when in the royal wing of the palace. She practiced speaking in baritone. She shortened her name to Ash and observed how the guards stood, studied how they laughed. She sewed her own loose tunics without frills or beautiful buttons and preferred them to the dresses she laced herself into while on embroidery duty.

It helped that Princess Damora encouraged her court to pursue hobbies. As to what they were, she didn't ask. She merely made sure to let them have ample time off. Ash knew that enrolling in the apprenticeship as a woman was forbidden, but she did so anyway, figuring if admissions was too stupid to know, she wouldn't volunteer the information.

She did her chores in the evenings, the shift a lot of the older ladies-in-waiting preferred not to take anyway since they had families to get home to. The princess was very independent; she brushed her own hair, scrubbed her own skin with oils and lotions, and pulled the sheet back fully on her own when it was time to jump into bed at night. Ash and the rest of the ladies were basically maids: tidying the chambers, sewing dresses and fixing hems, washing the stained riding clothes, refilling the pots of ink before they ran dry and, in Ash's case, also freshening up the wilted bouquets placed around her apartment.

It wasn't until the coat ceremony when Ash faced her princess that she thought her world would collapse. In truth, Princess Damora suspected the student looked familiar. But if she could be in a kitchen and judge cakes, why shouldn't Ash be there to bake them? Princess Damora simply assumed that Ash had gotten in on a merit she wasn't privy to and didn't question it. Not when she had a royal wedding to plan, a white dress to choose, and a baking competition to judge because her father thought it would get his estranged wife's attention. Simply put, she had too much on her plate to worry about what her ladies did on their own time.

What if you win?

The thought both thrilled and haunted Ash. Would she step into the limelight? Would her employer finally realize what was going on and put an end to it? Could the Crown revoke her certificate? Would she be allowed to continue employment in the royal kitchen? It seemed no matter how Ash analyzed the outcome, it would never be in her favor. Besides, who would patronize a restaurant run by a woman? Purple seal or not, there were prejudices in this city, and Ash felt she would only ever succeed if she was second fiddle to a man. She figured that man would be Noal.

It would be a dream, opening a shop with her best friend. But the trouble with being his shadow was that *she* wanted to pick the name. She wanted it to be, The-Name-of-the-Restaurant *by* Ash Birchwood. Dreams were dreams. Hard to shake.

"You did a fine job today."

Ash turned to find herself face-to-face with Alistair. She shrank back instinctively, as if she just noticed a snake too close, already poised to strike.

"Thanks." She turned away to make that the end of it.

"How'd you know?"

She couldn't help herself and looked over her shoulder. "Know what?"

Alistair let out a scoff. "Come now, Ash. You were the only one to pass the test. How do you know what the princess can't eat?"

His voice pulled her in, sweet as the candy off his cart. He smiled, his eyes crinkling at the corners, handsome laugh lines deepening around his lips. She couldn't help but answer, "I've lived in this city my whole life. People talk. I listen."

Alistair sat turned on his stool, facing her. They were nearly eye level, and it was now impossible to ignore him. Not for the first time tonight, someone wished Darce poured a little faster than he usually did.

"Sounds like you've got an unfair advantage."

At this, Ash let out a snort. "Me? How did *you* get into all this?"

"Perhaps the king noticed my talents." Alistair reached into his coat pocket and pulled out a pouch. He shook the contents onto the bar. Sweets of every color, shape, and size tumbled out. Wrapped in wax or clear cellophane. "Or perhaps you prefer peppermint?" He pulled out what looked like a cigar case, opened it, and presented her with the most gorgeous display of twisted shining peppermint sticks, the lacquer catching the old-fashioned candle lights above the bar.

"You think you can buy my secrets with candy?"

"I don't dare assume you would be charmed so easily. But, from one professional to another, it would be nice to get your opinion. Perhaps you'll be just as impressed as the king was by my talent."

Alistair nudged the box a little closer to her, and there was just something about the way the red and green ribboned around the white stick that made Ash reach in, pluck one out, and pop it into her mouth, half of it stuck out like a pipe between her lips. The explosion of flavor was unlike any peppermint she'd tried before. Hot, sweet, icy. She rolled it around with her togue, painting her whole mouth in the flavor. She finally pulled it out for inspection, unable to believe that all that deliciousness was contained in such a thin little stick. "Oh my."

Alistair broke into a grin. Ash noted his teeth were too white for someone who ate candy all the time. "It cleans your teeth, too," he said, as if reading her mind.

"It's enchanted?"

It was, but not to clean teeth. Alistair was no creature cursed not to lie. Still, he side-stepped the answer. "It's made with minerals good for teeth, and the saliva you produce from sucking on it naturally cleans."

"Candy that's good for you," Ash muttered, popping it back into her mouth. She closed her eyes. The booze, the sweetness...she felt herself relax, smile. She felt *wonderful*. Like she could kiss this stranger, kiss all the strange, foreign people at this bar and they would all be friends. What a wonderful place! She opened her eyes. "It wouldn't be fair for me not to pay you for this."

"I take no money," Alistair said, stuffing the box and bag of sweets back into his pockets. "A little friendship...that is priceless."

Ash narrowed her eyes. She could guess where this was going. "So is knowing the princess's allergies."

"Friends share secrets," Alistair coaxed, watching the peppermint flick from one corner of Ash's mouth to the other as she worked on it.

"I mean, they're not that big of a secret. She has really common allergies. Lots of people have them."

"Lots of people have allergies," Alistair agreed. "Nothing special about that."

"Plenty of people can't drink cow's milk."

"Truly."

"And gluten? Why, that's a strange one, but not unheard of."

"I know lots who can't have gluten."

"And eggs! Don't rob the hen of her babies."

"Truly cruel." Alistair waited for Ash to continue, almost afraid that speaking might break the spell. "What about...nuts?"

"Nuts?" Ash squinted into the distance, thinking. "Almonds are fine. But she might not like the taste of nuts. Maybe better avoid it?"

"It's for the best."

Darce set the mugs in front of Ash, who offered the coins with a wink. Darce blinked, confused. He looked at Alistair and then back at Ash and said, "I'm cutting you off."

"This isn't all for me," Ash said, rolling her eyes. She lifted the mugs and gave Alistair a nod. "Alright then, I'm off. Good luck."

Alistair gave a two-finger salute. "Same to you."

Ash made her way back to the table feeling like somehow, she'd won.

23

Deals Made

"What is that?" Noal asked as Ash approached, her lips still puckered around Alistair's sweet.

Gregor didn't bother being polite. He snatched the peppermint stick out of Ash's mouth and sniffed it. "It's a sweet!"

"You took candy from him?" Noal slapped a hand on his forehead. "That snake!"

"He gave it to me. He's nice."

"He *drugged* you." Gregor stuffed the sticky mess into his pocket. "He enchants his candies. Brimley confirmed it."

"Oh." Ash dropped into her seat, trying to comprehend fully what that meant through the pink feel-good haze in her mind. "What does that mean?"

"He put a spell on you," Noal hissed. "How do you feel?" He grabbed either side of Ash's head and used his thumbs to pull up her eyelids and inspect her eyes. He turned her head this way and that while she squirmed to get away.

"Lay off, I feel fine. I feel fantastic! You're overreacting. He's my *friend*."

Noal and Gregor each let out a frustrated groan. "You told him, didn't you?" Gregor said.

"Told him what?"

"The ingredients to avoid."

"No, I didn't. I just told him what the princess is allergic to."

"She's done for the night," Gregor said solemnly. "Come on, Ash, let's get you to your room."

"We can't take her," Noal insisted, then dropped his voice. "She's in a different wing than we are. We can't just go in where the ladies-in-waiting stay."

"By gods," Gregor groaned.

"We can just sneak her into our room," Noal offered.

"What would people say?" Gregor asked, scandalized.

"Ash is one of us, they won't suspect a thing. Oh, come on Gregor, nothing's changed, nothing really. We just toss her onto my bed, I'll sleep on the floor, she'll sneak back into her room before dawn. No one will be the wiser."

Ash grabbed at Gregor's legs as Noal spoke, trying to figure out which pocket held her prize. Gregor swatted her hand away. "I see you," he growled. To Noal he said, "Shouldn't we say something? Report this? It's a crime, isn't it? To enchant people without their consent?"

"Sure it is, but then they'll know Ash is...well, they'll find things out."

"How?"

"They'll probably take her to the hospital wing until the spell runs its course, and I'm sure they'll inspect her and whatnot."

Gregor sunk his face into his hands. "Gods, what a mess." His head popped up with an idea. "What about the monastery?"

Noal frowned. "I'll be honest, I'm a bit done with drinking..."

"No, I've got the sweet in my pocket. We can get Brimley to inspect it. He'll need to do it now in case the spell has an expiration."

"What if he's not awake?"

"Call his mirror."

"They don't have mirrors in the monastery."

"He's got his personal one!" Gregor roared.

"Oh." Noal broke into a grin. "You're right." He flipped his mirror open, consulted the parchment of runes, swiped about a bit, spoke into it, and Brimley's voice could be heard on the other end. Noal snapped it shut. "Alright, but we're taking a carriage."

Gregor slipped out of his seat, then paused. He reached for his mug and drained it. "Just because she's having the worst night doesn't mean I can't try to take the edge off."

Noal gawked at Gregor. "You trust that wasn't laced too, just in case?"

"Gods!" Gregor exclaimed. He hooked a finger through Ash's belt loop to steer as Noal pressed a hand against her back, pushing, and together they made their way out of the pub. Noal stuck his thumb out by the side of the road to hail a carriage while Ash pulled away to dance.

"Gods!" Gregor shouted and took off after Ash, who had broken his grip to spin in the downpour. He pulled his cloak over his head, trying to stay somewhat dry. A movement behind Ash gave him pause.

"Did you see that?" he asked Ash, who was spinning and must have. He raised his voice. "Did you see a dwarf? Run by? Just now?"

Ash stopped spinning and tried to focus on him. "I see about three dwarves."

"Oy, the carriage is ready," Noal announced, jogging over to them. He ducked under Ash's arm to hold her up. He could have picked her up and carried her, but how would that have looked?

"I saw a dwarf," Gregor said, sputtering, realizing what this meant. "The Luck of the Draw! He's here!"

Noal, thoroughly exhausted by this point, the adrenaline worn off and having not had nearly enough beers to glaze this whole mess in a film of humor, asked gently, "Are you sure it wasn't Gale? He was in there, you know, at Badger & Bard."

Gregor's astonished smile wavered. "Maybe." He looked at Noal, soaked through like an alley cat, and went to help put Ash into the carriage. They sat her between them to keep her upright, as the beer and the charm had worn off, and the ensuing crash drained her of just about everything else. She fell asleep and snored, completely unladylike, to Gregor and Noal's delight.

Brimley, who was reading, jumped when the trio burst through the door.

"You're barging in here like you're storming the damn palace!" Brimley clutched his chest, trying to calm his racing heart. He had been so absorbed in *The Medical Book of Everyday Ailments* that he'd completely lost track of time.

"Sorry, sorry," Noal muttered. "Ash needs to stay the night, if you don't mind."

"Too much ale," Gregor added, and set Ash down as gently as he could. Before he could catch her, she toppled like a log onto the woven bamboo mat on the floor. "Uh, Brimley, I have a request..." Gregor yanked out the peppermint stick, which had glued itself somewhat fiercely against the fabric lining his pocket. "Can you test this? We have reason to believe it is enchanted."

"Where's it from?" Gregor and Noal exchanged a look, unsure if they wanted to divulge everything to Brimley, but the look gave it away immediately. "Ash took candy from Alistair?"

"He was drunk," Noal offered, not sure if this somehow softened the blow. It made Ash look like a complete fool, but here they were.

"Did he do it because Ash won? Was he trying to get the truth out of Ash? Did he get the truth? Do *you* know the truth? Stop looking at each other like you've committed a crime and answer me."

"Can you run the tests for us?" Gregor repeated, pink in the face from being accosted by the questions.

"I can," Brimley said, taking the peppermint stick. He weighed it in his hand, thoughtful. "This is a big favor you're asking of me."

"For *our* friend," Gregor said.

"Sure, alright." Brimley scratched his chin. "But it feels a bit as if I'm left out of the loop, you can see that, right?"

"What are you saying, exactly?" Noal asked.

"He wants to know the allergens," Gregor said flatly. "How do you know we know?"

Brimley waved the peppermint stick at Ash. "I mean...it's a bit obvious what happened, isn't it?"

"What if he only told Alistair?" Gregor countered.

"Then I'm afraid it's not really worth my time then, is it?" Noal let out a frustrated moan, but Brimley just shrugged. "You want something. I need something."

"It's a bit different," Noal protested. "He was enchanted! Drugged!"

"Yes, well, that is truly unfortunate. But you're asking me to take time to do this for you, when *really* I need to be figuring out what allergens to avoid for the final round."

"If you demand this, you're no better than Alistair."

"How so?" Brimley asked, standing up straighter. "You're asking me to run experiments on my copper and time when you could be taking this to the authorities. Clearly you need discretion. *I* need to not be the only one in this competition floundering like a headless chimera. You've seen the mirrors, I'm sure. We're all being made out to be fools."

Noal turned his back to Brimley and whispered to Gregor, "We might as well."

Gregor threw up his hands. "Fine! But Elis doesn't get to find out. That's the condition."

Brimley clapped his hands with excitement. "Alright! Let's hear it."

24

Secret Visit

Mosley was never appointed to his position as Royal Right Hand (a title he gave himself) but rather claimed it by orbiting the king until King Varundil looked around for someone to give him answers and Mosley happened to be there, eager to supply them. Who to invite to what parties and where to sit the guests, which goods to slap import tariffs on, and then one day, who did Mosley think his daughter ought to marry?

Through his rank, Mosley recruited and established a ring of spies. That was how Mosley got his nose into every business and his toe through every doorway, quickly becoming the busybody that knew everything about everyone and all the happenings around the palace. Mosley also understood as soon as he saw the first enchanted mirror flicker to life in the king's chamber that they would quickly make his network of loyalists obsolete. Where Mosley would scrounge the severance pay when he let them go was a headache for another day, but what he knew for certain at that very moment was that if a universal all-seeing mirror could be created, he needed it. The king must have one, and by gods he would have one, too. He had a mirror that controlled all the mirrors he could touch, but he needed one to see into the mirrors beyond the palace walls. And a way to ensure no one could ever breach it.

Mosley needed a mirror bespelled in such a way that no one—not a soul—could scry into the medium, not the craftiest wizard trying to break in on purpose or the most powerful sorceress accidentally happening upon his channel. It required someone incredibly powerful, keen on spells and charms, like those employed by the Crown. But of course, it could not be one of the official royal sorcerers.

Inquiring around, Mosley eventually heard a name whispered through the stalls of the farmer's market, repeated in an echo through forbidden halls. That was how he found Remus Loftly, a sorcerer who had a reputation for silly things like love potions, hair replacement oils, and crystal magic. He sold those potions in the prettiest corked bottles at the farmer's market and read tarot to those who had the patience. He was very much a part of regular society, but Remus had skills far beyond what the average Everdorne housewife was privy to. She thought he was simply good at soil supplements, predicting if her husband was due for a raise, and determining if the barn cat was pregnant again, that hussy.

No, Remus Loftly was a retired sorcerer from a far kingdom; not *banished*, exactly—he hadn't stuck around long enough to be formally banished. A tattoo on his ring finger let those privy to such things know what he was capable of, and that he was for hire.

Mosley pulled his cloak closed against the warm summer storm rain. His boots were caked thick with the mud and muck of trekking out of the city, and he stomped on the stoop before he knocked on the heavy door of the cottage. The domesticated Heel Nibbler dragons trained to herd livestock poked their heads up over the low stone fence, then lazily put them back on their paws, uninterested in human flesh. A Fire Stoker, keeping watch on the roof, jumped down the chimney to alert its master.

"Password?"

Mosley faltered. He simply stared, dumbstruck, as the eyehole of the door opened then slammed shut. The great bolt on the other side slid aside and the massive wooden door swung open, revealing a half-giant who took up nearly the entirety of the entryway. "Mosley! Come in! Leave the boots, those are filthy, then come in!"

"Yes, yes," Mosley muttered, trying to slip off his boots as Remus, a man he'd in fact never met and never introduced himself to, untangled him from his soaked cloak. They danced a bit this way before Remus gave a final, frustrated tug and Mosley spun free of the fabric.

"Come! Mum's upstairs sleeping, so let's not make too much of a racket, eh?"

Mosley followed Remus past the staircase and through the house that boasted framed pressed flowers, damask patterned sitting furniture, bookcases with cats lounging on their shelves, and carpet that was in dire need of sweeping. It only took a few steps for Mosley's socks to become as caked with cat fur as his boots had been with mud.

Remus led them to the back of the house, into a room that was outfitted in more bookcases filled with leather-bound books, a small laboratory in the back corner, and a sitting area before a wall covered floor to ceiling in mirrors, all flickering with images from parlors, houses, and halls where shady deals were being made all across the kingdom. Mosley even noticed one portraying the live happenings inside the palace. Remus approached it, tapped the glass, and said, "Cash me out, boys, I'm calling it a night," then swiped the image away before the groans of the gambling parlor could reverberate through to this side.

"Quite the, eh, setup you have here," Mosley commented, motioning to the mosaic of mirrors. It was better assembled than the one he had made for the king, he noted with envy. He didn't want to *stare*, but how could he not? Why, there were eyes on gambling halls, like the ones Remus had just been participating in, and then there was the bidding at the merchant yards, a heralder making announcements, reruns of the Royal Bake Off. There were mirrors inside of dance halls and saloons, and even—and here, Mosley pretended he hadn't noticed but ooooh, he had!—mirrors in a gentleman's parlor, where exposed flesh was everywhere and heaving. The mirrors were all muted, but it seemed as if Remus had eyes behind every door in the kingdom. *This* was precisely what Mosley needed.

"Is this what you imagined you'd create?" Remus asked, watching Mosley marvel at his wall.

Mosley balked. "Not me, the king! It was all his idea."

"Yes, I'm sure it was. And I'm sure he's doing this all for the baking competition and to transmit his daughter's wedding to everyone, even the commoners. Truly a king of his people. It was such a good idea. Thanks to it, I'm rich beyond my wildest imaginations. I don't even know what to do with this much money! Buy off the king? Hah! I'm just joking, I jest! Please, sit. Whiskey? Rum? What's this—whew! Gin, I believe?" Remus took a swig of the bottle, made a face, took another, frowned, and gave a shrug. "Not so bad. It'll pickle a cucumber if nothing else. Wine?"

He poured two glasses before Mosley could protest. Mosley accepted the crystal and tried to sit, falling into a chair that swallowed his entire behind and raised his elbows to nearly his ears when he set them on the armrests. Mosley tried to tip the glass to his lips from this position, but it was impossible, so he set his hands in his lap instead, feeling rather small. This made him very uncomfortable, even as Remus did his best to put his client at ease. The big, burly, jolly half-giant was looming over him, and Mosley felt he would be crushed if Remus forgot he was already in the chair and tried to sit.

This proved not to be an issue as Remus sat in the twin seat. He kept his wandering right eye on the wall of mirrors and fixed the other on his guest. "To what pleasure do I owe this visit?"

"I, uh, well, speaking of mirrors," Mosley said, not sure how to ask, so instead picked up from the middle that had never started. "Do they all, ah, know their mirrors are enchanted?" Mosley glanced back at the one that didn't have clothes in its frame.

Remus smiled. "You know the answer to that. That's why you're here, isn't it? To have me enchant a mirror that can tap into any mirror, any time? Create one that shouldn't be?"

"No, no, it should—it *can* be, it's my mirror," Mosley sputtered. Then he remembered himself and sat up straight, puffed out his chest as best he could. "I need it for royal official purposes," Mosley snapped. "Now, I need to make sure it can't be ingressed. Not even by someone as good as you."

"I can always tap into my own enchantments—"

Mosley cut him off. "Okay! No one *but* you. And I'll pay you extra for your discretion to keep. Out."

Remus held out his hand. Mosley placed a tiny mirror inside of it, no bigger than a pinky nail. A spy mirror, Remus could tell. For inside the palace, he was sure of it. Maybe a lady's chamber?

Remus bit the question into his cheek. Curiosity was already gnawing at him. He didn't need the money, he meant it when he said he was rich beyond his imagination. But he loved the work. And while he said he wouldn't hack it...well, it was nice to know he would be able to if he wanted to. His insurance for keeping his name off his clients' lips was blackmail, and his clients feared it, suspected it, and didn't dare accuse him of it. "Funny, you're the second person this week to ask me this favor."

"Who was the first?"

"Nu-uh." Remus wagged a finger. "You expect the same discretion, do you not?"

"Touché," Mosley muttered, but his mind whirled. Who could afford such a task? Several names came to mind, which was unsettling.

"Give me a few minutes." Remus scratched a number on a piece of parchment and slipped it Mosley's way. He got up, went over to the ancient desk in the back of the room, and got to work enchanting as Mosley counted out the fat stack of coins totaling the amount on the parchment. He would expense it, of course, but he was still nervous watching the sum grow as he counted out the pieces.

Remus came back with the mirror, explained the spell, showed Mosley the motions to turn it on, off, and handed the piece over to him. As Mosley tested it, Remus swept the pile of coins into an open drawer, and Mosley wondered if he'd ever get around to counting it. Satisfied, he stood up, shook Remus's big, hairy hand, tossed back the rest of his wine, and thanked him for a job well done.

"Now don't go telling people what I did for you." Remus let out a guffaw, but then winked in a way that had Mosley unsure what he meant by it.

Mosley made his way back to his boots and pulled them on, clasped his cloak at his throat, and slipped out the door, anxious the whole way home, convinced someone had seen him. But even if they had, they would probably assume he had been there to purchase hair serum, maybe buy dragon eggs. Ordinary stuff.

25

Encounter in the Forest

The forest surrounding Mead Monastery was perfectly ordinary. Lots of kingdoms boasted "enchanted" forests, but the truth was, every forest had magic inside of it; one was not more magical than the other. One just had to know what to harvest.

Flowers that produced poisons and potions.

Barks that alleviated pain.

Fungus that filled the stomach or tripped the mind.

Roots that aided digestion.

Other assortments of flowers that could be brewed into incredible teas. The gifts amongst the trees were truly endless.

Most everything the monastery needed grew inside its garden. But Brimley wasn't sure what he was looking for, and so went foraging in the forest. He knew he needed to replace eggs somehow. After taking mental inventory of everything in the garden, he decided nothing in there would suffice.

Brimley set out as soon as Ash left the morning after his friends crashed his room. He wanted to make the most use of the sunlight that fought to peek in through the dense brush above. He wore his usual robes though traded his strappy sandals for real shoes to trudge through the underbrush, and set his favorite straw hat on his head, tied it under his chin. He had his woven basket in the crook of one arm, and he pushed aside branches, plucked this and that until he realized, suddenly looking up, that he was deeper in the woods than he'd ever been before.

This wasn't cause for alarm. He'd had few reasons to wander into the forest before, mostly to play hide-and-seek as a child, and then once as a preteen to sneak his first kiss, but he had been too afraid to go far, fearing beasts with fangs and venom. With the day's majority still ahead of him, and still a whole reper-toire of tunes to hum, Brimley pushed deeper, curious. Getting out wouldn't be a problem. Every forest had its edges. He was a tracker and could easily find his way whenever he was ready to turn back. Now it became a new game, not just foraging, but exploring. He saw birds' nests he'd never seen before, dens of animals he wished would come out and greet him. He didn't fear dragons; there were none in the forest. They kept to the city and the plains beyond, preferring caves and crevices to lush greenery.

Brimley had a vague idea of how deep the forest was and figured he was about in the center of it when his nose twitched. Smoke. Were there dragons after all?

He froze. If the forest was on fire, that was indeed dire. Forests had fires all the time; certain trees needed the heat to help burst open the pods around their seeds. But this smell wasn't a wildfire smell. It was...homey.

Curious, Brimley pressed on, expecting to creep upon a traveler roasting something for his midday meal. He didn't expect to find a darling cottage, squat and stone, its windows full of light, its chimney billowing smoke.

Brimley knew of the cottages on the far forest edge, which he thought maybe he'd arrived at, but looking around he saw he was still very much in the thicket, and the cottage stood alone. Quiet as a shadow, Brimley slipped closer and closer to the cottage until he had his back against the cool stone. Then he peered over his shoulder into the window and nearly fell over from the shock of what he saw.

Inside were two figures, both in crisp, black coats.

Chef coats.

One was Elis, Brimley recognized immediately, but the other...by gods! The other was Chef Eclin, but he had filled out. Certainly not Chef Toufie size, and not even pudgy, not even as round as Brimley. Just enough that Eclin's cheeks were not hollow, and his stomach was no longer concave. He looked...well, he looked downright healthy. Strong even, from taking up chopping wood for the stove fires. There was color in his face, his cheeks almost ruddy, and his hair was thicker than ever before. And they were cooking! Or baking? Brimley pressed his palms, then his nose against the glass, eager to see, wishing them to turn a bit more this way or that so he could see what business they were conducting in front of the oven.

Brimley concentrated so hard that he didn't see the shadow creeping toward the window. When Fergis the dragon popped his head into view, Brimley let out a startled scream and reeled back.

Elis and Eclin whirled around, saw Brimley through the glass, and had very different reactions. Eclin looked genuinely confused. Elis looked furious. "No!" Elis shouted, pointing a finger, and Brimley realized he'd been caught.

No point in running, Brimley made his way around the building until he found the front door, which was unlocked.

"What in goddess's name!" Brimley barged into the kitchen and ripped his hat off in excitement.

Elis held up a wooden spoon as if it were a sword. "You've nothing to see here!"

Brimley crossed his arms. "Right. Just the estranged royal chef and his protégé baking in the middle of the forest in a cottage in what I can only assume is an attempt at a recipe for the competition. Tell me I'm wrong, Elis."

"Brimley!" Chef Eclin exclaimed, going over and clapping a hand on his former pupil's shoulder. "Don't be mad, I would have helped you too if you would have sought me out at my darkest hour."

"Darkest hour?" Brimley looked at him, puzzled. "Chef, with all due respect, you've never looked better."

Chef Eclin let out a hearty laugh—a sound Brimley had never heard come from the man before—and steered Brimley to the table, forced him into a seat. "Tea?" Eclin nodded to Elis.

Elis scoffed. "Me? Make tea?"

"What, have you forgotten the basics?"

"Do we offer biscuits to trespassers as well?" Elis huffed.

"Biscuits? Or is that...cake?" Brimley asked, craning his neck to catch a glance at what Chef Eclin was pulling out of the oven. Fergis stalked over, sniffing noisily, just a tad less inconspicuous than Brimley, who had begun to salivate at the smell.

Elis ignored them both, busying himself with the kettle. He set cups in their saucers a bit too loudly, and Brimley just barely snatched his hands back in time as the tray slammed down on the table in front of him.

"Not *you* being upset over this, Elis! You're being trained by the greatest baker in all the kingdom." Brimley was amazed at Elis's audacity.

"No one was supposed to know," Elis said through gritted teeth.

"Is this cheating?" Brimley asked Chef Eclin, who steered the steaming loaf, iced and decorated with crushed pistachios, to the table.

"I've read the rules. Truth is, there are no rules." Eclin chuckled. "So, no!"

"Who found whom?" Brimley wagged a finger between the two.

Rather than answer, Elis, watching Chef Eclin cut the vanilla cake filled with orange marmalade, shouted, "You can't serve him this cake!"

"Why not? Fair is fair, is it not?"

"No allegiances." Brimley clapped, delighted. He patted his belly in anticipation as Chef Eclin served generous slices to each. "I suppose there's no egg, flour, or dairy in this."

"Not a one," Eclin confirmed, and Elis slammed a fist on the table with a bang. When they turned to glare at him, he said nothing. Instead, Elis took a bite and thoroughly enjoyed the morsel; their hard work had indeed paid off.

"Now, it would be unfair to tell you what we replaced the ingredients with, like fermented yongo beans for the egg replacement—"

Bang.

"—and cashew milk for the dairy. Mixed with confectioner's sugar, add a little vanilla and brandy, it makes the perfect icing."

Bang.

"Instead of flour, ground almonds?" Brimley asked.

"And flax seeds! Just to dense it up a bit."

"That's enough!" Elis cried. "Won't you show him how to make it, too? I've been here for weeks doing this."

"*I've* been here for weeks, you've been here for what, two days now?" Chef Eclin countered.

"Then why aren't you making the cake?" Brimley asked. "What happened?"

"I-I," Chef Eclin stammered. He sunk into his chair, steepled his fingers. "I'm a coward."

Brimley took a bite. "Mhmmh! But it's delicious!"

"*Now* it is. Now that I've had time to come into the forest and forage and experiment and test and taste. When I was asked to bake the cake, why, it seemed impossible! The mere thought sent me spiraling. It was unprofessional, I admit, but at the time I couldn't handle the task. And after running out like that...no, this is best. I pass the gauntlet onto you all, my star pupils. I've never been more proud of a graduating class."

Brimley felt wonderful. This felt like, why, like they were colleagues! And that Elis was there, fuming, made the moment all the sweeter. "Yes, thank you, I think I *will* have another," he said, raising his plate to receive a fresh slice.

26

Beans

When Brimley left the cottage, the leftover cake was packed into his basket. Elis trailed Brimley to the door. "Breathe a word of this to anyone and I'll—"

"You'll what?" Brimley cut in. "Tell everyone you discovered the allergens by secret rendezvous with our dearly departed ex-chef?"

"Just...don't," Elis hissed and slammed the door between them.

Brimley took off back in the direction of the monastery, humming to himself. He thought he ought to stay a little longer and collect yongo beans, but he was full and happy and thought he would burst from the excitement of the discovery if he did not walk it off.

He was just a few steps from the threshold when a rustling in the bushes caught his eye. Never one to be afraid, Brimley dove into the waving shrubbery to find not a rabbit, but a man in mid-transformation. Then the dog sat there paralyzed. Staring at each other, Brimley startled in recognition. "Ey! It's you! The taste tester!"

The dog turned and made to run, but Brimley grabbed it by its tail. It twisted and made to nip at Brimley, who had the basket ready and bonked him on the snout. Startled, the dog toppled over. Brimley let go and ran around to block his escape. "Turn back into a person!"

When the dog did nothing but whimper, Brimley tried another approach. "Turn back and you'll get cake."

At this, the lad obliged. Mercifully, he was a talented druid and retained a simple set of clothes on him; the fur shrunk back into breeches and a shirt.

"I'm Brimley."

"I'm Arosco."

"Here." Brimley sat down on a stump nearby and handed the lad the rest of the cake. Arosco sniffed it and wrinkled his nose. "It's made for the princess, isn't it?"

"That's right. Try it though, won't you?"

Arosco did, taking a nibble, then a generous bite. After he swallowed, he said, "They lied."

"About what?"

"Yongo beans. They didn't use those."

"Why would they lie? Is she allergic to them?"

Arosco shook his head. "They're very rare. They don't even exist in these woods. For this cake they used regular liverton beans."

"Is that so?"

"Well, they soak it, and then they whip the liquid it sits in. It whips into what looks like egg whites. Watched them do it myself."

Brimley could have grabbed Arosco and kissed him. "You're a *good* boy."

"Thanks," Arosco said, grinning. "It's very good cake."

"You've just been out here spying on them?"

"I come here a lot. Lots of people use that cottage, and they throw out yummy things. Being the princess's taste tester isn't any fun. Sure, I get to live in a nice palace and my mum's really proud of me, but the princess eats nothing but fish and vegetables."

"You don't test for the rest of the royals?"

"Sure, when there's a big occasion, but day to day they cook behind lock and key. When they have guests who bring their own chefs, that's when they get paranoid."

"You don't worry of being poisoned?"

"We have potions for that. Besides, no one wants to kill the king or princess. It's that foreign prince they're worried about."

"Why is that?"

Arosco paused, realized he'd said something he shouldn't have. He stuffed the rest of the cake in his mouth and shrugged.

"Arosco?"

Arosco stood up and started backing away. With a loud gulp he swallowed and said, "Thank you! I have to go." He pointed to the cottage. "I won't tell anyone." He tumbled backwards, transformed into a dog, and scurried off.

Brimley sat on the stump for a while, contemplating. It sounded like he needed to get some liverton beans and experiment. Speaking of experimenting, he had that peppermint candy of Alistair's he needed to test...

Brimley stood. A branch above him snapped, and he looked up. A large bird—*very* large—took off from a branch, which bounced tremendously from the relief of the weight.

When it was far enough away it circled back and peered down at Brimley. He stared up at it, squinting, and could have sworn it had the face of a woman. But Brimley had never seen a harpy before, and so he couldn't explain that was what he had seen. He certainly didn't recognize Harper Leewood of *The Harking Herald*. He shook his head, confused, and hurried out of the woods, lest the fading light cast more tricks on him.

27

Small Critters Menagerie

The Small Critters Menagerie was started by Princess Damora when she was young and scruffy and overlooked by her parents, who would wander off most evenings into the gardens holding hands, having eyes only for one another. Damora collected bugs and worms, eventually advancing to trapping a kitten, which was allowed in their apartment. Then there was also a rabbit, another kitten, and a squirrel with a twisted ankle. After that her father forbade any more animals in the palace. As a compromise they turned the greenhouse into the SCM, where a young Mosley was put in charge of healing, mending bones, and the general caretaking of raccoons, squirrels, possums, and the puppies of visiting aristocrats that got left behind.

Now the SCM trained rats for sniffing out pandemics, cats for hunting mice in the gardens, small monkeys for retrieving fruits from the tallest branches in the royal orchard, possums for keeping the flea and tick population in check, and a whole flock of pigeons that were in constant recovery from drunkenly smashing into palace windows.

It was from this pool that Mosley and Celeste selected their critters. They slipped little arms through knit sweaters, fastened reflective breastplates onto chests, fashioning themselves a mighty little army.

"You got the sorceress to enchant every single one of these?" Celeste asked.

"No, I had one big one that I smashed."

"And it kept the magic?"

"Yes. But it's not ideal because they can only capture, not project. Which is really all we need with them."

"I think I'll take one of these for my tabby," Celeste said. "Gertie wanders all over the palace, won't it be fun to see where she goes? I'll just attach this bit to her collar."

The flap on the door creaked and in walked the very tabby. "Gertie!" Celeste bent down and scooped up her cat, who immediately began to yowl in protest. "You've nothing to cry about! You're fat as a cow and as spoiled as the princess herself," Celeste scolded, and worked her nimble fingers to attach the mirror to the collar. "Alright, alright, go." She made to bend down, but Gertie was already coiled and sprung from her arms. She pawed at the rat cage just to remind them of her existence and took off back through the little door. Celeste pulled out her personal mirror and put two fingers against the glass and began swiping left, flipping through images until she let out a, "Hmm."

"What?"

"I can't find Gertie's mirror."

"That's because I have these mirrors especially locked so that no one can just scry into them," Mosley explained, and took Celeste's mirror. His fingertips danced across the glass before he handed it back. "There. I've given you permission to peek."

Mosley kept detailed parchments on which mirror saw what. While some enchanted mirrors could scry to see into other mirrors that accepted views, his mirrors were strictly locked from prying eyes and could only be accessed by the mirrors he drew a special rune on. He watched Celeste flip once more and finally saw a royal hallway. "My, she goes fast for a chonk."

Celeste gave him a glare before pocketing the mirror. She walked back over to the dovecot to wrestle more glittering sweaters onto pigeons.

Finally falling into a chair, Celeste reached into her pocket for her fan. She pulled it out along with the mirror, which she peered into. What she saw gave her pause. She watched as a stranger slipped out of one of the rooms of the ladies-in-waiting. She sat up, alarmed, and turned her mirror to Mosley. "Who's this?"

Mosley leaned forward, watched a few seconds. "Why, that's Ash Birchwood. One of the competing chefs."

"Why is he leaving the room of a lady-in-waiting?"

Mosley and Celeste looked at each other, and then Celeste jumped up, excited. "Get closer, you stupid cat!" she hissed at the mirror. To her astonishment, Gertie obliged.

Across the palace, Ash reached down and scratched the fat, old, mean tabby under her chin. "You're such a sweetie when you want to be," Ash cooed. She caught the flashy new accessory attached to Gertie's collar. "Huh?"

Celeste threw the mirror, and it was by Mosley's quick reflexes that it didn't hit the ground and shatter. "He can't see us, remember? It's one-way!" Mosley looked into the mirror. He watched the face of Ash grow bigger as she leaned in. He heard her say, "Huh, there's nothing etched into it, not your mum's name..."

Then Ash took off in a sprint.

Mosley didn't see that, just a dizzying swirl of palace wall and ceiling as the mirror swung back and forth on Gertie's collar. Then nothing but blackness as Gertie folded up into a loaf, watching, waiting, her thick neck spilling over the mirror.

"That felt..." Celeste wanted to say *invasive*, but she was trying to be positive about this whole kingdom-wide spying. "Clear. The image was clear," she said instead, and Mosley beamed with pride.

Mosley scratched his head, thinking. "Wait, what was Ash doing on that side of the palace?"

"Oh my, that's quite the scandal," Celeste said, giving Mosley a wicked grin.

Mosley finally understood. "So he's rendezvousing a lady-in-waiting. Is that taboo?"

"Men are strictly forbidden from entering that wing of the palace." Celeste clucked. "My, my, there will be more than baking drama happening around here."

Celeste placed two fingers on the mirror and began to swipe until Ash finally appeared in another mirror, this time being inconspicuously followed by a pigeon up in the arch of the ceiling. It followed Ash all the way out into the courtyard, where Ash met Lance.

Mosley cleared his throat. "It takes two, you know."

"I know," Celeste said, radiating with excitement. "Who do you think he's seeing?"

"You should know!" Mosley exclaimed. "Aren't you in charge of staffing and modesty? Making sure all the ladies are in line, showing up to work, and not being wooed?"

Celeste snorted and gave a dismissive wave. "It's always some guard or another they're slinking off into the alcoves with. Everyone suspects it, but now there's proof." Her eyes lit up with excitement. "Mosley, think of the opportunity this presents. Why, if this gets out, imagine the drama this will stir! Think of *who* would want to watch that drama unfold. *Women*." When Mosley merely rolled his eyes she added, "Mirrors are in a lot of businesses—businesses filled with *men*. But what about women? The beauty parlors? The knitting circles? You're so sure women aren't a threat? How better to get mirrors into women's private chambers than with a bit of gossip?"

"This is a *scandal*," Mosley hissed.

"Leave it to me," Celeste said, pocketing her mirror. "I've got a few ideas." She got up and followed Mosley to the door of the menagerie, which he opened with a flourish. Out poured the remaining squirrels, pigeons, possums, mice, and rats. Mosley and Celeste had to shield their eyes against the brightness of them pouring out like molten silver onto the lawn, dispersing into the shrubbery, the garden beds, and the skies.

"Fly, my little knights," Mosley bellowed, grinning like a madman.

28

Courtyard Confrontation

Ash burst into the courtyard. She wasn't necessarily looking for anyone, just needing to get out, out, *out* of that palace. She ran into Lance, who was sitting on a stone bench, scribbling onto some parchment. "Lance!"

Without looking up, Lance immediately pocketed his quill and began rolling up the parchment. By the time Ash strode up to him, it was tucked snuggly into his knapsack. He looked up, empty handed, as if there had never been anything there at all. "Ahoo! Hallo, Ash."

"C-can..." Ash set a hand on her hammering chest, realizing she needed to catch her breath. "Can I sit?"

Lance scooted over and motioned beside him. "Of course."

Ash sunk down heavily, looked at him, and started laughing.

"What is it?"

"You're going to think I'm crazy."

"I already do, from the way you're laughing. Better start talking."

Ash let out a few more fitful howls and then composed herself, wiping her eyes. "You'll never—okay, alright. Whew. I was just in the palace, and I thought that Gertie—well, there's this cat that's owned by—well there's this cat the prowls the halls." Ash was finding it rather difficult to narrate without giving too much away. "I reached down to scratch her and found a mirror on her collar! And for a wild second I thought the cat was sent to spy on me."

"Hah!" Lance said, a little too loudly. Then let out an actual giggle. "Funny you say that."

"Did you see the cat?"

Lance shook his head. "But I was sitting here, and I thought I saw a squirrel staring at me through those branches. There, right...there." Lance pointed at something Ash couldn't see. "When it climbed the trunk, I could have sworn it was wearing armor."

Ash looked at him skeptically. "Is that what you were doing with the parchment? Drawing an armored squirrel?"

Lance reached into his knapsack and unrolled the parchment.

"It's a rather good picture," Ash said, although it was quite a jump to go from a piece of mirror on a collar to a full-blown armor suit. She heard footsteps and looked up to find two groups coming in their direction: Gale and Harlowe from one end, along with a woman Ash had never met, and Noal and Gregor from the other. Gale, Harlowe, and the woman reached them first, but with Ash there, they simply stood around in awkward silence before Gale said, "Lance, won't you come have a word?"

"Don't tell me there's another competitor," Ash said, staring at the woman. Her black hair was wind-blown, and her purple cloak looked a bit soiled, as if she'd come from the forest. She stuck a hand through the slit of the cloak. "I'm Harper Leewood from *The Harking Herald*."

"The gossip magazine?" Ash asked, confusion spreading across her face.

"Well yes, there's definitely the gossip column, the celebrity sightings. But I'm covering the Royal Bake Off," Harper explained.

"A word?" Harlowe said to Lance. But before Lance could get up, Noal and Gregor arrived, a little winded, having hurried to catch up and see if Ash was alright. They had seen her run into the courtyard from the window of the dining room, where they agreed to meet to have a late breakfast upon her return from the monastery before their lunch shift in the kitchen. She was just supposed to change into fresh clothes and meet them, so what was she doing out here?

"Where did you go? You said you'd meet us—" Noal abruptly stopped, seeing the company they were in. "Are you...ready?"

Ash looked past his shoulder and noticed Alistair approaching as well. He paused, observing from a distance. She looked back at Noal. "I'm sorry, I—"

A twinkle caught her eye. She froze, raised her hand to hood her eyes for a better look.

"There it is!" Lance hissed, pointing where she was staring.

Everyone looked up and around, confused.

"There!" Lance shouted, and this time several of them saw it: a pigeon wearing armor. It headed right at them, then circled above, casting shimmers of light across their torsos. Lance ducked down and covered his head, then began sobbing, terrified.

Gregor pulled his sling out of his belt and a pebble from his pocket and aimed, let the pebble fly. It landed square on the pigeon's breast and bounced right off. "What in the gods!"

"Move," Harlowe ordered, and used one arm to sweep everyone aside. He pointed his staff and shouted a charm. They watched as a burst of green lightning shot from the tip, ricocheted off the mirror on the pigeon, and came back to hit Gale square on the chest. Gale fell back, hands and arms out like a starfish, snoring loudly.

The pigeon kept fluttering above, unbothered. In fact, it was a bit tipsy and the pummeling did nothing but make him more determined to keep the course, be a good pigeon.

Harper grabbed the edges of her cloak, gave a tremendous sweep downward, and with a jump transformed into a harpy. Her body morphed into a massive bird while her head remained unchanged, and she took flight after the pigeon. She easily plucked the bird out of the air. By the time she landed, she was back in human form except for one leg, the pigeon trapped in her talons. The pigeon put up a brief fight before slumping over, asleep.

Alistair ran over and crouched beside the hysteric Lance. While everyone was busy crowding around Harper, he pried Lance's teeth apart and popped a piece of taffy into his mouth. He pressed his forehead to Lance's. "Swallow," he ordered, and Lance obliged, chewing and swallowing the sweet before Ash glanced over and fully comprehended what was going on.

"Leave him alone!" she screamed and shoved Alistair aside.

"Woah, woah!" Harlowe shouted, turning.

"He was poisoning him!" Ash insisted, standing between Lance, whose eyes were back to focusing, and Alistair, knocked onto his back.

"I was merely giving him a piece of candy to bring him out of his panic spiral," Alistair insisted, pushing himself up onto his elbows.

"No, you give him *nothing*," Gregor growled, going over and helping Lance up. He turned to the others. "Alistair drugged Ash with a truth serum peppermint to get secrets out of him the other night."

"It was harmless," Alistair insisted. "All is fair in love and baking. Besides, what am I gaining here? I'm merely helping a friend in need."

Harlowe, who didn't have Gale's quick fuse to decide how he felt about a situation, decided to err on caution. "Thanks, but let's not try to medicate people without consent." He put his hands on Lance's shoulders and looked him in the eyes. "Are you alright now?"

"Yes. I-I'm not paranoid, am I?"

The two looked back at Harper, who presented the armored pigeon. "I bet there's more of these," she said, already looking up and around, sharp eyes scanning the trees. "He's the Crown's."

"How do you know?" Lance asked.

"I know him," Harper said with a shrug.

"Now don't start again," Harlowe hushed, wrapping an arm around Lance. "It's this silly baking competition. They want us to react. They *want* to see drama."

"We're not safe," Lance mumbled.

"Perfectly safe," Harper assured. "He's just got mirrors on him. No weapons. The worst he'll do is shit on you if he gets too close."

This confirmed what Ash had been afraid of. Gertie was also mirrored. She turned to her friends. "Let's go. I've had enough excitement for today. Lance, you'll be alright?"

Though a little pale, he nodded and let himself be led into the palace. The rest followed. Once inside, Gregor, Ash, and Noal peeled from the group and headed to the kitchen for their midday shift.

"Let's go see Brimley tonight," Gregor said. "I've got a feeling we're going to learn a lot more about what Alistair is hiding in his sweets."

They finished their shift in the kitchen and pulled on their summer cloaks, tossed the hoods over their heads, and slipped out of the palace, keeping their heads down, their profiles hidden from the mirrors that were scattered like stars throughout the halls.

29

A Plan is Hatched

"You come any more often they'll hand you a robe and a hoe," Brimley joked, greeting them when they arrived.

Brimley worked at a table covered in equipment he'd snagged from a liquidated apothecary years back. With mortar and pestle he crushed the peppermint and mixed pinches of it with fluids in bottles of various shapes and sizes. He watched the reactions, took notes, and wiped his goggles over and over as the steam from the experiments fogged them.

The three visitors sat on the other side of the makeshift laboratory, sipping mead which they had paid for by trimming the hops in the garden and pulling a few pesky, thorny weeds.

"There's a cat that prowls the halls that's got a mirror on its collar. And I'm not entirely sure the hired staff isn't flashing mirrors at us too," Ash lamented, having to raise her voice to be heard over the rumble of all the boiling liquids and hissing of steam out of contraptions. They scooted farther from the table and out of earshot of Brimley.

"Why would they do that when we're not baking?" Noal asked.

Gregor and Ash blinked at Noal. In the mountain, everyone knew everything about everyone. It was the same in the palace; gossip was currency, and the juicier the bits you procured, the higher your rank.

"Am I to worry they're watching while I brush my teeth? Or peeking through the window while I'm sleeping?" Ash asked. She reached up and pet the massive leaf of a griffin wing plant shading them. She could sense its peace; it was happy here, even though it was inside, and thrived in the cozy dimness.

Noal's eyes went wide. "Gods, what if windows are enchanted, too? Anything with a reflection?"

"Relax, Lance," Gregor muttered.

Ash laughed, but still looked worried. "Perhaps if we have nothing to hide, we have nothing to worry about."

"But you *do* have something to hide," Gregor quietly reminded her, nodding towards Brimley, who wasn't privy to her secret yet.

Ash gave a dismissive wave. "I'm not all that important, in the grand scheme of things."

"We deserve privacy," Noal insisted. Neither Ash nor Gregor could argue that.

"What if I get outed and can't compete? Or worse, banned from the kitchen? All my training, wasted!"

"Ash, don't take this as being insensitive, but what's the big plan here?" Gregor asked under his breath. "You're going to work in the royal kitchen and what, pretend you're a man for the rest of your life? What about when you serve the princess? All the ladies-in-waiting you worked with? Surely they'll figure it out."

"I can start an independent pastry shop," Ash countered.

"Run...by a woman?" Gregor asked.

"See, that's the thing." Ash wrung her hands. "I was sort of hoping one—or both!—of you would like to run it with me."

At this, Gregor and Noal exchanged looks. Rather than answer, Gregor countered with, "What did your parents say when you told them you're chopping off your hair and passing as a boy?"

"I didn't...tell...them." Ash burned with shame.

Noal let out a laugh. "Oy, don't feel bad! Gregor here only just now confessed to his folks that he's a baker and not an engineer."

"What!" Ash looked at Gregor with wide eyes. "You're lying, too?!"

Gregor threw his hands up. "I've told them!" He grabbed a fistful of his beard and tugged in despair.

"Wait, so you're giving me grief for living a double life when you have been, too? Hammer calls the anvil hard!"

"And here I am, just the keeper of secrets," Noal mused.

"Shut up!" both shouted in unison.

"Uh, guys?" They looked over at Brimley, who cut the heat. The whistling and bubble stopped almost immediately. "I can't get any magic out of this. There's like, an expiration to it or a one-time use enchantment or something."

Gregor scowled. "I knew it."

There was a knock at the door.

"Come in!"

The door cracked ajar, and Arosco in human form poked his head in. "It's not too late, is it?"

"Who's this?" Noal asked, watching the lanky lad walk over and drop a sack onto Brimley's table.

"You don't recognize the royal taste tester?" Brimley grinned. The three of them gaped, impressed. "It pays to have friends."

"Don't tell me he's also competing," Gregor lamented.

"No, just running an errand," Arosco assured. He went around, shaking everyone's hand, leaning in a little too closely each time to get a whiff. "A pleasure."

"I needed someone unrecognizable to go buy more candy."

"His cart is still up?" Gregor asked.

"No, but you can buy some off him."

"Lance was there," Arosco said. "Buying calming sweets."

"Gods," Brimley muttered. He opened the small sack and pulled out a whole variety of treats, including a peppermint stick like the one Ash had tasted, and began crushing it up.

"Good luck on the last round," Arosco said.

"We'll do our best," Ash said, grinning. Arosco looked at her funny, sniffed again, but thought better. He gave a little bow and backed out the door.

Ash let out a groan. "He knows!"

"He can suspect," Gregor said, dropping his voice again.

"Oh, he knows," Brimley said, and they all started shouting at once. Brimley chuckled. "Dogs can sense things. I don't know if it's the smell or what. But he knows. He can also talk to that cat, Gertie. They're good friends."

"No wonder Lance is medicating himself; one can go absolutely mad with paranoia," Ash seethed. "How long have you known?"

"About a day. You talk in your sleep, did you know that? Don't worry, I'm not telling anyone. But...makes sense now."

"What does?"

Brimley shrugged. "Some of your mannerisms. You hid it well, I'll give you that." He turned the flames back on and cranked them to full power.

"I think we should do it," Noal said, leaning back against the wall, feeling dreamy from the smell of the bubbling sugar, the heat from the experiments, the mead in his belly. "The three of us running a pastry shop! Wouldn't that be grand? It takes the pressure off, too. Now only one of us will have to win the seal."

"That does take the pressure off a bit," Gregor agreed. "Brimley, do you want to be part of our pastry business?"

"Nah." Brimley pushed his goggles up. "I'm going to bake bread at the monastery. Feed the poor and all that."

"You're really doing that? I thought you just didn't want to work in the royal kitchen," Ash said, looking surprised. "Not that it's not noble, it's just...well, won't the poor eat any old bread?"

"Do you hear yourself?" Noal hissed. He gave Brimley a sheepish look. "*Women.*"

"Honestly!" Ash punched Noal in the arm. "I'm sorry! I just...no, you're completely right, Brimley. Everyone deserves decent food."

Gregor's eyes narrowed, watching them. "Say, have you two...?"

"What?" Noal asked.

Gregor blushed. "Well, she's a lass and you're a lad. Are you two...*romantic*?"

Now it was Noal and Ash's turn to turn red.

"Come off it!" Noal scolded.

Ash, on the other hand, stayed more composed. "It's not like that," she said. "I mean, no. But also…I don't see him romantically because, well, I don't really *feel* romance."

"All girls are romantic," Gregor huffed.

Ash shrugged. "Not me. I'm just not interested in romance. I've been busy with better things. Besides, what's kept you two from chasing after girls?"

"Uh, well, that's a great question." Gregor tugged at his beard. "We've never talked about dating, have we? I suppose it was never on my mind, I was so devoted to finishing the apprenticeship. What about you?" he asked, turning to Noal. He suspected, after finding out Ash's secret, that they were in fact lovers all along. This new information had put his head in a bit of a spin.

"Oh, I've been on dates," Noal admitted sheepishly. "But it's not like you think! I'm not keeping anyone secret from you, I swear. My father would invite friends over for dinner and they'd bring daughters, but they were so boring! Needlework and potion brewing and talks of cultivating parcels of land and refurbishing abandoned palaces…I don't know, I appreciate their ambition, but all I want to do at the end of the day is talk about spice blends and enjoy the perfect cookie. I have that, between the two of you, so I never really felt like I was missing out on anything."

Gregor nodded. He looked over at Brimley and shouted, "Oy! You ever been in love?"

"Science is my passion!" A small bit of something exploded, sizzling Brimley's bangs. He shut the burners off and the heat immediately began to subside, to everyone's relief. Even the plants seemed to exhale. "Come closer so I can tell you what I discovered."

They obliged as Brimley stripped off his goggles and gloves and began to line up the various potion bottles before them, all varying in color. Then he pointed to each of them in turn and explained what they did.

"As we already knew, the peppermint stick is a truth serum. The lemon drop contains a drop of euphoria. Licorice rope has a memory charm encased in it. The caramel is for courage. The taffy is a calming spell, and this," he pointed to the bright pink liquid, "is sleeping spell gumdrops."

"What do we do with Brimley's findings?" Noal asked. "Suppose we can prove Alistair is spiking his sweets. Surely he'll get in trouble for not being a registered pharmacist to dole out remedies?"

"Remedies?" Gregor scoffed. "You're acting like he's doing good. Even if he was a pharmacist, he doesn't have the seal to sell!"

"He did help Lance come down from a panic attack," Ash vouched.

"He *drugged* you," Gregor reminded her. "Call it whatever, but at the end of the day, I think there are rules against giving people things that they're not fully informed about."

"You wanted proof, we have it," Brimley said, interrupting the squabble. "Now we need to make the trail of evidence lead to the culprit."

"I have an idea," Ash said, dropping her voice conspiratorially. "Those animals following us? We could give them the sleeping candy."

"Just sprinkle it around the palace and hope they get eaten?" Gregor asked.

"Have you known a squirrel who passes up sweets?" Ash asked, cocking an eyebrow.

Gregor's face lit up. "When the king's spies are all asleep, they'll ask questions and *demand* answers. We'll be ready with them. They'll see themselves the danger the king will be in if he's around Alistair."

"What if the dragons get to them first?" Noal asked. "They're notorious for their sweet tooths."

"And sleeping dragons won't raise alarms?" Ash asked. *See my point?*

"Alright, so we go buy all his sleeping candy," Noal said, brightening. "Send Arosco to buy more."

"Can't, today was his one day off, he's got to be back in the kitchens," Brimley said.

"He's certainly not going to sell any to us," Ash said. "Maybe Lance?"

"Elis," Gregor said grimly.

"I don't think—" Brimley began, but Gregor cut him off.

"He *has* to. He needs to be in the loop. For the good of the kingdom and the safety of everyone. We need him on our side if we want to get Alistair kicked out of this competition."

Noal groaned. "Are you sure we need his help?"

Gregor drained his mug. "I'm afraid I'm positive."

30

Right Place

"**A**re you sure this is the right place?" Gregor whispered, crouching below Noal as they peered through the crack in the door. Someone behind them pushed open the door they were hiding behind and the two stumbled into the dank, dark basement. No one seemed to notice, too engrossed in making their bets, counting out coins, and waving servers over for refills.

In this particular manor's basement, four high-top tables were set up in a row down the middle of the room, two stools at each, with four rings of uniform chairs around them for the audience, which was a step up from the last basement they'd investigated. That one had a handful of mismatched chairs around one table, and people were betting in coppers and trinkets. Gregor and Noal could tell from the glistening gold on the tables that this was perhaps the one they were after.

Sure enough, when their eyes swept the room they saw Elis, stripped down to his tight leather britches and boots, his torso naked and glistening, his hair sweaty and pulled back at the nape of his neck with a red ribbon. He had his forehead to his trainer's, who was wrapping his wrist and chanting words of encouragement. Not that Elis needed any. Elis never didn't believe in himself.

"Oy, it's a gold each."

"Each? For what?" Noal asked, flustered.

"Entry price. Price is a bet. Can't bet less than a gold."

"But the last place—" Noal began, but Gregor reached up and slapped two massive gold nuggets into the bouncer's waiting palm.

"That do?"

"It'll do," the bouncer said, and motioned them to two seats. Gregor had to drag Noal, who was stammering, in awe of what Gregor had just done. "That's got to be five gold coins each if you melt it down, are you insane?"

"Wine? Mead? A little something stronger?" asked a server, sashaying up with an elegant tray laden with decanters and goblets.

"Mead, and...?" Gregor raised his eyebrows at Noal, who had begun to sweat profusely.

"Um, yes, sure."

"Mead?" the waiter repeated, already handing Gregor his goblet.

Noal cleared his throat, willed himself to gather his wits. "Yes. Mead."

"Very good, sir."

Noal took his drink and watched Gregor drop far more reasonably sized nuggets onto the tray. He turned wide eyes to Gregor. "Well, this place isn't half bad!"

"I know these things are illegal, but I fully didn't anticipate some of these halls to be as dingy as the last place we stumbled upon," Gregor confessed.

"Did you see the rats?" Noal hissed, excited. "It looked like they'd been breeding with the dragons down there! And the smell! This place smells quite nice, for what it is."

A voice boomed through the room. "Positions!"

Elis broke away from his coach and took a seat at one of the tables. Once seated, the contestants set a figurine in front of them. The servers reappeared, and this time there were duplicates of the figurines on their trays instead of bottles and glasses.

"Your first bets, sir?" Gregor was asked.

"Elis."

"Who?"

Gregor squinted at Elis then nodded to the crown figurine. "Bet it all."

"Very good, sir." The server scribbled on a piece of parchment, tore off the bottom half, and handed it to Gregor. Noal shook his head, and the server moved on.

"If he makes us rich, I'm going to feel so conflicted," Noal muttered. "What about that big fellow? Why didn't you bet on him?"

"Where's the fun in that?" Gregor settled into his plush seat and sipped his mead.

It took mere minutes for bets to be placed; it seemed that everyone here was a regular, and they had their champions. Then the booming voice said, "Turn hands!"

Elbows dropped onto the tables and each pair clasped hands. They leaned in, kissed the back of their opponent's hand, and waited.

"Go!"

Nearly every face in the arena immediately turned red or purple from exertion as their muscles suddenly seized up and the arm-wrestling tournament began. Veins bulged, jaws flexed, and teeth gritted. Noal watched with rapt fascination as sweat rolled from their armpits down to their elbows. "Won't their elbows slip?"

"Shut up," Gregor whispered, eyes locked on Elis. Well, Elis's hand.

It didn't take long for hands to slam on tables. Gregor remembered to breathe again when Elis's opponent's hand hit the table. Cheers turned to roars of victory, turned to shouts that quickly got quelled when the servers appeared and began paying out winnings. Some guests left, making room for others who were waiting to be let in. Gregor looked around, feeling invigorated, caught up in the excitement that swelled in the room as contestants dropped out and others rotated in. Elis sat out a few rounds, but every time he competed either Noal or Gregor would wave a server over. If it was Noal, he pointed at the crown and then looked at Gregor, expectantly. After the second time he did this, Gregor asked, "Why don't you pay?"

"All I've got are coppers."

"So pay with coppers!"

"In a place like this? Are you insane?!"

Gregor glared at him. Noal reached for Gregor's pockets and got his hand slapped, hard. "Ouch!" He broke into a grin though as Gregor rolled his eyes and pulled out another nugget.

"But only this last round."

"It *is* the last round," Noal said excitedly and motioned to a server for a refill. "How much have we made?"

"I've made back the entrance fee tenfold."

"See? You're not so mad."

Gregor rolled his eyes, but he wasn't actually annoyed. He hadn't felt this relaxed since...well, since before he came to this strange, new land with its bustling, busy city. He wondered, guiltily, if he was having so much fun because Ash wasn't there.

"Hold on, it's hard to hear you, I'll scry you after," Noal shouted into the mirror, then pocketed it as the last two contestants took their seats. "Ash," he answered the assumed question. "Gods, if we'd bet on the big man in the beginning we'd still be in the positive."

Gregor watched the massive man they'd initially noticed sit across from Elis, twice the beautiful man's size. Gregor was nervous, but only a bit. He'd observed that when "Go!" was shouted, a lot of contestants threw themselves into the wrestling, seizing up in their arms and shoulders. Not Elis. He went rigid, completely down to the core, and his breath became perfectly even, measured, as if he suddenly entered a trance. He didn't lose because he simply wasn't there to lose, it seemed.

Sure enough, he wasn't going to accept a loss this last round either. It was like his competitor pushed and pushed against a boulder that just wouldn't budge. Then when he let his muscles relax for a second, to recoup and push again, Elis took his chance and slammed his hand down. His opponent looked genuinely shocked, as did half the room.

"There's no way!" someone shouted, and others joined in, completely flabbergasted. Elis slid off his stool, flashed the crowd a sly smile, and joined his coach in the corner, who began clapping his back with unbridled enthusiasm as Elis tried to shrug on his shirt.

Fans broke from the crowd and flocked Elis while investors swarmed the loser, scolding him.

"Gods, we'll never get a word in with him," Noal moaned, craning his neck to try to get a look at Elis, who had been completely swallowed by the crowd.

Gregor simply sipped his wine, unbothered, then beckoned the server over, who nearly tripped over his own feet in his haste. He bent down to let Gregor whisper in his ear. Then he straightened, went over to the crowd, which parted for him, and passed the whisper into Elis's ear. Elis's head snapped up, and he immediately found his companions in the crowd. Gregor raised his goblet in a salute. Elis broke into a grin, shook his head in disbelief. He gently pushed away the reaching hands of his adoring fans and went over to Gregor and Noal, straddling the seat in front of them and resting his chin in his palm. "I heard I have a new patron."

"You've made me very wealthy today," Gregor beamed, his nose rosy from the booze.

"So, to what do I owe the pleasure? Letting off some steam before the big baking contest?"

"Actually, we have a favor to ask you," Gregor said.

"Sounds like you owe me one, from the bulge of your coin sack."

Gregor took it off his belt and pulled out the largest nugget. "I need you to buy candy from Alistair."

Elis's eyes narrowed as he turned his palm up and accepted the gold. It was even heavier than it looked. "I didn't realize you had such a sweet tooth."

"Bring it to our dorm, we'll explain there," Gregor said. "Will you help us?"

"All I have to do is buy candy?"

"Yes," Gregor confirmed. "As big of a bag as you can get of the sleepy stuff. You can keep what's left over."

Elis pocketed the gold. "I'll get right on it. He's just over there." Elis nodded across the room, and the other two looked over, panicked.

Sure enough, Alistair sat in the thinning crowd, goblet in hand. He saluted Elis. Then he noticed the others and saluted them as well. Gregor and Noal returned nervous waves.

"Say, it was nice seeing you two here. Come anytime you like. Just don't bet on anyone else, promise?"

Noal grinned. "Not after what we saw. You're very good."

Elis swept a hand through his gorgeous blonde hair. "Of course I'm good, I have to be. My father cut me off."

Before Gregor and Noal could react to this news, Elis stood up and headed across the room toward Alistair. He didn't ask more questions because frankly he didn't want to know any more of what this whole scheme was about. He just knew that the gold in his pocket weighed more than all his earnings that night, and the less he knew, the easier this would be.

31
Secret Rendezvous

Following his victory, Elis followed Alistair out into the warm, balmy night. They walked at first along the river that had long dried up into a creek. It was constantly getting widened, mostly for cosmetic reasons. One king after another promised the return of otters to the kingdom, to *this very river*, but the dragon population was still very much out of hand. They were seen as vermin by many, and very few breeds were prized and bred for their intelligence and skills. They were kept for practical reasons or by the rich to imply their status. Hatchlings were cute, even Elis could admit to that. Out in the wide-open countryside, some grew to the size of mountains, with no enclosure and free range of sheep and other livestock to devour. Their wings grew as wide as the space around them allowed. Those were more myths; it had been decades since one so large had flown over the kingdom, and few witnesses swore they had even seen one that size with their own eyes.

Elis thought of himself as an otter, as one of a select few. Someone gorgeous, well-bred, but who also took great care of himself. Who minded his manners, studied up on poetry and the art of charm—both literal and metaphysical—and who came from a line of people who deserved things, and so therefore he did, too. Alistair was his adversary, and Elis didn't like it when people got in his way.

Elis followed Alistair as he took them through the turns and curves of town, walking expertly as if he too had grown up there. Elis's suspicion grew with each step, and he began to wonder if perhaps Alistair thought of *him* as a threat, to be eliminated that very night.

Past Gilded Bridge full of jewelry and finer things shops, beyond the town square, past the houses of worship, the Labor District with its blacksmiths, tanneries, carpenters, cobblers, stone masons. Past Lorde of Loaves and the other bakeries, butchers, spice stalls, and candle shops. Past Dragon Alley, which held all the different dragon handlers for hire and housed the breeders selling dragons for various professions: dragons bred for sensitive noses to exterminate mice and rats; dragons that could calibrate the correct oven temperature (these were perhaps the most popular for a common person to have); dragons for welding; for systematically burning forests and clearing unwanted brush; for the glass blowers and blacksmiths who could afford them. The royal seal ought to have been changed to two dragons entwined, but then dragons were so common, some felt it would cheapen the prestige of the seal.

The street began to fade from cobblestone to dirt and pebbles, and the houses began to lean, growing more and more weary as the city lamps grew more and more distance between themselves. Past even Slumber Mill, the inn at the edge of town where poor travelers stayed and where people from town spent the night with someone they didn't want their spouse to know about. It was here that Elis began to grow anxious, as he never came out this way, except once just to see what the end of the city looked like. Led down a narrow street with high walls festooned with overgrown vines, Elis was about to protest when Alistair stopped at a tall, elaborate iron door and knocked a pattern that seemed both mysterious and very popular. The eye hole slid to the side. There was an audible grunt, and the door was pulled open by a very short, cloaked man standing on an overturned crate. He waved the two into the courtyard and then stepped off and left. Alistair motioned for Elis, who noticed the infamous sweets cart parked inside, to follow. They walked past a bubbling fountain and a small table with iron chairs and approached another door, but this time Alistair had a key. The door, which looked as old as time, opened in total silence. There was reason to keep its hinges oiled, its swings silent.

They stepped inside a warehouse filled to the brim with bags of sugar stacked onto shelves lining the place from floor to ceiling, the yellow emblem on each glowering down at them like suspicious eyes. Alistair approached the man at the desk crunching numbers on a thick stack of parchment. "Ho! Hello, Tavis." He nodded over his shoulder. "This is Elis Goldstem."

Tavis pulled off his glasses and put the mirror perched on the desk into a drawer. He stood to shake Elis's hand. He was portly, dressed in fine merchant wear, eyes as sharp as a hawk's, and a bald spot eating its way down his head. His chest was another matter, as thick black tendrils of chest hair fought to curl out the top of his collar. He locked eyes with Elis as if he could read his soul through the irises, and Elis left his gaze wide open for him. What did he have to hide?

Alistair motioned Elis over to a chest on a shelf and flipped the lid open, revealing an assortment of candies. "It's a bit bare, I'm afraid. Busy with all that cake contest business...I've got lollies, taffy, a few bonbons...what ails ye?"

"Huh? What?" Elis tore his eyes away from the packed shelves.

"What do you need fixing? Don't tell me you just craved a bit of sugar."

"Oh, um, I can't sleep," Elis said, hoping this was one of the secret passwords to a sweet. Sure enough, Alistair scooped a fistful of gumdrops into a waxy pouch. "That's the last of them, so make 'em count."

Elis peeked into the chest. "What's all the rest for?"

"Anxiety...persuasion...hiccups..." Alistair pointed them out as he went. "Want to try a bit of each?"

Elis pulled out two silver coins—*not* the nugget worth his whole month's expenses—and flashed them in the dim light. Alistair snatched them from him, along with the bag, and filled it to the brim with the rest of the sweets. "A *pleasure* doing business."

"What's all this?" Elis asked, pocketing the candy and motioning around them.

"It's sugar!" Alistair gestured around the loft, the many bags all stuffed into their holding shelves, admiring it all.

"Yes, I see that. But for what?"

"This new prince." Alistair dropped his voice and pulled Elis conspiratorially off to the side. "He's planning on taxing sugar. Extraordinarily. Comes from a place of pearly white teeth, no diabetes, nothing. Absolutely absurd. He's going to want to outlaw it, but probably won't be able to. Says it's for the people's benefit. Imagine that! When I win this contest and get my seal, I'll have enough sugar to start up our business and corner the market."

"We're going into business?" Elis asked, amused.

"Of course! Think of it. You and I, we create our empire."

Elis walked around, intrigued. He composed his face into the perfect, neutral mask his father had taught him to wear in public, in court, and at all establishments where coins were gambled. "You're staying then? After the bake off?"

"Of course! This is where I've made a name for myself. And a few friends." Alistair nodded towards Tavis, who had gone back to scribbling on his parchment.

"Alright," Elis said, keeping a neutral tone. "I suppose we could make it work. Are you showing me this to get me excited? Or do you need something from me?"

Alistair threw his arm around Elis' shoulder, pulled him into a crushing side hug. "I'm certain one of us will win. We get the royal seal, gain glory, and there will be no end to the demand for our orders. Candies, sweets, cakes, whatever you like! When sugar becomes taxed and other shops can't afford it, we'll make ourselves a fortune. We'll be the two richest men in all the kingdom!"

Elis couldn't help but smile. He had been endowed with a trust fund before his father cut him off from the family fortune, but it was dwindling, and he had appearances to uphold. This would give him a running start out of the gate. And the pressure to win would be cut in half if Alistair was good on his word. Why wouldn't he be? He clearly saw talent! Elis remembered the bag of candy in his pocket and wondered what was so awful about Alistair that the others had sent him on this mission. "It sounds like a plan," he said, and Alistair clapped a hand on his shoulder, grinning a dazzling grin.

As Elis was let out the silent door, a tiny dragon tried to sneak its way between his ankles. "No, you don't!" Alistair swore and kicked it back into the street. "Those greedy little bastards. Make sure you keep the candy you don't finish in a jar with a ring of salt around it, just to be sure. They'll gobble it up if you're not careful."

After Elis left, Alistair strolled back to Tavis and settled onto the stool beside him. "Well?"

"He's a rich kid," Tavis said. "Nice clothes. Always has an impeccably clean coat. Holds himself apart from everyone else. He'll do it, alright. That you can trust."

"Good, good," Alistair murmured.

"Do you have the recipe ready?" Tavis asked, interrupting Alistair's thoughts of glory. "For the mind-control spell?"

"Yes, I do."

"You've tested it?"

"I have not tested that one specifically, but my truth serum worked like a charm, and the euphoria-inducing one worked as well. Put a man in a panic attack right to peace. Based on those, I was able to tweak the core formula. I'll be able to slip it to the prince no problem. I just need to win so I can get close enough. I need to be careful though. They're catching on."

"Who's catching on?"

"The other competitors."

Tavis scoffed. "Test the new formula on them. Make them forget. Better yet, make them release their suspicions."

"They don't trust me."

"Do they trust *him*?" Tavis asked, referring to Elis.

"I believe so."

"Then you chose a good second-in-command. You will succeed if you stay the course and stay careful. If that boy does not betray you."

"He's too selfish to lose."

"Good." Tavis's fierce eyes twinkled with excitement. "If this works, we'll rule the kingdom." He got up, placed the parchments into a drawer, and locked it. He beckoned for Alistair to lean in closer, and when he did, whispered, "I have the egg."

Alistair pulled away in shock. "Where?"

"In the back. The dwarf just left. Want to see?"

Alistair's eyes mirrored Tavis's excitement. "We won't need to use it, will we?"

Tavis shrugged, a smile tugging at his lips. "Better safe than sorry."

32

Under Scrutiny

In the royal residential wing of the palace, Ash sat in a common room doing needlework. She adjusted her headdress, which was frightfully hot but part of the uniform. It had also helped her go incognito since she arrived at the palace. She hadn't worried this much in all the years before combined. She had simply gone to class during the day and taken the evening shifts as lady-in-waiting, burning the candles to stumps as she mended undergarments, hems, dusted curtains, herded misplaced teacups into the kitchen time and time again. Her family was royal, and like other royal families in and around the kingdom, they sent their daughters to court to gain favor and alliance. Free domestic work in exchange for peace. It was silly, Ash thought, that the women tended house while sons stayed home and learned finance and how to reign and convinced their sisters and cousins to send home pictures of their coworkers so they might choose from them a suitable bride.

Ash's own mother had nagged her to send an updated portrait of herself. "Just pick up a mirror, we'll have your portrait painted here! You'll just sit still on your end and for goddess's sake try to smile! Men look at teeth, you know."

"I'm no mare," Ash had spat. She dodged the chiming mirrors and had long stopped replying to the letters home. For what? To be married? In her parents' defense, they thought all she was doing was waiting hand and foot on someone else. *Don't you want to be married, become a queen, and be the one who is waited on hand and foot?*

Ash had made sure to throw cloths over the few mirrors in the common room, which probably weren't enchanted—yet. This room was still lit by candles the old-fashioned way, not by stardust like the ones in the great halls. *Lamps filled with dust stolen from stars*, they had tittered when the sorcerers had arrived to demonstrate—and sell—the new forms of light. They were, for certain, magnificent, but the new technology made Ash's head ache. She preferred hearths fed by real wood and windows she could throw open.

This room was tranquil. She had arranged it to maximize energy flow and sat in a spot where the draft flowed in, took her troubles, and carried them right back out the window. Her hands fell into rhythm and her mind left the task to meditate on something else, replaying the excitements of the day.

Ash was so lost in thought that she jumped, throwing her needlework into the air and scrambling to catch it when Helva burst in. "Come quick!"

Ash looked around to see who she was talking to and realized she was all alone. She was flattered—she wasn't really in the sewing circles, since they preferred to include the chattier of the group. She happily got up and followed Helva into the next room until she realized Helva hadn't sought her out specifically, but rather had run around and collected everyone she could from all the rooms she found unlocked.

Helva pulled a massive mirror into the center of the room. Everyone paused their chatter to watch, eyes round with curiosity. Helva ran her fingertips across the glass to script a rune on its surface, turning the reflection of their faces into an animation of people who had never stepped foot in that room. Well, except one.

"Helva, what is this?" Brigni called.

"You must watch. Oh!" Helva squealed. "Celeste is out for the night. I don't think she'll mind."

"Is that the Royal Bake Off?"

"Finally! I can't believe they didn't let us suspend work for a few hours and watch," someone said.

Watch they did. Someone passed around bowls of snacks, and collectively they cheered and booed at the judges' critiques. Ash burned with embarrassment, convinced everyone could see how obvious she was, just standing there in plain sight, but it quickly became clear she wasn't the one catching anyone's eye.

"Look at his arms! Are all monks so buff?"

"I want to see Elis!"

"You just like his hair."

"Wait, are there mirrors in the dorms?"

Giggles erupted. Helva started shouting, trying to quiet the hysteric crowd. Ash ducked back into the other room to finish her needlework, hands shaking.

That was the thing, wasn't it? Being found out. Being scrutinized. Having people like Helva obsess over her. Ash gripped the fabric in her hands so tight it wrinkled.

Finally, when the clock struck late enough, she pulled the mirror from her pocket and scried Noal. Then she slipped out of her dress and into her tunic and trousers, covered herself in a cloak that sweltered in the summer night heat, and headed down to the other side of the palace.

33
Good Deed

Headed back to the palace, Elis felt as if the stakes had been raised, but not just for him. For everyone. They were no longer simply playing at a baking contest. Suddenly, there were plots holding up the backdrop. Political intrigue had entered the scene.

Elis knocked on the dorm door. "Come in." He pushed it open to find Ash, Gregor, Noal, and Brimley whispering with their heads together.

"What's this? An enemy strategy planning?" Elis glared at Brimley, who winked.

"Elis, we have to tell you what's going on," Noal began. "Alistair is going to do something bad if he wins, we're sure of it. The candies he sells have spells woven into them. If given the chance, he's going to lace the wedding cake. Or worse."

"What spells?" Elis asked sharply. "That's forbidden, giving people spells without their consent."

"You want to try it yourself?" Ash asked. "Show us the bag. I guarantee if you taste it, you'll believe it."

Elis pulled the sack of sweets out of his pocket. He thought there would be natural remedies in them, like lavender for sleeping and caffeine for alertness, but a spell was something else entirely. Ash snatched it out of his hand so fast he startled back. "Aha!" She pulled out a peppermint stick.

"What does that do?"

"It's laced with a truth serum," she said.

Elis scoffed and shook his head. "No, you're all paranoid. How would this even get past the royal taste tester?" But he took the stick and pocketed it, just in case.

"Arosco said so himself, he only taste tests if there are large festivals where foreigners visit, or if there's a new dish with unusual ingredients," Brimley said.

"You speak dog?" Elis asked, confused.

"He's a shapeshifter," Noal explained.

"You lot think Alistair is going to slip the king a few charms to loosen his tongue, and then what? Babble through dinner?" Elis tried to wrap his head around this new plot.

"A foreign dignitary asking the right questions with a mirror pointed at His Majesty might snatch a few Crown secrets for whoever's on the other side of that mirror. Bad guys can spy from anywhere," Noal said.

"This is *quite* the story." Elis sat down on the closest bed. "But...not implausible."

"Who is he, anyway? Where is he from? Does he have a master? A king he reports to? Or is he just a renegade, out to serve himself?" Gregor asked.

"How big does the web go?" Ash whispered, eyes wide. "I have to tell the princess."

"You can't," Noal said immediately. "You'd betray—" There he stopped, realized who else was in the room, and looked around sheepishly.

"I already know," Brimley reminded him.

"What? That you're an elf girl? We all know," Elis said, rolling his eyes as if the notion that she could fool him offended him. "You thought we wouldn't catch on?"

This horrified Gregor, that Elis knew without being told but he hadn't caught on.

Ash's jaw dropped. "This whole time? Then why did you accost me about where I'm staying?"

"Because I want to know where you're staying! I figured they'd put you in this shabby dorm with the lot of us no matter what you're hiding in your trousers."

"I'm in the ladies' wing. I'm still employed there. For now." Ash let out a giggle, then a full-belly laugh. "I'm a fool. Was it so obvious?"

"Not so obvious," Gregor grumbled but hurried to add, "You didn't let on that you were anything but a great chef. The rest, trifles."

"Well, let's hope the princess sees it that way," Ash said. getting up. "I'm going to take these," she said, grabbing a handful of candy.

"You think she already knows about your double life?" Noal asked, an amused smile creeping across his face. Ash let out a frustrated groan and stormed out of the room.

"Did he try anything on you?" Gregor asked Elis.

"He asked me to be his partner. Said if I win, he wins, doesn't matter, we could open a shop together."

"Are you going to be his ally?" Noal asked. Of course others would try to buddy up—hadn't they?

Elis looked at the candy spread across the bed. He inspected a piece of pink taffy, sniffing it. He'd be a fool to try it, but if he didn't, he had to take their word. And they were competitors, so how was this not a trick? "You better be sure of this," he said, looking at them sternly.

"We are," Brimley said, and while he was on Elis's shit list, he still held Elis's respect.

Elis blew an exasperated raspberry. "Alright. But if we're right and this goes all the way up to the king, I want credit for this. Glory."

"You'll certainly get it." Brimley grinned and clapped him on the back.

"When are we going to slip the sleeping candy to the animals?" Noal asked. "We've got the final round in a few days."

"I figure we can be at the ready if he somehow miraculously wins. Otherwise, there's no need to do it, is there?" Gregor said. "If he's out of the competition?"

"Suppose not," Elis said, and everyone nodded cautiously. Though they didn't seem convinced that Allstair would just slinker off into the shadows.

Gregor had a hunch that sooner or later, they would have to execute their plan.

34

Better Butter

The next morning Gregor made his way to the dovecote to see if a letter had arrived from the mountain. Passing a window in the hall, a pigeon, exhausted from its long flight, flapped its wings as hard as it could to make it through the hole and collided with the back of Gregor's head.

Gregor just so happened to be the person he was looking for.

Gregor picked the pigeon up and dropped it in a nest, pulled the letter from its parcel carrier, and was surprised to find it addressed to him. He looked around suspiciously and opened it, seeing no one and no mirrors.

Dear Greggy,

We're so excited for you to finish your moat and come home! There's lots to catch up on, some that can wait, but some that can't: The Luck of the Draw happened!

Your Da is all torn up about you not being here for it. He so hoped to pass on the throne to you, but I reminded him that we're not like other monarchs. That here, everyone has a chance to compete.

In the end, Minrol Pallad won the draw. He seems strong, he's definitely determined, and your father will get over his disappointment.

Minrol should pass through the kingdom at some point, so please keep an eye out for him! We've told him to look you up, we hope you don't mind. You must know it's intimidating, being in a big city like that, all alone. We're sure you got lucky with the friends you've made, and Minrol will be lucky to have you as his guide. We've enclosed a nugget of gold for the first round of drinks when you take him out. Your father thinks it's too much, but how is he to know what things cost in a metropolis? You'll be sure to tell us about it when you're home.

Lots of love,
Mum
& also Da

Gregor rubbed his head, understanding why the collision hurt so much after finding the massive nugget of gold the letter had been wrapped around. It seemed letters were taking as long as usual, and this one was sent before they received his confession letter. But Gregor had resigned himself—he had nothing to be ashamed of. He caught his reflection in the hall and smiled at it, the pin on his collar twinkling, polished that morning. He even gave a little wave to the glass, just in case his mum was watching, then noticed someone walking up behind him and coughed, embarrassed, before he hurried along to breakfast in the servant's dining hall. Long tables flanked with backless benches were set with bowls of fresh bread, blocks of butter in various stages of demolishment, salted meats, and elegant wheels of cheese. His friends looked up from a table and waved him over.

Gregor took a seat and a roll and pulled the butter dish closer. Before anyone could stop him, he scooped on a heaping glob and took a bite.

"Oh no, not that one," Ash moaned, watching Gregor's face screw up in disgust.

Panicked, Gregor closed his eyes, focused on the memory of a boulder biscuit, and finished chewing, finally swallowing the bite. "Bleh! What in the gods is that?"

"Vegan butter," Ash said, carefully pushing the dish out of reach. "The culinary students came up with it as their final project. It's a mix of oils, seasoning..."

"Coconut oil, apple cider vinegar, turmeric, and nutritional yeast," Brimley supplied, pulling the vile mess towards him. "It's very nutritious. The flavor takes some getting used to."

Gregor, wiping his tongue on a napkin, stopped when he understood it wasn't rancid, that he had consumed a deliberately made condiment. He rolled his tongue around, focusing on the lingering notes of flavor there. "It's...different. I wasn't expecting it."

"You could probably add some cinnamon, nutmeg, sugar, and make a sweet spread to better mask the vinegar. I think it would complement the coconut," Brimley added.

Inspiration dawned on Gregor, and he swiped the dish back from Brimley and began to doctor it just as he suggested, pulling closer the sugar jar and then the cinnamon shaker until he bit into something not bad, but a bit too grainy from the sugar. Replaced with powdered sugar, it could make a buttercream...his mind whirled with the possibilities. It was the perfect dairy replacement!

Noal watched the subtle excitement creep across Gregor's face in a way that only he noticed sometimes. He wasn't sure if he could ask, and when he did later in the test kitchen, Gregor just shrugged and said, "Oh nothing, I just had an idea."

"So it's going to be like that?" Noal asked, looking hurt.

"Like what?"

"Do you want me to bake on the other side of the room as well? So that I don't become privy to your secrets?"

Gregor rolled his eyes. "Noal, come off it. I just..." He sighed, realizing that they had to set a boundary, right then and there. "We can't make identical cakes. How about we talk about everything but baking? We're still friends, Noal, but we need to learn how to be competitors."

Noal frowned but nodded. He pulled his coat off the hook and then Gregor's, to show there were no hard feelings. Gregor thanked Noal and shrugged the jacket on, and they went to their usual table.

Gregor decided to start with a perfect cake recipe and swap ingredients out in increments. First the flour, that was easy. But the eggs were tricky. Eggs were the protein that bonded fats and liquid. Without it, the cake would lose structure, come out dense, flat, crumbly.

Water, oil, baking powder came the solution like a snap into Gregor's brain, a memory flinging itself to the surface. He would start with that and see how the cake turned out.

As for the dairy, why, there was almond milk, which was safe and would complement the flavor of the almond flour, but there were so many alternatives! He went to the pantry and flung it open to find all sorts of nuts: walnuts, cashews, pistachios, hazelnuts, pine nuts...Gregor ran a ringer down the line, recalling the flavors of each instantly as his fingers touched the bins. He had a phenomenal way of imagining how flavors would taste together and decided that cashews and baru nuts would complement vanilla best. He would try them as flour replacements and as milk replacements. A week between rounds seemed like ample time, but the sheer volume of combinations Gregor wanted to try and bake before the final competition made him absolutely dizzy. He made it back to his table and took a seat to steady himself, then began to grind, measure, and mix while Noal stole glances at him.

It wasn't until the bulge in Gregor's pocket banged against the leg of the table for the umpteenth time that he pulled the note-wrapped gold nugget out of his pocket and set it on the table. Noal nearly fainted with relief at the conversation starter.

"Your parents wrote you?" Noal asked, desperate to end the awkwardness.

"Aye, they did. Seems my confession letter didn't get to them yet. They told me Minrol Pallad had been selected for Luck of the Draw, and that he's coming to town. I'm worried about how he'll be able to find me. I'm not at the university, if that's where he goes to call on me."

"You could post a parchment in Badger & Bard," Noal suggested. "Ash could draw up something. She—" He glanced up at the enchanted mirror and dropped his voice. "*He's* very creative."

"I bet," Gregor muttered. So that Noal could hear, he said, "I wouldn't want to bother him, I know he needs to focus on the final round."

"I'm sure he won't mind," Noal said brightly, and before Gregor could protest turned and made the request of Ash, who leaned past Noal to confirm with Gregor. "Really? You'll let me draw up a poster?"

"Sure! Whatever," Gregor grumbled, and whisked with even greater fervor until the batter sloshed over the lip of the bowl, making a mess. He ripped his apron off and announced he was going for air.

He made it down the hall to his favorite window, the one that faced the university and, if he squinted and leaned out as far as he dared, he thought for sure that hill in the distance was Superstitious Mountain.

Gregor had initially been terrified of windows, especially this high up, but if he placed his palms firmly on the windowsill and felt the cool stone, he felt grounded, secure, and could enjoy the view.

He tore his eyes away at the sound of footsteps and saw Gale, Harlowe, and Lance approaching. He gave a friendly wave, and they mirrored it.

"Is everyone already in there?" Harlowe asked.

"Everyone but Alistair," Gregor said, and wondered if they would see him that week or if he had his own kitchen to practice in. The clear advantage of baking in the test kitchen was getting accustomed to the tools and the oven in there, plus the use of Crown-provided ingredients, but then they were also privy to everyone else's recipe unless they decided to curtain off sections of the kitchen, which seemed extreme, unless...

"We know which ingredients to avoid," Harlowe announced as if reading his mind. "We're not coming in to spy on you, if that's what you're afraid of."

"I don't reckon I could keep you out of the kitchen if I tried," Gregor retorted, eyeing Gale, who seemed to be sizing him up for a fight.

"It's flour, eggs, and dairy, isn't it?" Lance blurted, because he knew the prolonged tension would definitely do him in.

Gale let out a growl and Harlowe heaved a sigh, but Gregor nodded. "Yes, it is. How did you know?"

"That lady from the courtyard the other day? She's from *The Harking Harold*. We made a deal with her to find out for us," Lance confessed.

"What did she get for spying for you?"

"Interviews. *Exclusive* interviews," Gale said, as if this was as much a prize for them as it was for her.

Gregor tugged at his beard, thoughtful. "And if you lose?"

"Then I guess we all lose," Gale growled, and stepped past Gregor toward the test kitchen.

Lance followed him, but Harlowe delayed a moment to say to Gregor, "I don't even know if I want to win. The stress is so much."

"Then why did you come?"

Harlowe shrugged. "I'm not much for candy making. I wanted to learn more about these mirrors. Fascinating, no? One could really earn some fame with them."

Gregor gawked at him. "You like them? You want people to look at you through them?"

"When I was a wizard, people would hire me to do parlor tricks at parties. I rather miss it. I wouldn't mind doing them for a wider audience. What a time we're living in, eh?"

Gregor watched Harlowe follow the others. It was certainly a competition, but there were a surprising number of alliances. With that, he too made his way back to the kitchen and decided he would make a pact with Ash.

∗∗∗

The week went by in a flash. Eight of the nine competitors consistently showed up to bake in the test kitchen, experimenting with all the ways vanilla could be showcased in a cake.

Gregor loved that baking was a living, breathing art. Ingredients mixed and reacted, homogenized. The batter got fussy if some ingredients got added cold instead of room temperature. Sometimes it needed help rising, and there was a pinch of baking powder for that. It liked to bake at just the right temperature, uninterrupted, or else it would throw a fit and ruin itself.

It was why Ash whispered while she baked; plants liked to be coaxed, so why wouldn't yeast? Batter?

Noal tended to baking as if to an ill-tempered relative, always overcompensating by double-, triple-checking ingredients, the oven temperature, and the bake time. No one had more or better-quality kitchen timers than Noal, ones that chimed when they expired to make extra sure he noticed.

Gregor approached baking as if handling a dragon. Dragons were feared on the mountain, the Great Big Danger that was always on its way, to be braced for. But when Gregor arrived in Citeel, he found dragons to be pests that needed to be dealt with by a firm hand. Sweeping them out with a broom. Catching and tossing them out the window. Ushering them back up the chimney. Gregor had seen some of the bigger ones in shop windows, brutes the size of mares coaxing forges to extreme temperatures, but Gregor grew not to be afraid of them. All dragons had the same temperament, they just needed a bit more wrestling the taller they grew. And this vanilla cake he had to bake in a few short days, why this was what Gregor now imagined the Great Big Danger to be. And it wasn't so scary, when he broke it up into small pieces on the parchment. These beans instead of eggs. These nuts instead of flour. This strange new butter in exchange for regular dairy butter.

Most of all, Gregor loved to sample the cakes he baked, biting into each morsel as if tasting dessert for the first time all over again. *Sublime.* Knowing these were some of the best cakes in all the kingdom made them taste even better, sprinkled with that dash of pride.

When Ash finished the half-dozen posters for Minrol, Gregor went with Noal and Ash around town to stick them where they thought the traveling dwarf would easily happen upon them. This included one in Badger & Bard and another on the Official Palace Billboard that stood on the other side of the moat, a place where people liked to check for employment opportunities and tac up love notes for missed connections.

Minrol never called on Gregor. And Gregor quickly forgot about him, testing one batch of cake after another, made with vanilla bean, then vanilla paste, then vanilla extract, until finally it was time.

35

Morning Of

The day of the final competition, Gregor dropped onto the breakfast bench and immediately felt the tension. Ash gnawed her thumbnail instead of the muffin before her, and Noal kept swishing the same mouthful of oats around in his mouth, sipping coffee to rehydrate them his mouth was so dry. Gregor grabbed a blueberry scone and took a bite. It turned to stone in his stomach and he, too, found it hard to swallow the rest of his breakfast. He looked at Noal, who had deep purple bags under his eyes. "Gods, what happened to you?"

Noal opened his mouth and let out a tremendous yawn. "I couldn't sleep. Not last night, and not the night before, so I asked Brimley for a sleepy gumdrop but I lost it so I couldn't take it! You slept like a rock, it's not fair. I finally ran out of adrenaline and passed out in the wee hours."

"You didn't even bother changing your pants," Ash scolded, taking inventory of what he was wearing. "When's the last time you did laundry?"

"I've been busy," Noal wailed, and wiped his napkin on a stain on his thigh that could have been absolutely anything.

Elis dropped into the seat beside Ash, startling them all. "Good morning."

"What a surprise," Ash muttered, scooting away from him to escape the cloud of cologne that practically shone like a halo around him.

"I've put some thought into all this and honestly, I don't know what we're stressing about. The king has put all this effort into training us to be his perfect chefs. There's no way one of us isn't going to win."

"Are you saying it's rigged?" Ash asked, cocking an eyebrow.

"It would be *embarrassing* if we lost," Elis said, still not clarifying what he was implying.

Noal looked at Gregor, who squinted at Elis. "What deals have you made, Elis?"

Elis winked at Gregor. "I'm just feeling good. I'm on a winning streak!" He dropped his voice. "Plus, if *he* wins, you have enough evidence to put him away, don't you?"

Ash let out a huge sigh of relief. "There he is."

"I'm only worried about the lot of ya," Elis said, pointing at each in turn with his butter knife. He flashed a brilliant smile. "May the best chef win."

Some of the staff dropped by their table on their way in, confessing bets and wishing good luck to each of them. Elis pocketed a few coins, and Gregor had no doubt he had a pool going, but he wasn't entirely sure Elis was placing all his bets on himself, not even with that smile.

"I'd bet on you," Ash said to Noal as they made their way down the hall.

"He's cut off from betting," Gregor snapped.

"Oh, come on!" Noal protested. "You made out like a bandit the other night. I'd bet on you. Or Elis."

Gregor rolled his eyes and pushed the door of the royal test kitchen open.

✳✳✳

Nine competitors stood in stiff chef coats buttoned to the throat, tall, starched hats atop each head. Impeccably white aprons tied around their waists, eager for splatters and smears. They clasped their hands in front of those white aprons, feet placed hip-width apart in practical slip-proof black shoes. They stood behind their stations, facing forward, though none could keep their eyes from roaming.

Ash and Gregor stared straight ahead into the massive mirror.

Noal kept glancing at Alistair, itching with suspicion.

Elis glared at Brimley, who pretended not to notice.

Gale and Harlowe stared at Lance, who was sweating through his coat already though they hadn't even started, no flames were present, and in fact the room was kept delightfully cool by an enchanted fan not far above their heads.

"Alright, mate?" Gale whispered to Lance, but the door burst open. Chef Toufie marched in with his immense mug, trailed by Mosley and Arosco in dog form, as well as Celeste and Princess Damora. Mosley carried a gold-framed mirror before him, as if he was showing off a painting he was proud of, which he set on the desk. He peeked into it and rubbed his chin, smoothed his eyebrows. Toufie slurped his mug and inspected a parchment.

"Alright," Chef Toufie said, but Mosley cleared his throat, pointed him to stand a little bit...there. "Perfect. Carry on."

"We have a guest competitor," Chef Toufie announced. The room, as expected, erupted. Chef Toufie simply smiled and sipped his coffee until everyone regained composure, catching on that he would not engage in their complaints. He nodded at Mosley, who took this as his cue and pulled out his pocket mirror, traced his finger over the surface, and spoke into it. A moment later a man walked in, and Mosley shouted his name into the table mirror. "Sorren Weaver!"

Standing before the contestants was the head pastry chef of Demure Delicacies, the most famous wedding cake bakery in the neighboring city. He was also devastatingly beautiful, which had helped catapult his bakery to success.

Ash made a choking sound. She hated this surprise.

Sorren, looking around the room, nodded at Elis, whom he'd met at the pubs when he visited town. Noal's blood ran cold when he recognized him from his older sister's wedding all those years ago. He nearly burst from the desire to turn to Gregor and scream this at him.

The others, if they recognized Sorren, didn't betray their thoughts. Sorren took his place at the table beside Ash, who looked so embarrassed she made Lance, who was near collapse, look composed.

Chef Toufie cleared his throat. "For this round, you will be paired up. When I call your names, please grab your nameplates and rearrange yourselves beside your partner.

"I have Elis and Harlowe, Ash and Gale—"

"Gale?" Mosley interrupted. "No, I believe Ash is paired with Sorren."

Ash slammed her hands on the table to steady herself. Sorren looked at her, amused, and when she stole a peek at him her whole body flashed hot then cold. It was a feeling Ash had never felt before. She'd never been around anyone so famous. She'd read profiles on Sorren, seen his face in *The Harking Herald* for years. His was the only picture she'd traced her fingers down, snuck kisses to. She was reckoning her obsession with him, right then and there, and she could hardly compose herself as she was. Standing there, right next to him, just being in his general vicinity would certainly be her demise. Hearing them bicker over whether or not she would be paired with him, she found herself praying she would be his partner, but also desperately hoping not to be.

Mosley was whispering harshly. "No, I specifically invited him to be—"

"It's *my* say," Chef Toufie finally snapped. He then looked directly into the mirror, as if imploring the powers that be beyond them to back him up.

Mosley relented. "Fine," he spat. "Carry on."

"Gregor and Alistair, Noal and Brimley, Sorren and Lance. Your goal this round is to bake the *tallest* vanilla cake." He paused a moment here for the detail to sink in. Chef Toufie was impressed by the unflinching, stoic stares. "You'll have twenty minutes to work together to prepare your recipe. Then Fergis will light the oven, and you will have two hours to complete your cake. Find your stations."

Shuffle, shuffle, shuffle.

Mosley looked directly into the mirror. "Ready...set...*bake your best*!" He turned the first hourglass. Twenty minutes to plan.

Everyone jumped into action.

Mosley watched gleefully as quills raced across parchments, some of which were fought over and ripped, causing waterfalls of profanities. He hadn't planned on roaming the room until the real action began, but he was dying to know what all there was to fight about. He pulled the framed mirror off the desk and wandered the room, flashing it this way, that. Some didn't notice. Some looked irked, and Gregor was having none of it.

"Back it up, I can see my nose hairs," he growled.

"What's your tactic?" Mosley repeated, only to be ignored. He was about to move on when a crash had him and the rest of the room whirling around to find Lance collapsed.

There was a brief moment of pause where no one dared break protocol. Then they decided some things were more important than winning a contest. Nearly everyone—except Elis and Alistair—dropped to the ground beside Lance, offering help.

"Make way, make way!" Chef Toufie boomed, shooing them aside. He put one hand under Lance's neck and with the other slapped his cheeks—not too gently— until his eyes fluttered open. His face was white as flour, cold, and drenched in sweat. "Come on now, lad, you're just baking a cake."

They all knew it was more than that, of course. It was immense pressure, the eyes of the kingdom upon them thanks to those cursed mirrors.

"I-I," Lance sputtered, fighting to sit up. Ash swooped down with a mug of water, which Lance gulped down. He didn't look any better, but his eyes were at least focusing. "I'm sorry, I'm a bit stressed."

"We're all a bit stressed, lad," Toufie said gently. "Do you want to go to the medical wing, or would you like to continue?"

"You can't quit now," Gale insisted. "You're better than that."

Noal reached into his pocket to retrieve a handkerchief. It was sticky and stuck to the lining of his pocket, and he had to tug hard to pull it out. A bean flew out with it and skittered across the floor, but Noal and everyone else ignored it as he offered up the soiled hanky. Ash snatched it away before Lance could accept it. She gave Noal a glare before stuffing it in her own pocket, lest he try to be helpful and offer it to anyone else.

Lance looked past them all to Alistair, as if making to ask something, but before he did Alistair gave a short, brief shake of his head and looked away, ignoring the scene. Gregor saw this and suspected what Lance had wanted.

"He'll be alright," Sorren said. "He's a fine baker. We'll do just fine."

A ring rang out as the final sand slipped through the neck of the hourglass. Mosley reached for the much larger one beside it and turned it, beginning the two-hour countdown. Final words of encouragement were hurled at Lance before they all returned to their stations. The show had to go on.

Nuts and oats were pounded, sugar weighed, beans—which beans?!—were counted, crushed, soaked, whipped. Vanilla pods were boiled, steeped, sliced open. Mosley went down the line, trying to ask, "What's your tactic here?" to deaf ears.

Lance seemed to be the only one not in perpetual motion as he stood holding his refreshed glass of water, sipping, letting the color seep back into his face.

Eyes glanced at the second, much larger hourglass as it dripped grains of black sand from one belly into the other, and they swore each speck went down faster than the last.

The intense concentration was finally interrupted with a, "Where's Fergis?"

Every head popped up as if finally breaking the surface for air. They swiveled around nearly in unison towards the great oven, which was still cold. Then panic broke out as they raced around and no one could find the dragon.

"Gods, he's asleep!" Elis announced, happening upon the dragon snoring on the bottom shelf of the pantry and poking it with the toe of his shiny shoe.

Ash reached him next, and she booped Fergis on the nose. Dragons had a reflex there to open their mouth, but his stayed shut. She remembered that something had skittered across the floor earlier and looked around for it. Her eyes landed on Noal instead. "Come here," she hissed, and he did, shuffling over at the awkward pace between a walk and a run that desperately didn't want to look like a run. "What?"

"What was in your pocket?"

"A bean! I think?"

"It was your sleeping pill," Gregor realized, slapping a hand to his forehead. He looked over to Brimley, who slapped *his* hand over his mouth in shock. Brimley whipped around to glare at Alistair, who pretended to ignore the whole business while sneaking glances out of the corner of his eye.

"What's wrong with him?" Mosley asked, and was already hurrying over with the mirror, Chef Toufie at his heels.

"He's asleep," Elis said matter-of-factly.

"So wake him," Mosley replied, confused. It took one look at the snoring beast before Toufie, who knew dragons were mischievous but not lazy, understood this dragon wouldn't be rousing.

"I'm going to get the one from next door," he announced, and lumbered out the door. The other contestants took this opportunity to keep measuring, mixing, and folding.

It didn't take long for Toufie to return, without the dragon. An apron was wrapped around his forearm, and it was blooming red with blood. "I feel a bit woozy, I-I'm going to go to the medical wing," Toufie announced and did just that.

"Can we pause that timer?" Lance asked, his voice a full octave higher than usual.

Mosley and Celeste locked eyes, both vibrating with excitement. "Afraid not," Mosley said. "It's enchanted."

"So is the oven," Harlowe shouted, who was standing beside it with Sorren trying to make sense of the inscription chiseled into the brick.

"Is this part of the test?" Elis asked, crossing his arms. "Because if it's not, I'm not helping."

"You're useless anyway," Brimley muttered, shoving him aside. Ash followed him to the oven, and between Ash's meager summoning of fire and Brimley's tinkering skills, they got a flame going, then roaring. A few more incantations from Harlowe and the oven was tuned into more or less a decent temperature to bake. "Four hundred, boys," Ash announced, grinning at their applause.

"I'll take it," Gregor shouted, and nodded to her in thanks as she returned to her station.

Hot cakes came out, loaves beautifully baked. It seemed that baking was the easy task; assembling would be the challenge.

Competitors began to side-eye the pairs around them, wondering what their stacking tactic was.

Brimley spun glass out of sugar, blowing balls that he then stacked in between layers, giving their cake height and a cloudlike effect.

Sorren rolled pillars of tempered chocolate to stick in the cake to stabilize it.

Elis and Harlowe cut and stacked their cake tall and narrow.

Gregor kept waiting for Alistair to pull something from his pocket, perhaps a spell to make the layers levitate, elevating them to the tallest height, but that didn't happen. He and Alistair had agreed to bake layers of different densities to help with stabilizing, but as they stacked their cake it could only get so high before it started to wobble, sliding over the dairy-free buttercream Gregor had whipped up and slathered between the layers. Alistair grew visibly frustrated. They needed support.

"Not tall enough," Alistair said, and Gregor was about to snap something unkind his way when he had an idea, watching Sorren and his chocolate pillars.

Boulder biscuits.

"I can't explain, I just need you to trust me," Gregor told Alistair, who dutifully began gathering the ingredients he was listed. Oats. Barley. Lentils. Molasses. Nuts. These biscuits were hearty, dense, and stayed preserved until just about the end of time. Gregor stretched the sticky mass into a rope and tossed it directly into the oven's flame, and within minutes it hardened beautifully into what they would use as support beams. He took a dough cutter and, using the force of his entire weight, chopped it up into perfect-sized bits. He passed them off to Alistair, who shoved them into the cake, instantly stabilizing it. They stacked the next layer, then the next, smearing buttercream on as they went.

With the timer nearly completely out, Gregor shoved the last of the boulder biscuits into the final layer and looked around to see their cake stacked just a few inches higher than the rest of the competitors. He stood back, grinning, as Alistair leaned in to pipe on what was left of the buttercream.

"Time!"

36

Winner

One by one, pairs were called and cakes were presented, same as the last round. "Ash and Gale."

This cake was barely baked in time. They had squabbled, Ash wanting to play it safe with almond flour, but Gale had insisted on baru nuts, which unfortunately absorbed the moisture of the batter, drying the cake out in the oven. The final loaves came out cracked and crumbling. Copious amounts of whipped bean meringue did its best to glue the disks together, and it was decorated with a beautiful spray of edible flowers that Ash had tastefully arranged to cascade down the side of it. But as soon as Gale set the cake on the presenting table—a little too heavily—the bottom layer of the cake split in two. The top layers slid off the side of the cake in an avalanche of melted meringue, which had been slathered on while the cake was still piping hot, having run out of time to let it cool completely. Ash looked about ready to cry, and Gale grumbled, "We might win on taste yet."

They did not. But the princess did get the chance to taste it. And spit it out.

Brimley and Noal's cake looked celestial, and Celeste said so, delighted. She gave them full marks, although the judges squabbled a bit over whether or not the hollow sugar sculptures gave or took points away. The best part of it was that it, too, was edible. In fact, every single cake was tasted that day.

Elis and Harlowe's cake was very tall. It was glued solid with vanilla pastry cream coated with granulated sugar and torched until it created a shiny, crispy shell. Princess Damora questioned whether the tall and skinny tactic could translate to a cake that would feed six hundred guests, although it got full marks for flavor.

Lance shook like a leaf as he walked with his and Sorren's cake to the front. It was covered in vanilla bean buttercream—Sorren had perfected a dairy-free recipe a decade ago— and piped elegantly all around the edges of each layer. It was also five layers high, one layer higher than Elis and Harlowe's cake, held steady by the hidden chocolate pillars.

Everyone held their breath.

Lance nearly made it to the front when he suddenly sneezed, and the gorgeous white cake dropped from his unsteady hands and crumpled atop his shoes.

Everyone gasped, Celeste screamed, and Mosley howled with delight. "They'll replay this in slow-motion," he chuckled, running over with his mirror to capture Lance's horror up close. Arosco darted over and began wolfing down mouthfuls of the cake before Princess Damora grabbed him by the collar and scolded him, forced him to sit between her feet. From the way he wagged his tail, it looked like there was a clear winner in Arosco's heart. Lance looked over at Sorren, terrified, but he was clutching his chest, laughing. Any publicity would be good publicity for his bakery.

Taking note, Gregor and Alistair took their cake together, eyeing the top, but it didn't wobble despite it towering far above their heads. Set beside the others, it was the clear winner, at least height-wise. Gregor couldn't help beaming up at it, his heart swelling with pride. *He had made that.* He gingerly cut the pieces and watched Alistair dish them out. Then his eyes shifted to the princess, the one—perhaps the only—opinion that mattered most. She poked the cake, turned it over, sniffed the buttercream, which was a few shades lighter than the one smeared all over the floor thanks to the few drops of purple dye that Ash had discovered and taught him and Noal to use. Finally, she took a bite, and Gregor had to remember to close his mouth as he watched her chew, swallow. Her eyebrows raised and she looked over at Celeste beside her, who mirrored her reaction. Princess Damora quickly finished the rest of the cake, nodding approvingly at the pair of chefs standing anxiously at attention before her.

"Taste was wonderful," Damora said, finally setting the plate down. "The vanilla shines through wonderfully. Less nutty than the others we've tasted."

"And that color!" Mosley interrupted, holding up his barely touched piece, inspecting it from all angles. "Although a bit more decoration would have been nice."

"And so moist," Celeste added, ignoring Mosley's criticism. "Easily the tallest, too."

Gregor couldn't keep the grin off his face. He turned to Alistair, who gave him a respectful nod.

Points were calculated, taking into consideration the previous round, and Princess Damora stood.

"Based on this round alone, we have Alistair and Gregor at the top. After calculating in the other rounds, we have our winner."

Princess Damora turned and smiled right at him. "Gregor Brimstone."

Half the room exploded into cheers, as Ash, Noal, and Brimley broke into celebration that it was *one of them*. They hugged their friend and clapped him on the back. Even Elis came over and shook his hand, as did the others once Gregor could break away from the crushing embrace of his friends. Sorren nearly tripped over Fergis, who had roused from the noise and was making his way over to help clean up the dropped cake. Arosco let out a growl, but Fergis ignored him, happily munching away.

Princess Damora stopped clapping and the room fell silent. "Thanks to everyone for your participation. It has been an honor. Those who have newly joined the employment of the royal kitchen, you'll be reporting directly to Gregor and aiding him in the preparation of this cake. You all have my utmost confidence."

Princess Damora motioned for Gregor to approach. Then she pulled out a velvet case, opened it, and presented the royal seal. Gasps rang out around the room. Gregor stood hypnotized by the golden otters swimming in the amethyst hexagon.

"To be given to you upon your success," Princess Damora said, and held the case open another moment for him to admire—and for Mosley to get a close-up of—before she slammed it shut. "You are dismissed."

In pubs all across the kingdom, groans filled the air, coins were exchanged, and fights nearly broke out. Would Gregor crack under the pressure on the big day? Of course not, he was a dwarf! They're made to withstand immense pressure! And so new bets were scratched, new wagers were cast.

In ladies' parlors all across the kingdom, women sat enraptured on their couches, clutching cushions, swooning over Sorren. Celeste had paid him a handsome sum of gold to make an appearance. She'd dropped hints of his upcoming appearance here and there, at the hairdresser, the tailor, the cheese stall at the market, the dragon groomer. It didn't take long for royal sorcerers to be summoned to the most lavish private residences to enchant gorgeously framed mirrors.

Celeste sat at the judge's table, lost to the images she swiped through in her palm, finally seeing inside the homes of socialites she'd only ever dreamt of being invited into. Little did they know she would now be entering whenever she fancied. She rubbed Arosco's head absentmindedly, a sinister smile spreading across her impeccably painted face.

The chefs left the test kitchen and broke off into groups in the hallway. Noal turned and scooped Gregor into a fierce bear hug, burying Gregor's face against his abdomen. "I'm so relieved! It's like when I could finally say nutmeg again."

"You can finally say nutmeg?" Ash was clearly relieved; the holidays had been rough the past year, trying to get him to "pass the spice that's the one you can't say."

Gregor tolerated the embrace for another moment, then, as gingerly as he could, pulled away, gasping for air.

Noal ran over to the window Gregor liked to look out of and shouted, "Nutmeg!" It felt so good he did it again and again until Gregor joined him, and then Ash, and they did it until it didn't mean anything anymore. They finally broke the chant with fits of giggles.

Alistair, who had been lingering in the hall, stepped up to Gregor and reached out a hand to shake. Gregor took it without pause and enthusiastically echoed Alistair's words of congratulations. Before Alistair let go, he leaned in and whispered, "I suppose I'm the alternate. Should...anything happen."

Gregor jerked back and stared at Alistair, horrified.

Alistair let go and winked. "I'm just joking."

But from the way he said it, Gregor wasn't so sure. After all, as first alternate, didn't Alistair have every reason to hope he failed?

37

Sprinkle of Sweets

With the previous letter sent, the next one was a lot easier for Gregor to write. Perhaps it was the glow of victory that fueled him.

In any case, he took a seat at his desk and, ignoring the loud snoring of Noal—he always snored louder after a night of robust drinking—wrote a letter to his parents.

Dear Mum & Da,

I have exciting news to share: I've won the baking contest!

It feels validating that all my hard work has paid off. I will be awarded the royal purple seal and then I'll be able to open my own shop here.

All my dreams are about to come true.

The royal wedding will be held on the summer solstice, which is sentimental and nice and all, but will be terrible for a cake. I'm stressed, but I'll have my friends to help me plan and bake the cake. Even Elis, who isn't such a good sport.

Speaking of the wedding day, I'd like to invite you both. I hope you'll come, as it would mean a lot to me. And you'll get to taste my cake! I'd like nothing better.

I've kept my eyes out for Minrol, but he hasn't come calling. I've gotten no letters or anything from him either, but with these drunk pigeons, it's hard to tell if it's lost or late.

Sorry again I lied and I hope you say yes,

Greggy

Gregor folded and waxed the letter and left Noal to sleep off the night. They had stayed up into the wee hours scheming at Badger & Bard and had come up with a plan, which Gregor was about to execute. After attaching the letter to the pigeon who looked the least inebriated, he made his way down to breakfast.

As he entered the hall, the kitchen staff poked their heads in, and all came over to shake his hand and congratulate him. Gregor waved them off good-naturedly and took a seat at the empty end of a table, the other end occupied by a group of gardeners half-asleep over their steaming mugs. They saluted him and he gave them a smile. Gregor was friendly, but he wasn't *outgoing*.

Gregor reached for a plate from the stack in the center of the table. That seemed to set off an invisible bell and a server appeared and offered him a cup of tea? Coffee? Juice? Ale?

It had made him laugh, the first time he'd been offered ale that early, but upon further inspection he noticed the flasks on hips, the night shift getting off work just as others sat down preparing to take on the day. Time didn't matter in the dining hall, and it was one of the reasons Gregor loved it.

"Er, coffee. No, tea. A nice herbal one, if you've got it."

"We have *everything*," the server reminded him and glided away.

As Gregor began piling his plate high, a familiar figure swooped into the seat across from him, still in her purple dressing robe and slippers, eyes hooded, half-asleep. "Hello, Gregor."

"You're staff?" Gregor asked, blinking at Harper in disbelief.

"What, only staff get to eat here?" Harper asked, reaching for a plate.

"Typically. The fancy staff eat out in the main hall with the royals."

"Oh no, then I definitely belong here."

The server was back with a mug of hot water and an array of teas arranged on a small plate. "Miss?"

"Coffee, darling, a bucket of it."

The server nodded and left. Harper used her knife to scoop a glob of butter and began slathering it all over her ripped-apart roll. "I'm starving. Those pigeons sure know how to party!"

Gregor didn't know what to say to this and instead went for a wedge of cheese. He carved off a chunk for himself and for Harper, which she snatched from him greedily. She moaned around her mouthful when the coffee, served in a mug the size of Chef Toufie's, was planted in front of her. She loaded it with cream and sugar and dunked the rest of her buttered roll in it. She licked her fingers, wiped them on the napkin in her lap, and then slurped down a few gulps of coffee. She perked up and smiled at Gregor over the brim of the mug. "What an exciting time."

"Yes, I'm...very pleased," he said, not sure if this was the beginning of an interview, and if it was, if it was on or off the record. Not that he knew the difference, he'd never been interviewed in his life, not even to enter the apprenticeship, which he had been told was mandatory for everyone else. He tugged anxiously at his beard before remembering the hot water before him. This gave him something to busy himself with as he dunked a bag containing spearmint and lemongrass into his mug.

Harper watched him, but Gregor seemed perfectly content with the silence and wasn't about to crack. She finally asked, "How do you feel about giving me an exclusive interview? I'm sure the public would love to know all about you."

Gregor had anticipated this. He knew of Harper and knew she was very much on the job. They'd discussed her over celebratory drinks last night, and how that might be to their benefit.

"Once a gossiper, always a gossiper," Brimley had said and held up the bag of sleepy gumdrop candy.

That bag burned in Gregor's pocket. He had suspected he would run into her here, or in the dovecot he just came from, or perched on some gargoyle somewhere. He watched her rake an elegant hand through her hair. The feathers sprouting at the roots gave her mane truly astonishing volume.

"You're a journalist," Gregor said carefully, as if putting a toe of pressure on a rock to see if it would hold. The hint of a smile tugging at her lips indicated this was a point of great pride for her. "Don't you feel..." Gregor let out a raspberry. "As if these mirrors, they're competing with you?"

Harper's smile froze. "What do you mean?"

"Don't you want to be the sole source of coverage of this royal wedding? Your name on everyone's lips when asked, 'How did you find out?' These mirrors, they're letting everyone see and hear everything all the time. What does the public need you for? Who needs a carefully crafted column, a blurb, a by-line from a *trained reporter* when people can just tap their mirrors to eavesdrop and make any assumptions they like? No one is guiding them through the story here! It's..." Gregor's voice waivered, realizing that Harper was leaning clear over her mug, her hooked nose nearly in his face she was listening so intently. He gulped and finished with, "*making you obsolete.*"

Harper ingested each of his words so meticulously that it took a few seconds after his voice faded for her to fully consume them. She slumped back into her seat. "You make a fair point."

Harper sipped her coffee and considered what he said. Gregor, beginning to tremble with anticipation, had to focus hard on chewing each bite as he willed himself to let her lead this next bit. He nearly dropped his butter knife when she finally said, "Do you have an idea of how to stop this nonsense?"

"In fact, I do," Gregor said, and pulled the bag of gumdrops out of his pocket.

38

Just a Peek

Mosley sat in his chamber nibbling his breakfast and staring intently at the mirror he had Remus enchant. It was displaying the view of a teeny-tiny mirror secured around the neck of a gimey lizard that was carried by a pigeon. He was soaring above a maze of empty hallways, and then suddenly Ash was getting closer and closer until...*plop*. The pigeon dropped the lizard, which landed lightly on Ash's shoulder. She was in such a hurry she didn't notice, muttering under her breath the speech she had rehearsed as she headed up the tower to the princess's chamber. Mosley watched in awe. He had hoped to catch a peek at Ash's lover, but this? Was he romancing the princess?

Lots of lore like to put princesses in tall towers, but that was based on truth because a lot of them loved to read the stars, decipher horoscopes, and write astrology-based advice to their friends and subjects. Some went on to be queens who blessed or dissuaded the unions of their children based on where the stars lingered. To be able to do this, seeing them through a telescope from a tall tower was paramount.

Whether or not the former queen approved of the upcoming nuptials based on the betrothed's star signs had not been confirmed publicly. But from flicking through a mirror of Celeste's—who suddenly had access to nearly as many mirrors as Remus, Mosley discovered—it seemed there were a lot of women in the kingdom who had read the stars and were weighing in on the matter, speaking their predictions into mirrors to whoever happened to swipe and catch their transmission.

Mosley was still baffled. The intention had been to enchant the public's mirrors to receive the channeling of the royal wedding and to be peered into by a select few such as himself. But it became apparent that nearly everyone who called a royal sorcerer to enchant their mirror had also requested they be reverse-engineered to channel out instead of just in. And people weren't afraid of being watched; they welcomed it! Where once families used two-way mirrors to scry each other, suddenly people were using them to talk to no one in particular!

On quiet evenings tucked early into bed, Mosley swiped through his own mirror and caught sight of a woman reading off recipes for po-tions—*swipe*—the royal dance troupe in practice—*swipe*—Madrigola, the fa-mous opera singer performing for a full audience, which one could watch live, just like that!—*swipe*—a butcher telling the mirror how to best pick a piece of meat based on what it would be made into for supper. There were even investment recommendations to watch!

And now, he was using his handheld to get to the bottom of the mystery of a certain royal chef.

Ash entered the princess's chamber and removed her cloak, hung it on a hook before taking a seat across from where the princess was sitting on her sofa, sipping her morning tea.

"Oh gods," Mosley gasped, seeing Ash in a dress.

Celeste, who sat beside him, looked up from her needlework. "What is it, Cousin?"

"It's just, I mean, I didn't think, why this is quite..."

"Spit. It. Out."

"He's not rendezvousing with anyone. I think..." Mosley turned the mirror to Celeste. "I believe he *is* the lady-in-waiting."

"What? How can that be? We don't hire men." Celeste's eyebrows raised to her hairline. She snatched the mirror and watched it closely. "That's Ashlynn," Celeste said, amazed. Her fingers danced across the glass, rewinding the frame, zooming in, then back out again. "My, you could really convict anyone with evidence like this," she murmured.

"No, it's the other way around," Mosley said, sinking his face into his palms.

"One of your chefs is a *girl*." Celeste understood. Then they looked at each other as the gravity of what they just saw sunk in. "Are you sure she's the only one?"

"What do you mean am I sure? I just found this out!" Mosley slapped a hand onto his forehead.

"What about that dwarf he—*she*—hangs out with? You never know with dwarves. The women have beards, too."

"Do they?" Mosley blinked, baffled. Gregor was the only dwarf he'd ever met. "You're saying the royal kitchen has been infiltrated by women? This whole time?"

"On *your* watch?"

Mosley realized what she was insinuating. "In that case, we keep this a secret."

"Is she about to confess?"

"Shhh." Mosley motioned for Celeste to be quiet. He tapped the mirror, whispered an incantation, and the fuzzy whispers suddenly boomed from the mirror. Mosley cupped his hand around his ear to be sure he caught every word.

"He's not a doctor," Ash insisted. "He spins spells into his candy. He's up to no good. He might yet try to sabotage the wedding or harm you or the rest of your family."

"Do you have proof?"

Ash pulled out a peppermint stick and set it on the table. Princess Damora picked it up and inspected it. "What does it do?"

"It makes you spill all your secrets. Think of the damage that could do."

Damora pursed her lips. "We have a new pharmacy apprentice who could look into this," she said and pocketed the peppermint.

"How did he come to enter the contest, anyhow?"

"My father found him," Princess Damora said. "Well, Mosley did. Funny fellow. His cousin, Celeste, is a bit wicked. I like her. She's been introducing me to all these mirror magicians."

Mosley dropped his toast. *Oh no.* He was now associated with Alistair and a possible treasonous crime. Enchanted sweets!

Princess Damora took a sip of her tea before becoming serious. "I'll have to investigate this candy business. Unfortunately, it's a bit your word against his, and you haven't, er, been totally honest."

Ash blushed. "I thought for sure you knew when you judged my strawberry lemon loaf."

"Oh, my suspicions were confirmed then. I suspected since your second year. You made a comment at breakfast one day about a pastry not being flaky enough."

"And you said nothing?" Ash gasped.

"For what? To lose a perfectly good chef to needlework and idle gossip? I can make you my personal baker now," Damora said with a wink.

The image became wobbly as the gimey lizard began to toddle over to something. A bug? *Dammit, you simple creature*! Mosley shook the mirror as if that would do anything. It didn't, of course. The gimey lizard made it to the open window, lost its footing, and the next thing Mosley saw was sky, a lot of it, until there was a frame of green on the edges and then the mirror went still. The lizard had fallen out of the tower and landed in a tree, staring up at the sky.

Mosley set the mirror down and pinched the bridge of his nose, rubbed his temples. Oh, what a disaster!

39

Impostor

Meanwhile, Helva sat alone in Celeste's sitting room, dolloping sweet cream onto a scone. She figured Celeste wouldn't mind her being in there. The two were getting along rather well lately, bonding over the mirror magicians, listening in on the tips, tricks, and gossip around the city that dwarfed the drama of the baking competition.

Well, not completely.

She swiped her fingers across Celeste's mirror until she saw through Gertie's collar mirror the entrance to the wing that housed the princess's tower. That was as far as the mirrors went, even as far as Gertie the cat was allowed, who was stopped by the guards posted at the entrance. Helva watched now as someone came towards her—well, towards Gertie. She recognized the person walking down the stairs as Ashlynn, wearing the royal purple dress of the ladies-in-waiting. She seemed distracted and didn't notice the cat watching her as she made her way down the hall into the common area. Gertie, who loved to chase an unsuspecting gown hem, crept after in full prowl mode until the purple cloth vanished behind a bathroom door. Gertie waited patiently, as if in front of a mouse hole; what went in must always come out. Except, not the same thing came out. In her stead was Ash Birchwood.

Helva spit her tea in a spray across the table. She jumped up and pumped a fist in the air. "I *knew* there was something amiss," she cried and ran to the royal wing. By then Ash was long gone. Helva panted to the guards, holding the cramp in her side from sprinting across the palace, that she needed to speak to the princess, it was a matter of kingdom security.

The posted guards weren't alarmed by this display of hysteria; since the mirrors became popular, everyone was trying to tattle on someone. The ladies-in-waiting were no different, though not as bad as the gentlemen-in-waiting, who would throw one another in the dungeon over a bad hand of cards if the guards didn't wave them away. But the morning was slow, and the princess was taking visitors, it seemed. One took out a mirror, rang the princess, and Helva was waved through.

Nearing the top of the stairs, Helva dragged herself up one step at a time, holding onto the banister for dear life, wondering who in gods' names decided *velvet* would be the best cloth for dresses?

"Your-your Majesty," Helva sputtered, falling through the door and catching herself against the back of a chair. Her thighs burned, her knees wobbled, and her face was so red Princess Damora insisted she sit, won't she have a glass of water?

Helva took the glass and chugged, clutching her still-heaving chest. She gave the empty glass back with a tremendous groan and said, "My lady, I have discovered an impostor!"

"Oh dear," Damora said, settling into the chair beside her. Damora was used to such hyperbolics, especially from her ladies, who liked to work each other into a tittering ball of anxiety over the littlest things. "Who?"

"Ashlynn! Or Ash! She is a *he*. He is the baker! In the competition!" Helva nodded, eyes wide, waiting for the princess to mirror her excitement or show some sort of astonishment.

Instead, Damora disappointed her with a smile. She took Helva's sweaty hands and said, "My dear Helva, I am aware of this."

"You are! As of when?" Helva sputtered.

"I *appreciate* what you are doing here. I *understand* you are simply looking out for me. As princess, you must understand I have just a bit more resources than my ladies do. I keep guards not just for decoration but because they are my eyes, my informants. I am aware of what is going on in my own palace."

Damora knew not to deter good intel, but Helva was never one for repeating anything but gossip ad nauseam. Perhaps this would hush her up once and for all. From the look of disappointment on Helva's face, Damora was betting it just might.

Helva gulped and nodded. "Of course, my lady. How silly of me to think that I knew something Her Highness did not." She took her hands back. "May I be dismissed?"

"Yes. And Helva? Thank you. You do a great service to the Crown."

Still beet red, Helva gave a sharp nod and ran back to her room as fast as she wished she would have been able to run up those stairs. "No good deed," she muttered and threw herself onto her sofa. Before long, she pulled her mirror out, raised it nearly to her nose, and became wholly absorbed in it.

40

Fergis Finds Dinner

"**I**'ve covered the grounds, the halls, the menagerie, and even the princess's windowsill, just for good measure," Harper reported, taking a seat with Ash, Gregor, Noal, and Brimley in the dining room.

"They're not going to assume they're dead, are they?" Noal asked, suddenly concerned.

"No, it's a simple sleeping spell," Brimley assured.

"The princess is informed," Ash announced. She watched Harper scribble into her notepad. "You'll tell people, won't you? That I'm, you know, a girl?"

"Do you want me to?"

Ash looked at her with surprise. "I thought you had to write the truth."

"Of course I do. But omitting facts isn't the same as lying. I'm simply narrowing the scope of my article," Harper said.

"Then I'd rather you not," Ash said. "I don't think it's anyone's business."

"What about your lady-in-waiting duties?" Gregor asked and bit off a chunk of turkey leg.

"I'm resigning at the end of the summer. The princess has officially accepted me into the royal kitchen staff with the rest of you lot. Until I earn my own purple seal," she added with a sly smile.

Noal gave Gregor a proud shoulder bump. "To victory!"

They all raised their mugs and clicked obnoxiously. The staff around them rolled their eyes. In the beginning, they had been the celebrities in the palace. Now, they were all but forgotten. It was the weather wizard everyone really wanted to speak of. Harvesting lightning? What was the decibel of a roar of thunder? How fast did clouds move? *That* was the really exciting stuff.

After dinner, they strolled into the courtyard. That was where they witnessed the first bit of evidence that their plan was in motion. It was a squirrel, in its shiny armor, lying on its side in the grass below a tree. They went to investigate. Ash gently removed the mirrored garment and passed it to Brimley, who pocketed it. "What? Do you know how expensive these are getting?"

A little later came the next bit of evidence, though this was far more disturbing. A possum had taken a lick of the sleeping candy and collapsed, still holding onto the branch by its tail. While unconscious, it was discovered by Fergis the dragon, who, as they watched, sniffed it curiously. Then he blew a scorching breath and lit the possum on fire.

"Fergis, no!" Gregor shouted and made to run at him. Fergis, who was not about to give up a tasty snack, turned and sprayed a warning ring of fire around himself. Gregor fell back against Noal, who clung to him. They watched as Fergis roasted his dinner alive, covering their noses against the stench of burning fur.

"It's going to turn into a feeding frenzy!" Ash exclaimed.

"Oh no," Harper gasped. "The pigeons!" With a whip of her cape, she transformed and took off.

"Oooh, this is bad," Noal whimpered. "We didn't think this through."

"It's fine," Gregor snapped. "We'll just run around and collect the bodies and put them somewhere safe. The menagerie!"

A scream erupted behind them. They turned to find Helva holding a mirror in her quaking hand, trying to aim it at Fergis's barbeque session. "You did this!" She pointed the mirror at Ash. "You're not who you say you are! Now everyone in the kingdom will know!"

Ash raised a fist and shook it in warning at Helva. "Go! Get! Back to your pincushions!"

"The princess will hear of this!" Helva screamed. It didn't matter that in the next moment it occurred to her the princess might already know. And not even care. But it felt good, yelling that.

Ash reached out and grabbed the mirror and tried to wrestle it out of Helva's hand. The two ended up jostling themselves to the ground, where they struggled over the mirror.

"Should we jump in?" Noal whispered, unsure what he was watching. It wasn't exactly fighting—they weren't punching or scratching. In fact, it was rather polite and mild-mannered, just hands grabbing at the mirror, slipping, trying to pry fingers away.

"This...isn't our priority," Gregor said, unsure what exactly the struggle was over. The mirror? Ash's secret? In any case, it seemed that Ash would inevitably win, wearing trousers instead of a heavy dress, which seemed to be slowly wrapping around Helva's legs, cocooning her. They eventually averted their eyes, beginning to feel a bit funny about the whole thing.

"So, um, the menagerie?" Gregor asked, clearing his throat.

"Wait, wait!"

They looked up to find Mosley pushing his way through the crowd that had begun to cluster around the pathetic wrestling match. Mosley pulled up, panting slightly, and easily plucked the mirror out of the hand that was clutching it, barely holding on from all the sweat. "I'll take that, thank you."

"Hey!" Ash pushed Helva down and got up. "It's not—"

"I know who the culprit is, no need to point fingers," Mosley interrupted. Then, remembering something, he cleared his throat, turned that mirror on himself, and repeated himself more clearly, adding, "This is, surely, the workings of a nefarious man. Alistair Alimar!"

Everyone looked at one another in wonder. Ash reached down and pulled Helva up and whispered in her ear, "You best not make this your business." Helva hiked up the hem of her dress and took off running.

"So...it's settled," Noal said, clasping his hands together. "Alistair's the one...doing what, exactly?" He wanted to hear it spoken aloud on record.

"That scoundrel!" Mosley said, shaking with passion.

"Yes," Gregor whispered, egging him on.

"He-he—why, he's poisoned my animals."

"Um, well, he's charmed them. Sleeping spell," Brimley quipped quickly. "They'll be fine."

"But to tamper with royal animals!"

"Oh yes, dreadful. He should be disqualified," Noal urged.

"Disqualified! He's going to the dungeon! If only you knew how much time—how much care—how hard I've worked..." Mosley's voice quivered and cracked. The pressure and stress weighed heavy on him, and this was all too much. How could someone be so ungrateful, undoing all the work he had done?

Just then Alistair, who had been keeping an eye on his competition this whole time, marched out into the courtyard. "What's going on here? Am I getting accused of something?"

"You certainly are!" Mosley spat, pointing a finger in his face so close he nearly tickled a rogue nose hair. "Bespelling my animals! How dare you!"

Alistair snorted, then looked around and realized from the stony faces that Mosley was serious. He squinted over Mosley's shoulder, sniffed, saw Fergis grilling what looked like it had once been a...possum?

Suddenly a pigeon, in all its shiny armor, fell from the sky and landed between them. Mosley, in near tears, scooped it up and clutched it to its chest. "You'd better hope he's just dazed. I'm having you arrested."

"I'll need a judge and a jury," Alistair snapped.

"You'll have the king! Now come, or else I'll call the guards," Mosley shouted. Alistair gritted his teeth and followed Mosley back into the palace.

"What now?" Noal asked, suddenly afraid that this triumph hadn't actually happened.

"Now," Gregor said, motioning for Noal and Ash to follow him, "We are going to design a stunning wedding cake."

As Brimley watched them go, an idea came to him. He pulled a whistle from his pocket and blew it. Fergis paused his possum charring for a moment before losing interest. Seconds later, Arosco came bounding out of the palace on all fours.

Brimley leaned down and spoke into his ear. Arosco transformed. "I'm not a retriever," he protested.

"Please," Brimley begged and pointed at the tree where Fergis was now chomping on the crisped carcass. "If you don't, there's going to be a lot more crispy critters."

Arosco rolled his eyes. "Where do you want me to take them?"

"The royal menagerie. You should be able to spot them easily before dark, they're covered with mirrors and probably sparkling from the sun."

Arosco, ever loyal to the Crown, transformed back into canine form and bounded away.

***

That evening, Mosley fell back in his chair, exhausted by the day's excitement. It was the first time he'd ever had anyone arrested! He reached for the crystal tumbler of amber liquor but stopped as he noticed several mirrors on the wall before him displaying the same image. He got up, pulled on his robe, and made his way down to the menagerie.

There, a pile of sleeping mirrored animals rested on the stoop. Mosley looked around, wondering where they had come from. Who had deposited them? He unlocked the menagerie and quickly began to bring them inside. He stripped them of the mirrors and handled them gently into their nests and beds, whispering thanks for their service to the Crown. The guilt he felt was tremendous and still rising. This whole mess was getting wildly out of hand.

<h1 style="text-align:center">41</h1>

Four Weeks Later...

The official test kitchen key was formally handed over to Gregor to become his creative culinary sanctuary, and although he couldn't look at Fergis the same way after the possum incident, the dragon was at Gregor's beck and call anytime he needed the massive oven lit.

He and the other pastry chefs spent the next four weeks forming a recipe for a cake the princess could eat that six hundred guests would also enjoy. And although he initially resisted, Gregor let Ash and Noal fight over control of the massive mirror that had been hung over the chalkboard. It was enchanted to always transmit, but after some convincing, Mosley called in a royal sorcerer to charm it to also receive.

They turned it on as background noise as they labored, pausing on occasion to gawk or yell at it if anything truly entertaining flickered on. They liked to change up the channel from musicians putting on performances in concert halls to interviews of dignitaries on the dilemmas the marriage might cause—although only Ash liked to listen to these—to the live stream from inside of Sorren's bakery, which was apparently widely viewed. Perhaps even more viewed than their test kitchen, Gregor suspected. Lately they were scrying into the mirror of a very popular weather wizard, who was none other than Harlowe Langston. It seemed he had found his true calling after losing the baking competition and hadn't returned to his cousin's shop after all.

"Lance is his mirror man. Less pressure being behind the glass. He really cracked during this competition," Ash explained, moving the volume dial up until Gregor snapped an irritated, "Enough!"

"What happened to Gale?" Gregor asked.

"He's back at his family's bakery," Noal said. "They're making an absolute fortune with the festivities."

Working so closely together, Gregor and Ash discovered they liked a lot of similar things. They enjoyed listening to the same bards perform. They liked discussing politics together and got into a friendly debate over whether or not Superstitious Mountain should be governed by the Crown. And they got along really well perfecting the dairy-free buttercream recipe. If Noal felt smug about this progress, he didn't let it show.

Gregor opened his notebook. The cake recipe was completed, the design was drawn and approved, the layers were calculated, the taste tests done. Now, the day before the wedding, they were doing prep work in the royal kitchen: making mountains of frosting and baking a few layers. Tomorrow they would finish the baking and do the assembly during the wedding ceremony. Elis was due to come by and help, though he was running between cake duty on one side of the kitchen and actual wedding feast prepping on the other.

A knock at the door startled them. They looked at one another, unsure who it could possibly be. Elis always just barged in, as did anyone else who wanted to peek in, though they were hastily shooed away.

Ash finally called a tentative, "Come in!"

The kitchen door creaked open hesitantly to reveal two dwarves clad in chainmail, leather, and wide-brimmed hats, their eyes wide with curiosity.

Gregor dropped the whisk he had been wielding and threw his arms wide at the sight of his parents. "Mum! Da!"

"Greggy!" His mother squealed and rushed to embrace her son. His father shuffled in after, shaking first Ash's hand, then Noal's, who was about as excited to finally meet his best friend's parents as Gregor was to see them.

When Gregor's father came close enough, his mother let go. Gregor and his father stood gazing at each other, absorbing the lines of change that had etched into one another's face. Then the senior dwarf reached around and clapped his son so hard on the back that Gregor stumbled forward into the bear hug his father had been dreaming of giving him for so long. "I am"—*sniff*—"so proud," he mumbled into Gregor's ear.

Gregor's eyes began to shine, and his two friends turned away, embarrassed to be caught in such an intimate moment. Then the senior dwarf let go, took a step back, and cuffed his son playfully on the chin. "What, no cakes waiting for us? After all this walking?"

"Now Dominus," his wife warned, but she too looked about curiously, squinting against the harsh overhead light. "You'll show us around, won't you?"

"He must, Amrie! He's the head chef!"

"Well, um, not quite," Gregor said with a laugh. "All I get to do is bake a cake."

"*The* cake," Ash threw in, unable to extract herself from the moment.

"Noal!" Amrie exclaimed, suddenly seeing the others. She lunged for Ash, whom she thought was the phantom of her son's letters come to life.

"Um, *that's* Noal," Ash wheezed from the strength of the hug. "I'm Ash."

"That's alright." Amrie pulled away and looked over at Noal, who gave a shy wave. She grabbed Noal and pulled him into an equally bone-crushing embrace. "It's so *good* to finally meet Greggy's friends," she gushed, beaming at them both.

"My two *best* friends," Gregor confirmed, giving Ash a little nod. It was the first time he'd acknowledged her like that, and she set her hand on her heart without meaning to.

When they all left to troupe down to the dining hall for treats and tea Ash went with them, Amrie clinging onto one of her's and one of Noal's arms, chattering excitedly the whole way. Gregor walked with his father behind them, bashfully explaining his smoky quartz sunglasses.

42

The Dungeon

Deep in the dungeon, in a cell outfitted with a cot, a lavatory, a desk, broken quills donated by the monastery, and a plate with the crumbs left over from a breakfast of a fresh cheddar biscuit and fried bacon, sat Alistair, scribbling away in a notebook he had snuck in four weeks ago when he was arrested. He was in the best shape of his life thanks to the discarded exercise equipment lying around and had even tried his hand at painting, but the oils were old, and the fumes gave him a headache.

Alistair wrote letters on the pages he tore from the notebook, continuing to scheme with Tavis as they were forced to pivot from the original plan. Thanks to a pigeon, he and Tavis kept in regular touch.

Alistair was sentenced to the dungeon until the day after the royal wedding. They figured he was only a menace until then, after which he was ordered to return to whence he came. But Alistair didn't plan on staying locked up that long. He was breaking out the day of the wedding, when all the guards would be busy posted around the castle, stretched too thin to worry about the largely forgotten prisoner.

Today was that day.

The two guards stood at the top of the steps leading down to the dungeon, leaning against their spears. Each held a mirror in their hand, completely absorbed in what they watched except for the occasional nudge to one another to look, look at that!

"Whatcha looking at?"

The guards looked at each other and grew confused when they realized it wasn't the other that had spoken.

"Hey! Me, look at me," Alistair tried again. The guards shuffled down and peeked in through the bars, half afraid the prisoner was mid-defecation, as some liked to do when they felt the breakfast—or really, any meal—had not been up to par. They both relaxed, seeing Alistair fully clothed. "Hello, boys."

"You alright?" the one on the left asked. "You finished with the plate?"

Alistair looked over his shoulder, then back at them. "Not quite. I was just wondering...what are you watching?"

Left and right exchanged looks, embarrassed.

"Oh come now, I haven't seen anything outside of these four walls in four weeks, and I get released tomorrow! I'm practically a free man, it won't hurt," Alistair coaxed. He *was* a charming man, and his smile *did* dazzle, and so reluctantly the two flipped their mirrors around to expose the inside of a brothel. Alistair could have laughed—so predictable!—but didn't want to embarrass them. "Any news?" he asked in an indifferent tone.

Relieved, the guards began flipping their fingers over the surface of their mirrors.

"There's this weather wizard..." Right turned his mirror to show Harlowe Langston in his full wizard garb on a cliff's edge, pointing out cloud formations.

"Hah! I know him. He was in the baking competition."

The two guards looked at each other, confused.

"Don't tell me you've already forgotten about the Royal Bake Off? For the royal wedding cake?"

The candle went on in one brain, and he nudged the other, gave a little grunt, and then the other candle lit itself with remembrance. "Right! Gosh, it's been so long since anyone's tuned into that. There's just so much other stuff to watch in these mirrors," left said. "That's why you're in here, isn't it? You cheated?"

"Something like that," Alistair said with a dismissive wave. "Won't you bring it closer? I think I recognize those clouds."

As the two guards shuffled forward, Alistair reached into his pocket, produced a handful of white powder, and blew it into their faces. The effect was instantaneous: the two felt sparks like lit phosphate go off in their brains, and then they swayed, fell against each other, and collapsed in a heap, snoozing a slumber neither had enjoyed since they discovered the late-night channels on their mirror.

Alistair crouched, grabbed the end of the tunic of a guard, and tugged. He dragged the body towards him until he could reach the belt and remove the ring of keys there.

The palace was busy with guards stationed all around for security. These two were the skeleton crew that stood watch in the dungeon, because they were unionized and so had to be paid to be down there, even though Alistair had been the first and only prisoner in years. So, while he didn't anticipate anyone coming to check on them, Alistair hurried, trying each key (there were only three) in the lock until he set himself free.

Alistair stripped the tunic off the guard, shrugged it on, and grabbed a spear just for effect. He thought about rolling the guards into the cell and locking it but knew the powder was potent enough to have them snoozing through the rest of the day. He did snatch a mirror before he hurried up the stairs and found the station that it should have been on permanently: surveillance mirrors in the hall outside the dungeon.

No one would think twice about Alistair; no one even remembered him, it seemed, as he hurried as fast as he could without raising suspicions down the corridors and out of the palace.

43
Preparation

The big day had arrived. Her Royal Highness Princess Daroma Varundil, heir to the throne of the Kingdom of Everdorne, was marrying her betrothed, Prince Eadwine Norsdorf of the Kingdom of Galloway.

In the most lavish chamber in the palace, Mosley helped King Varundil get ready. The king was freshly barbered, and his undergarments were already on, but Mosley was having terrible trouble getting the rest of him dressed as the king stared into his mirrors, eagerly awaiting the arrival of his estranged wife.

"What a day! One always dreams of a day like this, do they not?" The king giggled and finally stood still long enough for Mosley to jump and get the tunic over his head.

"Sit," Mosley ordered. He buckled the polished shoes. "Stand."

Mosley helped the king shrug his ceremonial robe on and belted it at the waist. "Crown!" An attendant nearly tripped over his feet rushing over with the pillow it perched on. As Mosley set the crown on the king's curls, which were carefully combed over the ever-growing bald spot, a knock came from the door. "Go see who it is."

The servant came back and whispered into Mosley's ear. Confused, he looked over his shoulder to find, sure enough, Celeste peeking through the crack in the door, curling one finger her way in a 'come hither' motion.

"Finish this," Mosley instructed, dropping the cologne bottle into the attendant's hands, and shuffled to the door. Mosley stepped into the hall and closed the door. "Don't tell me she got cold feet," he hissed.

Celeste blinked, confused for a moment who he was talking about, and gave a little laugh. "Oh, you! That was funny. No, no, look at this, dear Cousin."

She turned her mirror to show flashes of Alistair's face passing though different checkpoints of the palace.

"Is that...?"

"The one and only prisoner this palace has seen in decades," Celeste mused. "Aren't those guards unionized? Shouldn't they be good at their job?"

"No, your mirror! How are you tapping into those mirrors? Those are locked surveillance," Mosley sputtered.

Celeste gave a dismissing wave. "You're not the only one who's paid Remus a visit."

Mosley really didn't have time for this. "We need to get him!"

"You'll do nothing. Let him leave, isn't that what we want? Him out of the way?" Celeste asked. "I just thought you ought to know. Since it is, after all, *your* jurisdiction."

"Yes, yes," Mosley muttered. "You'll rub it in my nose tomorrow, won't you? Now I've got to get back, His Majesty will never make his cues if I don't drag him to each spot myself."

"Do you have any idea what he's up to?"

"He's trying to win back the queen. This whole elaborate thing has been to get her into the kingdom and woo her—"

"The *prisone*r."

"Oh! Right. Of course. Er, no."

Celeste gave a "you're useless" wave and marched off. Mosley turned back to the king.

King Varundil sat in a chair, reading a column, which, as Mosley got closer, he saw was *The Harking Herald*.

"Have you read this?" Varundil asked, waving the page. "It's got all sorts of insider scoops on the palace, the baking contest, and the wedding preparations. I wonder who their source is?"

"Your Majesty, wasn't the whole point of the mirrors to get everyone in on the scoop?"

"Yes, but *I* wanted to be the mouthpiece to the kingdom! Everyone is tuning in to watch *me* and listen to *me*. Now we have this"—Varundil squinted at the fine print under the header—"Harper Leewood telling people all about the things I've been planning."

I've *been planning*, Mosley thought, gritting his teeth. He pinched the bridge of his nose and forced his jaws to relax. "Everyone will have their eyes on the ceremony today. Nothing will be missed," Mosley assured the king and motioned for him to up, get up! Let's go!

44

Hex His Highness

Crystal Quench was a hip, witch-owned bar that touted its vibrant-colored cocktails in hand-spun crystal glasses. It wasn't the sort of place Alistair would patron, but Tavis had promised that it was inconspicuous and, since it had a mostly female clientele, probably wasn't outfitted with mirrors.

Well, he was wrong, Alistair realized, trying to hide his face in his hands as he sipped something called 'Hex His Highness.' It was bitter and overpriced and what they brought out when Alistair had panicked and said, "I'll have whatever you recommend." On the plus side, there was no one he recognized, and with any luck, no one here would recognize him.

Alistair tried to distract himself by focusing on one of the four massive mirrors strung up around the cocktail lounge. One showed the promenade of guests entering the palace, tuned into the royal ceremony as mandated by the king. Another showed a kitchen witch preparing A Feast to Serve Your Closest Friends. The third showed a female commentator scrutinizing the fashion of the ladies pouring into the Grand Hall, and the final mirror was tuned into that stupid weather wizard, that twerp he'd had to compete with.

Alistair got so engrossed in what Harlowe was saying about atmospheric pressure that he nearly collapsed off his stool when a hand clapped him on the shoulder.

"On edge, old boy?" Tavis grinned, dropping into the seat across from Alistair. The other chairs had been swiped away, and it had taken a near fight to keep this one as long as he had with patrons insisting that Alistair was being greedy to leave it open when others had to stand, his imaginary friend nowhere to be found.

"I was about to book it," Alistair growled. He motioned for a waitress, who was having trouble enough elbowing her way through the packed crowd.

Tavis scoffed. "Go where? Do what? No, your whole life has been leading up to this. Thank you, dear." Tavis grabbed two goblets off the tray circling the room and replaced them with nickels. He could have tried to swim his way to the bar to order something specific, but paying for a mystery drink was infinitely easier. "I bet they're serving the sweet stuff at that wedding."

"Don't rub it in," Alistair muttered, accepting the fresh drink. They clinked their glasses together and drew long, deep gulps. Alistair's shoulders dropped and Tavis let out a languid belch. "If this goes well, we'll be more powerful than the king himself. Remember our original plan? Getting you to audition to be in the royal kitchen and then sneak spells into the prince's meals to convince him to pass that sugar tax? How small our ambitions were! Now we'll steal the king's mirror and tap into all the mirrors the Crown has enchanted. We'll see and hear conversations about trade, gambling, marriages, business negotiations. *Think of the power.*" Tavis pounded a fist on the table in excitement.

"There's got to be an easier way," Alistair said, speaking what had been on his mind ever since he escaped the palace, convinced that by now his profile was sent to every mirror in the kingdom, alerting every citizen to watch out for him. He half expected his image to flicker across one of the mirrors in the bar, but alas, it had not. Now to sneak back into the palace? Alistair tried again to persuade Tavis of an alternative plan. "There must be a sorcerer who bespelled the king's mirror. That's who we need to find."

"You don't think I've been searching?" Tavis replied, irked. "I have tried to bribe every fellow and lass who has ever uttered even the measliest of spells to coax out who has that sort of power, and all are mum. *No.* We'll put the lot to sleep, then you will sneak in and steal the snoring king's mirror. Do you have enough powder?" Tavis asked.

"Enough to put the whole kingdom asleep." Alistair patted his pocket. The sleeping powder would put everyone to sleep, and then he would steal the mirror off the king, tossing the powder at any guards who pursued him. In and out, simple as that.

"Good, good. Didn't even take much to convince those pigeons to smuggle it in. They're the real breach in security, let me tell you."

Alistair smiled. "Something to keep in mind, should this plan fail."

"You won't fail." Tavis raised his drink, and Alistair clinked his to it before they drained their glasses.

Tavis pushed a fist-sized package across the table. Alistair took it and slipped it into his pocket. He didn't need to check to know it was the dragon egg. "I've cast a cloaking spell over it. When it's time, read off the incantation on the parchment. It will reveal the egg for its mother to find. You won't have much time after," Tavis warned. "She's already been spotted just past Mead Monastery."

The egg in Alistair's pocket was warm, nearly ready to hatch. It should have been with its mother by now, but since it hadn't been delivered, she was on her way to find it, and she was likely angry.

They clasped hands, gave each other a nod, and then Alistair was out the door, weaving his way through the crowd, his expression grim. *He would not fail.*

45

Short on Sweet

"What do you mean we're out of sugar?" Gregor asked, flummoxed. "I had more than enough yesterday, and now you're telling me we're fresh out?"

"We did not have enough yesterday," Noal whispered, too afraid to admit he had been worried about the dwindling supply all week.

Gregor looked around the massive royal kitchen. His team of bakers had their own designated area to build the monstrosity that was the wedding cake. Twelve layers were planned to feed the nearly six hundred guests. His eyes darted to the other side of the room where the other royal chefs were baking the breads, rolls, and tarts for the rest of the staff's daily meals. "Have you tried....?" Gregor motioned with his eyes.

Noal shook his head. "They have already used their sugar ration. Trust me, I tried to bribe them."

Gregor sighed. He took in the giant mountains of frosting, whipped extra light to add volume and spread it further, sitting in massive buckets awaiting assembly. Cake loaves cooled on racks. Sugar sculptures Elis had blown—not quite as good as Brimley's—waited on shelves. A fine film of sugar covered the floors, as if winter itself had blown her way through the room. Looking back at Noal, Gregor saw there were even tiny sugar crystals settled on his lashes and on his arched, worried brows. "Elis?"

Elis looked over his shoulder, saw Gregor beckon. He glanced back at the batter he was mixing, gave a great sigh, and walked over as fast as he dared, considering the state of the floors. "Chef?"

"Are we low on sugar?"

"Nope. We're nearly out."

Gregor's eyes blazed. Elis shrugged. "I'm not head chef, am I?"

"Order more," Gregor barked. When neither moved, unsure whom he was talking to, he turned to Noal and growled, "Order more!"

Noal clicked his heels together in a salute and ran off to find a pigeon. Gregor looked back to find Elis giving him a skeptical look. "We're coming down to the fine hairs here."

"I know," Gregor growled. "Go back to your station."

Elis frowned but clicked his heels and returned to the giant bowl of batter.

It didn't take long for a whole wheelbarrow of sugar to arrive, to Gregor's amazement. It was almost as if it had been anticipated. This piqued Elis's suspicion as he followed Gregor over to the door to receive it.

"Where'd ya want it?" the delivery man demanded.

"Right over—"

"Hold on," Elis said, stepping in front of the wheelbarrow. He recognized the familiar yellow emblem. It was the same one he had seen on the bags of sugar at Tavis's. "Huh. So that's why." He motioned for Gregor to come closer so he could whisper.

"I need payment on delivery," the man said loudly.

Elis glared at him. "A moment, please."

"I gots other deliveries!"

Elis ignored him and turned Gregor by the shoulders, so they faced away from the wheelbarrow. "Do you know where this is from?"

Gregor beckoned Noal over. "Where's this sugar from?"

"Uh, I don't know, honestly. I told the pigeon to find sugar. He found sugar."

Gregor looked at him, dumbfounded. "Pigeons can't just find sugar! What address did you send it to?"

Now it was Noal's turn to look confused. "What do you mean they can't find sugar? They know the whole city! The whole kingdom, probably. Of course they know where to find sugar. Look! Did it not find sugar?"

"What do you mean?" Gregor shouted. "It's a *pigeon*! It needs an *address*! It doesn't know words like *sugar*!"

It finally dawned on Noal why Gregor was confused. "Oh, you think they're *pigeons*."

"What the bloody demon else bird is it? A *mocking* bird?"

"They're shapeshifters," Noal explained with a laugh. "That's why they're drunk all the time! They work hard and then hit Badger & Bard after. Harper hangs out with them all the time. But they're in a union, so there's nothing the king can do to curb their off-hours habits."

Gregor looked as if he would punch a wall. With his head. Just bash it right through, this was so ridiculous to him. He wiped a hand down his face and took a breath. "Alright. Fine. Now I know. Great. Okay."

Elis jabbed a thumb over his shoulder. "That sugar is from Alistair's friend. I don't know what funny business they have planned, but I'd be wary if I were you."

Gregor's eyebrows furrowed. "You think it's charmed? Do we have a squirrel lying around to taste test? I'm kidding, just kidding," Gregor muttered, but then remembered the dog. Was this not Arosco's job? He scratched his head, feeling pushed into a corner.

"Smaller cake?" Noal suggested. The two glared at him.

"My legacy won't be a smaller—"

The throat clearing behind them made them remember the impatient deliveryman. "I'm goin' to leave if you don't pay."

Gregor looked between his two friends one last time before he said, "Actually, we're not in any need of it."

"Beg pardon?"

"We don't need the sugar," Elis said more firmly. "The pigeon must have been drunk."

That got the effect they hoped for. The man started yelling obscenities, but not at them, rather the pigeons. "When I get my two hands on one of 'em I'm going to wring its neck so hard..."

Still muttering, he hoisted up the handles of the wheelbarrow and grunted his way out. The three chefs watched him go, wincing. Elis pulled a flask from a pocket deep inside his uniform, a pocket that was not standard design and definitely not sewn into the others' coats. He took a swig and passed it around. Even Noal took a half-hearted gulp. "Now what?"

"Let's do a walk-through, see the inventory we have," Gregor suggested. They did just that, calculating how much this grand cake would have to shrink from its original size to accommodate their dwindling ingredients.

46

Alternate Plan

Alistair stood at the edge of the moat surrounding the palace, far enough from the bridge to avoid the loud clattering of the traffic to and from the main gate, but close enough that he would be ready when the signal was given.

A signal *was* given, just not the one Alistair had anticipated. He watched in horror as the wagon came back across the moat, still full of sugar bags. The plan was to have the spiked sugar baked into the cake, not sent away.

Now on his side of the moat, Alistair fell into step with the deliveryman, heard his story. "You could have pushed a bit harder," Alistair scolded.

"For what? I get paid whether the delivery is accepted or not."

"Can't you go back? Surely you can convince them."

"Couldn't if I wanted to. It's already been stamped."

"Stamped?"

The deliveryman pulled the tarp back to reveal that each bag had been given a bright red 'REJECTED' stamp.

"Gods," Alistair muttered. "There isn't one that hasn't been stamped?"

He considered, for an instant, dressing in one of those bags and demanding to be wheeled back in, but doing that seemed idiotic the moment the thought congealed in his brain. The deliveryman shook his head, and Alistair let out a curse. He peeked around the building corner they were hovering behind. The guards were vigilant. The plan had to be altered; the alternative plan burned in his pocket. Alistair had dreaded this. Having everyone fall asleep would have been so much easier, then he would have just sauntered into the palace and taken that blasted mirror. Now he had to summon the beast, get everyone in the palace to evacuate, and pick the king's pocket out here. And there was only a small window to plant the lure...

The trumpets sounded, signaling it was time for the ceremony, and Alistair's heart began to hammer. Time was running out!

Alistair paid the deliveryman and made his way back across the moat and around the palace, looking for the perfect place to throw from. He'd spent a lot of his time in the palace scoping out exits and entrances specifically in case it came down to this. He found his spot and crouched down, doing his best to look inconspicuous. He pulled the egg from his pocket and read the inscription off the parchment. He felt the egg vibrate once, and then the golden shell shined as if a thousand suns awoke inside of it. Alistair nearly dropped it in surprise and quickly threw the cloth back over it. It now emitted a homing beacon to its mother, who was already on her way in search of it.

Next Alistair opened the burlap sack he brought along. From it he pulled a coil of rope, a small net, and a jar full of grey Endless Putty. He unscrewed the lid, pulled out the sticky mess, and began sculpting it into a hook he could loop the rope through. He whispered the magic spell and it hardened, ready to use. He looked up, gauged the roof, and tossed the rope with all his might. The hook fell short, catching brick and scraping back down, a failed throw. He tried a few more times, moving a few paces here then there to find a better angle until he came across a gargoyle. With one mighty throw, Alistair tossed the rope so that it looped around the gargoyle's neck, the hook catching the rope and securing the hold with a mighty pull. A pigeon that had been resting on its shoulder fluttered off, annoyed. Alistair tugged the rope to be sure it would hold before scaling the wall.

When he pulled himself up onto the roof, Alistair found a group of young men sitting around smoking pipes. Empty bottles of wine littered the roof around them. They looked just as surprised as Alistair was.

"Oy, are you here to clean the roof?" one asked Alistair.

"I'm, ah, the chimney sweep. Know which one leads to the Royal Banquet Hall? I've got to get it spruced up before the ceremony's over."

"Better hurry then, they're nearly man and wife," another said and pointed to a roof not far off from where they were. "Say, where's your broom?"

Alistair opened his mouth, found he didn't have an answer, and took off running.

"Oy!"

"Should we stop him?"

"Who is he?"

"Get up lads, he's clearly up to no good!"

"Wait, is that a dragon?"

A moment later Alistair found himself being chased by a cloud of pigeons. He made it to the chimney and reached into his pocket, turned, and threw a handful of powder at the birds. They instantly dropped to the ridges, dead asleep.

Alistair pulled the egg back out and uncovered it. It glittered in the sunlight, which flickered as an enormous body eclipsed the sun, making slow, searching circles above him. Alistair set the egg inside the net, lowered the net down the chimney, and secured it inside with the repurposed Endless Putty. He looked up, shielding his eyes, to see Mother Dragon hunting for her lost egg.

Mission complete, Alistair collected the pigeons and tossed them through a turret window, determined no one would get hurt.

Then he lassoed the rope around the gargoyle again and scaled down the palace wall to be swallowed up by the growing crowd below.

47

So Romantic

"What a service! What a delight!"

Mosley steered the king by the elbow into the next room, trying to keep to the schedule he had so meticulously set.

"Did you cry, Mosley? Be honest. I think I saw a bit of a tear creep into your eye. How could you not? It was so romantic. *So* romantic! Why am I standing here?"

"Sir, you must acknowledge and thank all your guests."

"Now?" King Varundil looked stricken.

"Your Majesty, you must! It's royal protocol. You know this, you're the embodiment of the law."

"It's not that I mind, I'm just hungry. Haven't you got any snacks? It's been so long since breakfast. Breakfast! I forgot to eat breakfast, silly me." King Varundil chuckled. He patted his pockets to see if he had any sweets or snacks forgotten in his robes, but they were freshly laundered garments and had not even a crumb on them. Sticking his hand in his pocket, he found the one item he now always carried on his person: a mirror the size of his palm, like the ones everyone else had. Except, no mirror was quite like this one. He pulled it out and swiped the surface of the glass until his daughter's face at the altar reappeared. He paused it and admired her blushing face, elbowed Mosley to look. "Everyone in the kingdom got to experience this magical moment with us. Isn't that grand? I unified the entirety of my people to celebrate this moment."

Mosley had his own mirror out and had just cursed under his breath, watching the dragon with the green armor—*not* the blue one, dammit, he had put a lot of gold on that ruddy little sky sausage!—cross the finish line. He glanced up at the king and quickly pocketed his mirror.

"Oh yes, Your Majesty, surely everyone has been sitting in front of their mirrors, entranced."

No one in attendance had been allowed to use their mirrors. The king found it a bit odd, in fact, when the druid conducting the ceremony (at his estranged wife's request) had gone as far as to make an announcement for all to hide their mirrors, should the reflection from them catch him in the eye and make him stumble. There had been a chuckle, and then a pause as everyone realized he was, in fact, serious and wouldn't begin the ceremony until every hand was clear and clasped in their laps. Even the king was tapped on the shoulder and told to pocket his mirror, and he did so after being assured that the man hired to hold the enormous mirror was a professional who was sure to catch all the best angles for everyone to see in the live transmit.

King Varundil stood where Mosley instructed him to and couldn't keep the smile off his face as he shook each hand and thanked the guests for being there that day. Mosley stood hunched beside the king, whispering introductions into his ear.

Once all the guests were ushered into the Royal Banquet Hall and seated, the massive bell was pulled, and the happy couple burst in and took their seats. Speeches were made, and once the king had made his, Mosley waved the server with the wine decanter over and finally allowed the king's goblet to be filled. *Now the king can get as ruddy drunk as he likes*, Mosley thought and gulped down his own glass. He motioned for more. "Don't stand too far unless you want to tire yourself out," he warned under his breath, and the waiter filled his goblet to the brim.

48

Mother Dragon

Noal pulled his apron up to his face, balled his fists, and screamed. No one around him turned. They couldn't afford to, lest they too let out a frightful display of panic. The air was already too charged, too tense, and it was one more scream away from causing some sort of metaphysical avalanche to roar down upon them. Gregor shoved Noal into the freezer. He pulled a chunk of steak off the shelf and slapped his best friend cross the face with it. Noal froze. Then he gave a bit of a shudder, and his eyes went back into focus. "Thanks, I think I needed that."

Gregor grumbled and made to return the steak but caught himself. He shoved the freezer door open and shouted, "Where's Arosco?" The dog gleefully galloped over and accepted the steak.

The sugar situation hadn't been fixed. Instead, a few cake layers had been omitted and the frosting was as thin as it could be without giving away the chocolate color of the cake inside. From far away, it was turning out picture-perfect. Perhaps it was only because Gregor was minutely scrutinizing each scoop of frosting leaving the bowl.

He hadn't promised a certain number of layers, yet he knew they mattered. Every. Single. One.

Because there were those like Harper Leewood who would count and set the record straight. Everyone would wonder, was it big enough? Was it bigger than the cake from the last royal wedding? What about the kingdom over? All Gregor knew was bigger was better. And that it had to feed all the guests. Everyone was expecting a monolith, for certain. Would they be impressed?

Noal could have a meltdown in the freezer all he liked, thaw out the whole entire chamber if he pleased, but every chef wasn't watching Noal out of their peripherals. All around the kingdom, everyone was eagerly awaiting Gregor and his big reveal.

Forget the princess, Gregor's parents were here, and he simply could not disappoint.

Finally, the last dairy-free white buttercream flower was piped. They loaded up the layers onto the cart and Gregor went to get Noal. "Are you quite done?"

Noal straightened his hat, pulled his coat into place, and nodded, determined. He followed the cart into the Royal Banquet Hall, where guests were seated and served their first course of strawberry poppyseed salad. The display table was ready for them, a small ladder placed in front. One by one they layered cake slab atop cake slab, pushing in pillars of boulder biscuits as needed to stabilize the towering confection.

When they were finished, applause rang out, and Gregor turned on his ladder and gave a little bow. He found the princess and her new husband, and then his parents in the crowd, beaming with immense pride. This was the greatest moment of Gregor's life. Noal's name was shouted, and they turned to find the Lord of the Royal Copper Mint waving at his son, beaming with pride.

Unfortunately, the moment was cut short by a blood-curdling scream.

"*Dragon!*"

Everyone looked around, confused. Protocol was broken as mirrors came out of pockets and gasps fluttered around the room.

"Is there really a dragon?" Noal asked and began to shake like gelatin pudding all over again.

Guests whispered in confusion until the roar of the great beast trumpeted down the chimney, preceding a blast of fire that ignited the cosmetically arranged logs.

It being the summer solstice, the last thing the packed hall needed was a roaring fire. The temperature of the room soared, and Gregor, flushed, looked over at the massive wedding cake to see it glistening with condensation. "Gods, it's not going to make it."

"Should we roll it back into the kitchen?" Ash asked, wringing her hands.

"Greggy!" his mum shouted. Gregor found her in the crowd and saw her point to the hearth, wherein glistened a golden egg. *The* egg.

"*Gods*," Gregor exclaimed. He looked around at the chaos around them. Guests rushed for the doors. Guards clustered around the royals, trying to escort them out of the hall first. Gregor looked at Ash, Noal, and Elis, all waiting for his command. "I've got to get that egg back to its mum."

"What egg?" Elis asked, then noticed it. "For gods' sake, how did that get there?"

"It was planted," Gregor concluded. "And I think we all have an idea of who did it." He climbed down the ladder and began tearing off his coat, his hat.

"You're not serious," Noal protested. "You're going to fight the dragon?"

"Absolutely not," Gregor scoffed. "I'm going to return its egg and finish what that stupid dwarf didn't. I'm going to complete the Luck of the Draw." He stood before his friends in an undershirt and butter-smeared trousers, his belt with a sling in it, and non-slip black shoes. This was hardly battle gear, and Gregor would stand about as much chance against the dragon's flames as a wax candle.

"Son, take my armor," his father shouted, having already removed his chain-mail.

Unfortunately for Gregor, he had eaten an awful lot of sweets in the last two years, and his tummy was more rotund than it used to be, rounder than his father's. Try as he might, the chainmail got stuck around his chest, trapping his arms above his head. He tugged it back off. "I'll be back," Gregor shouted, and ran from the room.

He started for his dorm, then realized he would never make it there in time. He wasn't even sure his old armor would fit; he hadn't put it on in so long. He needed to improvise.

He pivoted and burst instead into the royal kitchen and began to assemble makeshift armor by bending ordinary kitchen tools around his body.

A colander on his head, a baking sheet wrapped around his back, and a muffin tin strapped to his chest using baking twine. He punched his arms through cylindrical cheese graters for gauntlets. With a meat pounder in one hand and a rolling pin in the other, he ran back into the banquet hall, clinking and clanking all the way.

"I can't believe," Gregor grunted, shoving the rolling pin and meat cleaver into his belt to grab the egg, "I left the mountain just to face a dragon after all." He motioned for water, and those who had stayed behind all helped extinguish the fire. The smoke plumed up and out of the chimney, irritating Mother Dragon. She leapt off the roof and circled around the black cloud. It was the window Gregor needed to climb up.

"You'll be alright?" Noal asked, grabbing the handles of the colander to look his best friend in the eyes.

Gregor flashed him a brave smile. "I'm a dwarf. I was born to do this. Climbing tunnels is in my blood. This one just happens to go up."

The smoke burned his eyes. Gregor closed them as he stepped onto the smoldered logs. His lungs burned, but it was like being back home, inhaling the coal dust down in the mines; with each breath he wheezed out the toxins, just as every dwarf in his bloodline had been bred to do. Holding the egg in the crook of one arm, Gregor braced the other arm against the flue, the grates of the cheese grater giving him tremendous grip. He stepped up with one foot, then the other, and climbed his way out.

Gregor emerged from the lip of the chimney and with great effort pulled himself out, tumbling onto the roof. He thought for a second he had taken so long it had turned to night, but that was just the enormous vermilion body of the dragon eclipsing the sun. Gregor looked over the edge of the roof and saw what seemed like the entire kingdom down below, watching with bated breath.

Gregor gave the egg a good rub to remove the soot and held it up. In a moment the sun reappeared and poured over the golden shell, glittering brilliantly. The enormous dragon landed on the roof before Gregor. Her massive wings fell around her then tucked in tight. Her long neck extended, head the size of a whiskey barrel, nearly touching Gregor, and she sniffed his offering.

She began to chitter.

Gregor slowly crouched and set the egg before him, then backed away. His hands hovered near the rolling pin and meat cleaver, at the ready. The sound in Mother Dragon's throat grew and she tossed her head back and let out a thunderous caw.

Gregor smiled. He knew enough about dragons to know this was no roar, no call to war. He lowered his gaze and held still as a statue as Mother Dragon scooped up her egg and pushed off the roof. She soared high into the sky and disappeared amongst the clouds.

49

Pigeons to the Rescue

Down below, applause broke out as the guests realized the dragon was leaving for good.

The wedding cake had been wheeled outside to save it, and for the most part it was unharmed. The side that faced the fire had melted quite a bit, but the guests didn't seem to mind as they accepted generous slices on napkins and ate the cake with their hands.

A thief stalked through the unsuspecting crowd.

Alistair spotted the king and spiraled his way closer and closer until he brushed past him, fingers dipping in and out of the pockets of his robe. With the jostling of the crowd and the excitement distracting him, King Varundil never suspected a thing.

Triumphant, Alistair wove his way out of the crowd. But he couldn't help himself; he pulled the mirror out and turned it over to look at it. Staring back at him was Mosley.

Alistair froze. He looked over his shoulder to find, sure enough, a bewildered Mosley staring into his palm. Mosley looked up and locked eyes with the thief. Alistair ran.

Mosley grabbed his king by the shoulders. "Your Majesty! Your mirror!"

The red-nosed king burped. "Hmm?"

"Guards! Guards!"

The already excited crowd began to shriek as guards tried to push their way to, then away from the king, unable to fully comprehend what the shouting was about. This gave Alistair the chance to run across the moat's bridge. He pulled the rest of the powder out of his pocket and threw it in the air behind him, where the sweet particles floated, waiting to be inhaled.

"Don't walk through it!" Elis shouted. He had spotted Alistair as he took off running and chased him to the bridge, where the guards now piled up behind him. They tried motioning to the guards on the other side, who saw Alistair run by but hadn't thought to stop him.

"What do we do?" a guard asked.

"I've got an idea." Elis pulled out his mirror. He flipped through the channels, past Harlowe pointing out an especially shapely cumulus cloud, past the image of the chefs in the kitchen breaking out the booze, and finally found Harper's face, chatting away into the mirror with an update on the royal wedding. Elis drew a rune on the glass to get her attention. "I need your help!"

"Yes, I see that," Harper said, breaking character to address Elis. "What happened in there? Is everyone alright?"

"It was Alistair. I don't have time to explain. He's escaped and we must catch him. Where are you?"

"I'm not close enough, but I have a few friends who can help," she said, and with the flick of her fingers switched from receiving to transmitting.

***

Alistair hurried through the city, laughing with each step; he was free!

A flash momentarily blinded him.

Alistair stopped, put his hands up to shield his eyes, and looked around. Nothing. He kept going.

Looking back down, he noticed lights dancing on the cobblestone before him. He looked up again and this time saw the flock of pigeons circling. *Maybe some dragon had jumped into their tree*, Alistair thought, then realized why the birds were shimmering—mirrors! Alistair burst into a sprint, the cramp in his side intensifying. There was a battle cry above him as a pigeon transformed into a man mid-flight and landed with incredible accuracy onto Alistair's shoulders, tackling him to the ground.

Tum braced his legs out and landed expertly on his feet as Alistair hit the ground. Alistair landed flat on his chest, the wind knocked out of him.

Harper caught up a few minutes later and landed elegantly beside them, her wings transforming into the luxurious purple cloak. She reached out and shook Tum's hand with gusto for a job well done and flipped her pocket mirror open, positioning the captive in the background.

"Harper Leewood here with The Harking Herald *reporting live from the royal wedding. The perpetrator that gave chase has been caught..."*

Alistair made to get up, but Tum placed a clawed foot on his back and put pressure between his shoulder blades. "I wouldn't if I were you, pal."

Moments later Elis and a handful of palace guards caught up to them. The guards picked Alistair up by the armpits and stood him on his feet.

"I haven't done anything," Alistair spat.

"Sure, maybe," Elis said. "But you sure ran like you did." He patted Alistair down, found a mirror stamped with the royal seal in his pocket, and handed it to a guard. "Was this your plan? Steal the king's mirror? And do what with it?"

Harper stepped closer, her mirror aimed directly at Alistair's face.

"I'm not saying anything."

"Not without a little help you won't, I'm sure," Elis said, and pulled out a truth peppermint. Alistair clamped his mouth shut. Elis reached over and pinched Alistair's nose, cutting off his air. He winked over his shoulder at Harper. "Just...give it a minute..."

Sure enough, after he went from red to purple to blue, Alistair let out a gasp for breath. He tried to suck in a fresh lungful quickly, but Elis was ready, the stick poised right against Alistair's lips. He jammed it into Alistair's mouth as soon as they parted.

"Give that a swirl...If you spit, I'm going to tickle your tonsils with it the next time it goes in...that's a good lad." Elis smacked Alistair on the back. Alistair coughed, then instinctively swallowed, and the spell made its way to his stomach, tackled his mind. Elis turned to the guards. "I think you'll find he'll sing like a sparrow now."

"I'll tag along, if you don't mind," Harper chirped sweetly. "I feel I earned this exclusive interview." She followed the group as the guards dragged Alistair away.

"That was his grand plan? Steal the king's mirror? Then what?" Noal asked Elis through the mirror.

"What do you mean, 'then what?' He would have had eyes on every person in the kingdom!"

The realization sunk in. Alistair, at full power. Wouldn't that have been terrifying!

"Do you suppose this has earned us a purple seal? Saving the kingdom and all?" Noal asked, turning to Gregor.

"I think it's definitely earned us that." Gregor clapped his friend on the back. "Now let's eat cake."

Epilogue

Noal was right. Shortly after the royal wedding, before the princess and her new husband went on their honeymoon, they held a ceremony to award Gregor Brimstone the royal purple seal. He was exclusively interviewed afterward by Harper Leewood, who became a chief producer at *The Harking Herald*. Gregor's parents couldn't have been prouder and were the talk of the mountain when they arrived back home, their son joining them for two weeks before he returned to Citeel. Minrol Pallad was never seen or heard from again.

Unfortunately, a heavy sugar tariff was eventually passed to restrict the amount of sugar entering the capital city in an effort to curb the dragon population, which had gotten completely out of control. This led to many bakeries and sweets shops eventually shuttering their doors. Some bakers left Citeel to relocate to other parts of the kingdom where they could bake in peace with sugar that may or may not have been smuggled by pirates.

Gregor, Noal, and Ash eventually opened a pastry shop together in Bambrough, a tourist town at the edge of the kingdom near Superstitious Mountain. While they sell all the usuals—cakes, cookies, tarts, and pies—boulder biscuits are also on the menu, and many dwarves visit the shop to buy them during the festival season of the Luck of the Draw.

Harlowe became the Official Royal Aeromancer and was well-known and respected by the farmers, ranchers, and gardeners of the kingdom. With the help of his assistant Lance, he also started a successful mirror show called 'Magic or Illusion?' where they debunked spells and curses that claimed to cause earthquakes, thunderstorms, rainbows, and all sorts of other weather-related mischief.

Tum the shapeshifter was awarded command of his own fleet of patrol pigeons. They formed a sobriety club to help their fellow feathery friends recover from booze abuse. They meet on Wednesdays at Badger & Bard. It's going so-so.

Remus? Who's Remus?

King Varundil's estranged wife did, in fact, attend the royal wedding. She stayed late and they chatted long into the night, where they finally decided they were better off as friends after all.

Mosley is still in the service of the royals, having lost so much money to dragon racing that he will never in his lifetime afford to give up his post, and retiring early is absolutely out of the question.

Elis works in the royal kitchen, transmitting tutorials on the basics of baking. He's got quite the following. Due to demand he's had to cut back on his after-dark activities and hasn't sent a letter to his father asking for money since he graduated the apprenticeship. He's hoping to find a nice gal, settle down, and have some children in the countryside.

Brimley opened a successful soup kitchen at the monastery. It is one of the few places where sweets are still being served, thanks to the *alleged* secret sugar cane field out back amongst the hops.

In the end, they mostly lived happily ever after.

Except Alistair, who's probably still miserable in a cell somewhere.

The End.

Acknowledgements

Gregor came about as I was baking for my real-life job as a self-employed French macaron baker and my husband barged into the kitchen and demanded I make up a character for our upcoming D&D game. Flustered, I yelled, "Dwarf!"

"What's his name?"

"Gregor?"

"What does he look like?"

I surveyed the mess in my kitchen and immediately imagined a dwarf with a colander on his head, decked out in armor made of sheet pans, wielding a rolling pin.

The rest, as they say, is history.

Thank you to that sweet husband for leaving me alone to write (carving out time as we entered parenthood), for reading the first draft, and for encouraging me to share this story with the world.

Thank you to Sarah Faeth Sanders, my editor, who took my hallucinated cast of characters and saw them as the real bunch of pastry chefs I envisioned them as and helped round them out and polish their story to perfection.

A huge thank you to Adrian DKC who designed the cover. Fergis is perfect.

And a massive thanks to you all, who see this cover, pick up this book, and join me on this wacky adventure into Everdorne. I have so many more characters to introduce you to, I hope you'll come along!

About the Author

Bo Huffman lives in a cottage overgrown by roses and overrun by perfect pets. She has been a lifelong writer and reader of all things fantasy and romance. Her favorite things include rabbits, being a coffee snob, hunting for speakeasies, visiting grocery stores in foreign cities, and eating a perfect croissant.

Website: bohuffman.com

Instagram: @AuthorBoHuffman